Leaning on the Lyrics by Linda Hebert

FreeLanceLinda@yahoo.com

Published by Digital Publishing of Florida, Inc.

Copyright © 2012 by Linda Hebert

Reprint 2013, 2014, 2015.

All rights reserved. No part of this book shall be reproduced, stored in a retrieval system, or transmitted by any means, electronic, mechanical, photocopying, recording, or otherwise, without written permission from the author or publisher.

ISBN  978-1-937183-44-8

Cover Design: Danette DeRouin & Laurie Kornilow

Cover Illustrations: Chris Shephard & Hugh Mackay Hebert

Editing: Bill Baranowski & Brigid O. Nawrocki

Printed in the United States by Digital Publishing of Florida, Inc.

**Disclaimer:** This book contains hundreds of song quotes by hundreds of artists and because of the sheer impracticality of the notion; those artists were not consulted prior to this printing. Based on the "Fair Use Doctrine", referring to rights when using quotes, no artist was disparaged and nothing contained here jeopardizes their continued revenue stream. The messages in this book are about empowering song lyrics and all references to them are full of praise and gratitude. **It is my hope and intention to compliment these artists and bring them even more fans while benefitting some very worthwhile charities.** Please contact us for requests for participation in contributing to fund raising events for your cause.

Book proceeds benefit:

The Wounded Warrior Project

## Foreword

When downsizing had me feeling down-hearted, it was actually song lyrics that reminded me to see the serendipity in my situation. As I found myself relating to certain refrains, I realized how much I really appreciated hearing how somebody else has walked in my shoes. Then, as I made a habit of leaning on lyrics in this way, my journey of self discovery through recession recovery, led me from melancholy to "Margaritaville".

This experience has made me see how I started living my life like a song, a long time ago. It has also helped me realize that the best songs come from the best places (Jimmy Buffett calls it Margaritaville, but explains that this is a state of mind). And in my opinion, good songs come from their creators' highest and best mindsets. Those who write moving lyrics, speak to the human condition, & those who deliver the words, sing from the heart with spirit. It can be a true expression of mind, body & soul. It all somehow becomes more powerful & more memorable when a good voice puts good thoughts to good music. While each contribution is excellent, putting them together makes the whole greater than the sum of its parts.

Bob Marley spoke of "one Love, one Heart", a theme that many others have embodied. His son, Ziggy sings about a "Higher Vibration". While some may claim that his high could be more due to a substance commonly found at reggae (& probably most other) concerts, what if he's actually speaking about real substance, like meaningful, mood altering, inspirational, sometimes even life transforming songs, produced through sound vibrations, shared collectively by any who are ready to tune in?

It is this collective energy, like that put forth by a flash mob or a patriotic band or a church choir that can sometimes catch us off guard & compel us to stop & watch & listen & in that moment, all who are present are focused on one theme & the true power of music is present. Most of us enjoy being caught up in that moment but in time, the sights & sounds we witnessed fade. What doesn't usually fade however, is the memory of how the whole scene made us feel.

Sometimes it happens on a more personal level, when a lone voice on the radio reaches us in the stillness of our room or accompanies us on a road trip. When music carries a meaningful message, especially when we hear it at significant times in our lives, the feelings evoked can often subconsciously creep in & make an imprint on our psyches. For many of us, for the rest of our lives, every time we hear that certain song, that same feeling we had the first time we heard it, comes rushing over us, often without us even realizing it. Some of these feelings can invoke nostalgic memories bringing a smile to our face. They can conjure up thoughts that make us laugh or ones that stir our souls. Sometimes they just serve as a brief distraction from the present day. In this way, music somehow seems capable of permeating our senses & our memories more than other forms of communication

Through my personal experience amounting to decades of relating to & reflecting on song lyrics, I have reached the conclusion that the best songwriters & singers are true artists & often even philosophers. And whether we acknowledge it or not, I believe they have some power to influence society. I've been listening to songs so long that somewhere along the way, I started talking back & thinking of this as an interactive process. When I think about it, I can easily quote a song lyric for just about any situation in life. Occasionally these artists can even produce works that seem larger than life. Their messages have sometimes fallen on deaf ears, but it is my hope that through this book, I can share some of my favorites therefore reviving them, and possibly in some small part, reviving those who choose to listen.

On a more superficial level, Jimmy Buffett has a song referring to "A Smart Woman in a Real Short Skirt". Keeping that in mind, a friend of mine told me, "the length of a book should be like the length of a woman's skirt...long enough to cover everything, but short enough to keep your interest"* So here is my short, bittersweet tale.

I'll begin this story by inviting you to tune in with me & look/hear songs through my eyes/ears. I hope that something here strikes a chord with you. Then I'll invite you to stay tuned to all the ways that music can make a difference in life so I'm also including a link to my site containing short lists & short stories relating to certain song subjects (when you see **RTA**, it means: **Refer to Appendix, @www.LeaningOnTheLyrics.com**) & While I consider my picks to be superlatives in their category, **since the music world seems to be an ever changing & growing entity**, with your possible participation, **these lists will likely have lots of additions in the future..** I want to apologize in advance for the multitude of great songs that were not yet included here, but as this "Parrot Head Looks @ 50", these are only "events I have happened to witness!" Also since this book was written throughout a 7 year period of time & in a very conversational tone, **please allow me the indulgence of often digressing** (as various tidbits pop in my head even though some of them didn't happen exactly at that point in the story) & when I'm ready to return to the topic at hand, I'll insert an, **"Anyway"** (just like Ellen Degeneres does after her show's credits & just as if you & I were sitting & chatting). Jimmy Buffett's signature salutation to his fans is, "Fins Up!" I'd like to put a spin on this and say, from one music fan to another, **Fans Up!**

---

*Stacie Harmon, from her book, "Secrets Men Share".

# Dedications

To my husband **Hugh**, Thanks for confirming what I knew 20 years ago, "You could be the perfect partner"*
& "I'm better for the smile you give"**

To my sons, **Hugh and Eric**, Thanks for letting this "Full grown woman get to learn from a child"***

To my **Parents, Siblings, and Supportive Friends (especially Diane & Stacie),** Thanks for helping me to "Keep smiling and let my family & friends show me the best of what this world can be"****

To the **Make a Wish Foundation ®**, Thank you for making one of my biggest dreams comes true and for continuing to do so for so many more deserving others

To the **Wounded Warrior Project ®,** Thanks for rising to the challenge because "We all need a little tenderness or how can Love survive in such a graceless age?"*****

To The **Writers & Singers of all of the Songs Quoted,** Thanks for being a continuous source of joy, comfort & inspiration throughout my life.

A Special Thank You to **Teri Sullivan**, For your time and encouragement from the beginning!

*Jimmy Buffett's, "She Could Be the Perfect Partner" ** Genesis', "Follow You, Follow Me" ***Jimmy Buffett's, "Good Guys Win" **** MacMcAnally's, "Until Then" *****Don Henley's "Heart of the Matter"

# Leaning On the Lyrics

### (The Buffett Rules)

Linda Hebert

# Contents

Chapter 1 - Tune In……………………...p.13

Chapter 2 - A New Lease on Life……….p.43

Chapter 3 – Af-*fin*-ity……………………..p.71

Chapter 4 – The F Word! ………………..p.101

Chapter 5 – False Cents of Security…… p.125

Chapter 6 - The Perfect Storm …………p.151

Chapter 7 – My LOT in Life……………. p.189

Chapter 8- Encore…………………….. p.221

# 1

# Tune In

(Once there was a way to get back homeward)

The Beatles

They say that writers need to find their voice and identify their muse. I know that my muse is music and my voice is a collective one echoing the many songs stuck in my head. You see, since I was a little girl, I've paid close attention to the songs on the radio and somewhere along the way I subconsciously began storing memorable lyrics in the back of my mind, supposedly in case I might need to refer to them later. By the summer of 2007, "later" had arrived in my life.

At that time, my personal experience with the housing crisis left me feeling lost. A post-hurricane, impending housing market crash left me stumbling in a whirlwind of confusion and debt; and when I didn't know where else to turn, I began paying closer attention to some of those voices singing in my head. Surprisingly, their wisdom brought me solace and inspiration.

While developing the theme for this book, one of my writing colleagues accused me of being disingenuous about how music could have made such a difference in my life. When I referred to the way musical lyrics soothed me through tough times, she couldn't make the connection between melodies and money woes. But the truth is that when I felt most lost, the first signs of hope and comfort did come from a song. Her hesitation however, did help me to realize that maybe not everybody *gets it*. Maybe not everybody is *in tune* to getting the messages in the music. Maybe some people need to *adjust their dial* and become more receptive to the benefits of...The Beatles, Bach, Bon Jovi, Buffett or any music that may get through to them.

This realization lead me to wonder, how did I acquire this skill so naturally and how far back did it start? I do not come from a musical family. None of us owned instruments or received musical instruction. I was not taken to concerts in my formative years. Participating in music was neither a hobby nor a potential career path for me. I couldn't even make the cut for the church choir (in response to that, I hear Jimmy Buffett telling me, "Sister Mary Mojo so hard to trick", from his "That's My Story and I'm Sticking to It" song). *Anyway*, at what point could I remember music becoming so important in my life? How did I become such a devoted listener, and how has life trained me to be such a good music follower?

I then reflected on my childhood and realized that musical awareness started early for me. I'm the sixth child in a family of seven, with the oldest being eleven years my senior. Sharing a bedroom full of bunk beds, my younger sister and I were lulled to sleep each night by the mellow rock of the seventies coming from our older siblings' hi-fi stereo. My dad had the only decent singing voice in the house; and while I was growing up, he would occasionally break into song sharing with feeling, one of his favorite fifties classics. And every year on my birthday, he wouldn't miss the chance to treat me to a serenade of the songs that were the inspiration for my first and middle names, "Linda", by Ray Noble and "Maria", from the musical, *Westside Story*. The likeliest starting point however, must have been when I observed the twinkle in his eye particularly when he sang, "When Irish Eyes Are Smiling."

Being an Irish Catholic family, one of our weekly traditions was attending Saturday five o'clock mass (far from Alan Jackson's five o'clock ritual). And there, I recall fond memories of how certain joyous hymns, like my favorite called, "Glory to the Father", brought camaraderie among the congregation. For us kids though, our real joy was coming more from the anticipation of the treats awaiting us at home.

Mom always remained behind to have dinner on the table as we returned. Then it was time for a night of our favorite television shows and our one weekly ration of soda and a bowl of dad's special popcorn (this was no microwave popcorn). The smell of that melted butter wafting through the house and the escalating sound of kernels popping as we all took our places coveting our own tall 16 oz. glass bottle of Coca-Cola, got us primed for the Saturday night line-up.

We were all watching and listening as Mary Tyler Moore tossed up her hat into the cityscape sky while being serenaded with her theme song, "Love is All Around", by Paul Williams. Then the Partridge Family would take over, traveling through town in their musical bus. Even the Brady Bunch got in on the act as their story line led them into a brief musical career. And who could forget The Monkees, led by Davy Jones, with their British accents and boyish charm that even made a devoted fan out of Marsha Brady! I actually caught most of their episodes on Saturday mornings as they sang, "Hey, hey we're the Monkees; people say we monkey around, but we're too busy singing to put anybody down".

There were no MTV, VH1 of CMT channels back then. We didn't have shows such as, "American Idol", "The Voice" or "Glee". And the fact that we do now have shows like, "Singing Bee" and "Don't Forget the Lyrics" proves that lyrics do stick in our heads. Think about it, can you recite "Jenny's" number? How about if I tell you that the first three digits are 8-6-7? Is there anyone out there who cannot supply the "5-3-0-9"? You may not be able to get past the first line of the Gettysburg Address or Martin Luther King's I Have a Dream speech, or maybe even the first couple digits of your number when you were growing up, but I'll bet you'll never forget Jenny's number and many other lyrics that are most likely stuck in your subconscious. When I was growing up, we did have shows like, "Name that Tune" and the "Gong Show" and "Donnie & Marie" (who claimed to be "a little bit country and a little bit rock and roll), which may have paved the way for music permeating prime time programming today. And commonly aired commercials of that era also got in on the act. Catchy, repetitive jingles like, "If I were an Oscar Mayer wiener, everyone would be in love with me," gave our generation plenty of food for thought.

When dad took control of the TV, (this was in the day before remote controls, when you had to actually get out of your chair and turn the channels), the one television set in the house was tuned into "The Lawrence Welk Variety Show". As Mr. Welk signed off at the end of each episode, he would approach the front of the stage, look directly into the camera and say, "Keep a song in your heart". At least back then, I was used to doing what I was told, so I guess I started taking this instruction to heart! After all, if my idol at that time, Nadia Comaneci, the gymnastic star of the 1976 Olympics, could have her own theme song (an instrumental borrowed from the daytime series, "The Young and the Restless"), why couldn't I? My favorite childhood activity was gymnastics, therefore, as I practiced my stunts on the make shift home equipment that my dad made for me, I would borrow her song and play it as a continuous source of inspiration. I'd also whistle along to the Globetrotters show theme since back in that day, I was naïve enough to believe their story lines when every episode resulted in a basketball game challenge as the solution for settling any score. Then as the Miami Dolphins lead an undefeated season in 1972, my dad, my two brothers and it seemed everybody else in town, was singing along to the team's fight song. So as my interests turned to sports, music continued to be ever present. And in the years to follow, I watched *Rocky* and the runners in *Chariots of Fire* achieve victory with the accompaniment of their triumphant tunes.

Before long though, my preteen years brought new developments and I no longer had the petite stature optimal for gymnastics. That's when I began noticing boys and paying more attention to love songs. One of my first exposures to ballads was through a friend in my sixth grade class named, Kerry Quinn. When her parents had a new baby girl, they repeatedly played, "Little Miss Magic", Jimmy Buffett's ode to his daughter, Savannah. When she in turn shared that sweet song with me, I was hooked. All I wanted to do from that point on, was to grow up and marry a sentimental man who would adore me and our children that way.

**The next Buffett song I recall hearing was, "Come Monday", the song that put this singer on the charts and from that point forward, forever in my heart.**

However, it was never one of those teen idol crushes. It was nothing like this generation's Justin Bieber craze. If the girls of that era were gaga over anyone, it most likely would have been David Cassidy (as confesses one of my present day friends), or Rick Springfield or Jack Wagoner as those two each made their debuts on "General Hospital". The song from "General Hospital" that still haunts me is Christopher Cross' "Think of Laura". I must confess, in addition to musical idols, Laura Weber's character took over where Marsha Brady's left off, as far as actresses I identified with. But I was never bold enough to let myself fantasize about actually associating with real celebrities. It never occurred to me to subscribe to <u>Tigerbeat Magazine</u> or to find space on my crowded bedroom walls for any kind of pin up poster. And even if I had wanted to, I would not have found Jimmy Buffett there. I didn't know anything about this singer personally. It was more like I was developing an affinity for the qualities his lyrics personified…fun-loving, sentimental, spontaneity. And those became the qualities most important to me in any future relationships.

My best friend, Diane certainly had those qualities. To get some comic relief from those strict nuns in our Catholic school, she and I spent hours amusing one another with our own silly private jokes. I've heard that Andy Rooney, famous for his "Sixty Minutes" commentary, said, "No matter how serious life requires you to be, everyone needs a friend to act goofy with". Diane was that friend for me. People used to get irritated being around us because we were constantly giggling and practically spoke our own language. With time on our hands at that age, we spent night after night watching John

Travolta transfer from a Sweathog named Vinny Barbarino on "Welcome Back Kotter", to the dashing big screen star, Danny Zucko, as idle summer hours allowed us to see the musical, *Grease*, thirteen times (once for every year of our lives)! This had us crash dieting with dreams of fitting into those skin tight leather pants that Olivia Newton John's character pranced around in, as her flawless beauty and angelic voice wooed the boys of our generation. I guess that movie was our generation's version of *High School Musical*.

When we weren't at the movies, Diane and I were back home calling in to the radio station to play one of our requests or trying to be the "bazillionth" lucky caller to win whatever promotional trinket was being offered. This occurred on a rotary phone before such luxuries as speed-dial. On one lucky night, fate shined upon us, and my older brother, Don called home from his friend, Paul's house across town where he had gone to play pool to congratulate me as he heard my name being announced from Paul's game room stereo-- "Linda Sullivan is tonight's winner of the album of her choice"! Later in the week, Don drove me down to WQYK to pick up my top choice, the double album *Soundtrack from Grease*, of course!

Then one day, Diane's dad got transferred from our hometown of Ft. Lauderdale to Cincinnati, Ohio, and she had to move. As far as we were concerned, Cincinnati was on the other side of the world and being separated like this right before high school, was a cruel twist of fate. That summer, I wore out my *Best of Bread with David Gates,* eight track as the tearjerker song, "Everything I Own" did its job of bringing on the waterworks whenever I needed a good teenage cry. Diane's parents felt so guilty that they actually let her live with our family for the summer while they settled into their new home in Ohio. But on that awful day when her dad knocked on the front door and it was time for her to go, I plopped myself on the floor in my room alongside my giant teddy bear and sobbed for hours.

Some of my siblings felt sorry for me and tried to distract me. Knowing how much I listened to the radio, my brother Don made up an interesting activity. He would walk up to me and blurt out song lyrics; only he would not sing them. He would speak them as if in a conversational tone. For example, at any given moment, he might enter a room and say, "When the cupboard's bare, I'll still find something there with My Love" (Paul McCartney) or "I Shot the Sheriff" (Bob Marley). At first this was all a bit confusing to me until I caught on and sharpened my lyrical knowledge enough to come back with the correct reply which in the latter case would have been, "But I didn't shoot the deputy". I probably owe him much credit for my musical memory to date. To partially fill the void in my life, I must have listened closely when Bill Withers sang, "Lean On Me when you're not strong and I'll be your friend. I'll help you carry on". Only I think that I began to think of music itself, not this singer as a friend. And fortunately, Diane soon discovered that her dad's new job also came with a Watts Line which provided her with unlimited long distance talk time, so we made good use of that over the next decade.

Another question that I've pondered in this self analysis is my tendency to be so analytical. When I searched for reasons why I might have become so serious minded, even as a young child, it dawned on me that there was a period of time in my formative years when I observed a lot of death (not violent or on a grand scale) but several within our own family within a short period of time. As I recall, I attended three funerals of immediate family (a grandparent, an uncle and an aunt) within an eighteen month period. Simultaneously, my older sister's best friend and her two brothers were killed in a car accident and my older brother's best friend became the victim of a mysterious crime. It wasn't so much my personal loss at the age of eight that year, but watching my family members (especially my mom) in such anguish. Two songs that haunt me from that time period are, Dion's "Abraham, Martin and John", which speaks about assassinations of leaders with the following lines that give me chills: "He freed a lot of people but it seems the good, they die young. I just look around and he's gone" and Joan Baez's "The Night They Drove Old Dixie Down" with the lines: "All the people were singing. They went, 'Na, na, na'...Now I don't mind choppin' wood and I don't care if the money's no good. Ya take what you need and ya leave the rest. But they never should have taken the very best". One season on "American Idol", one of the finalists was given this song to sing and I found myself having a strong reaction to it. It had nothing to do with his performance. It was just hearing that melody again after almost forty years that made me feel like I was being kicked in the gut. My husband had never heard the song before but he was certainly surprised at my reaction. He said my eyes seemed to become glazed over and I got an eerie blank stare on my face. This ability of a song to put you right back in the place when you first heard it, is what I was talking about in the introduction to this book. Also around that time in my life, the tearjerker songs, "Honey" by Bobby Goldsboro, "Seasons in the Sun" by Terry Jacks, "Wildfire" by Michael Martin Murphey and "Shannon" by Henry Gross, (which are all full of melancholy mourning), were being constantly played on the radio. And later came along Billy Joel's "Only the Good Die Young" to add to this list of songs on this topic. It also probably didn't help that I saw movies like *Love Story* and *Sunshine* (I'll describe their heart wrenching themes in detail later) when they were played on TV. No doubt, this subject matter was very heavy for an eight year old, but I was always trying to keep up with my brothers and sisters. Consequently, since I seemed to have so much first hand exposure to tragedies, I guess I became particularly sensitive to songs about serious topics.

But fortunately for me, life went on and once I recovered from these losses and Diane's move and all of the melodrama of adolescent hormonal changes, music helped me rebuild my social life with the plethora of party tunes ushered in with the eighties. These tunes (many of which were the Bee Gees' hits which accompanied John Travolta's dance moves on the *Saturday Night Fever* soundtrack) gave us all disco fever and many causes for celebration KC and The Sunshine Band had us shaking our bootys, and Michael Jackson had us imitating the Moonwalk while Donna Summer had us wanting to get in that "Last Dance". During most gatherings, the boys would stand around and try to look cool while the girls would dance together in a circle and shout out the refrains to the current hits (but TY Kenny Costello for being brave enough to attempt to teach me how to disco dance back then!). Upon the looks of it, not much has changed at present day school dances!

**Strangely though, even back then, while all of my friends were bopping to the beat, I was always asking,**

**"What is this song about?"**

According to the website, *The-top-tens.com*, the top-ten bands that had the kids I grew up with in the 70's & 80's rocking, were: On the 70's list: Abba, (it is appropriate that they are first on this list, especially with a song that says:

**"Thank you for the music, the songs I'm singing**

Thanks for all the joy they're bringing

Who can live without it, I ask in all honesty

What would life be?

Without a song or a dance, what are we?

So I say thank you for the music for giving it to me")

Led Zeppelin, The Jackson Five, Pink Floyd, The Allman Brothers Band, Aerosmith, and Black Sabbath. And the 80's List: A-ha (which had a cool computerized graphics video for their song, "Take On Me", which was constantly being played during the early days of MTV, along with Peter Gabriel's "Sledgehammer"), Journey, Guns N Roses, Metallica, U2, Bon Jovi, & Van Halen. Before anybody reacts in disbelief because their favorite band is missing from these lists, let me clarify that the following three bands made both lists, awarding them top ten status for both of those decades: AC/DC, Queen & Heart. And if you still disagree with the lists, you can log on to that website and vote and express your opinions. My only hesitation in doing so is that I just know that I'll inadvertently leave out some very deserving band because we were so fortunate to have so many greats of our era!

**"I may be old but at least
I got to see all of the good bands!"**

Others I recall being commonly played on the radio in those days are ( in no particular order): The Rolling Stones, The Guess Who, Bob Dylan, Ted Nugent, Jimmy Hendricks, James Brown, James Taylor, Jefferson Airplane/Starship, Simon & Garfunkel, The Eagles, Reo Speedwagon, Bob Seger, Supertramp, Stevie Wonder, The Steve Miller Band, Steve Winwood, Bad Company, Neil Diamond, John Denver, Air Supply, Elton John, Billy Joel, Paul McCartney & Wings, Foghat, Firefall, Fleetwood Mac, Chicago, Crosby Stills and Nash, Loggins and Messina, America, The Little River Band, Phil Collins & Genesis, Prince, The Doobie Brothers, (especially their song, "Listen to the Music") The Cars, and Bob Marley. During a recent countdown of the all time top artists on CMT, one of the commentators credits Bob Marley for bringing reggae to the masses with his larger than life persona with a legacy that seems timeless.

Fast-forwarding to my adulthood, music continued to remain in the background of my life, and eventually I realized that some of those songs were not about anything at all. Many of them were just ramblings of silly nonsense providing a great beat that got everyone moving and sharing some brief breaks from reality, like the following poem that some silly "friend" posted on my Facebook wall this morning! ---

### "Roses are Cars, Violets are Buckets,

### This Poem makes no sense-
### BOOBS!"

(I'm Not Right in the Head.com)

On a deeper more personal level though, other songs have evoked real emotion and contained pearls of wisdom from wise songwriters which took me years of life experience to relate to and understand. Some of these concepts became clearer as I progressed to college, first in the mountains of North Carolina at a small college in a dry town called, Brevard (which was ironically for music majors, even though I only took general curriculum courses there). That is where I first became introduced to forest parties. Since this dry town allowed no alcohol, the student population quickly learned what mountain trails to take a keg and a boom box to for a bonfire and their form of what I had previously know as a beach bash. These gatherings are where I learned to climb a rope swing and slide down a waterfall and enjoy the tunes of Loverboy, 38 Special, Billy Squire, The Scorpions, The Police, John Cougar Mellencamp and Lionel Richie.

Then in my third year, since I could no longer stand the winters out of the state of Florida, I transferred to the University of South Florida in Tampa, where I majored in Mass Communications. Unfortunately though, I never had a class addressing the communicative power of music. This was a lesson I had to figure out for myself. My college years had me shying away from karaoke bars but not being able to resist those dueling piano places especially when they played the songs that I knew all of the words to. Since the days of grade school field trips and family cross county car rides, I never could resist a good sing along. On the college campus, I appreciated when the Sun Dome auditorium hosted concerts, as my cocktail waitressing job at a nearby popular happy hour spot, the actual first *Chilis* restaurant, then managed by a woman named, Debbie Ivers (who decades later partnered with Jimmy Buffett in his *Cheeseburger in Paradise* chain of restaurants), had me greatly profiting from the pre-parties. In that way, music aided my college fund. I probably should have majored in Music Appreciation, but instead I ended up spending close to a decade as an elementary school teacher.

As I began my teaching career, my old friend, music followed me into my classroom and served as an efficient teaching assistant. I can barely even read music, but I found a way to use music in teaching reading. As a matter of fact, I found it very helpful to incorporate music and movement into the curriculum whenever possible in order to create some memorable lessons on various subjects. After all, I grew up watching "Schoolhouse Rock" segments in between Saturday morning cartoons. I think "Lolly, Lolly, Lolly, Get Your Adverbs Here" & "I'm Just a Bill on Capitol Hill" were my favorites. And I invested in all of the addition, subtraction and multiplication rap tapes I could find for my classroom.

During one stint at an inner city school, I actually implemented an upbeat Ziggy Marley song called "Give a Little Love" into our opening ceremonies each morning. Getting that group of fourth graders to sing along using the song chart that I posted at the front of the classroom, resulted in some subconscious reading lessons and more important bonding lessons. As any early childhood teacher most likely would tell you, breaking into song and getting the kids to join in, is a very effective classroom management technique. I recently heard about a teacher who chimes out the first half of an ad jingle like, "ba da ba ba ba…" and challenges her students to complete the phrase with the corresponding counterpart, which would be: "I'm lov'n it!" (McDonalds' jingle) in order to regain focus in the classroom.

Of course, in those years, I was no different than my students as June rolled around each year, when I'd hear Alice Cooper's "School's Out for Summer"! Although, I never did take a summer off (I stuck around to teach summer school or run a summer camp), so for me it played out more like Jimmy Buffett's more recent release, "Summezcool". And if my reality had been more like that song describes it, I never would have gotten burned out after a decade in this occupation. So in this way, I also carried music into my work life. And whether you're like Elton John's "Rocketman", or like Billy Currington, you're best skills are that you're, "Pretty Good at Drinking Beer", I'll bet music in some form accompanies you to work each day too. If nothing else, advertisers know that a.m. & p.m. drive times, are the best way to reach working commuters. And a station in my present day town, 95.3, "The River", boasts, "Music that makes you feel good at work" as their slogan.

I met my husband, Hugh, through a teaching friend. One of our instant bonds was our mutual love of Jimmy Buffett music along with a "Margaretville" mindset. The night we met, I remember him asking me what kind of music and what kind of food I liked. That night we danced to "A Pirate Looks at Forty" (Buffett) and the next night he made me a scrumptious seafood dinner. Four months later, we danced to our wedding song, "Bigger than the Both of Us", (also by Buffett). Two years later our first son was born, followed by our second son, twenty two months after that.

When my boys were babies, I rocked them to sleep with lullabies and shared silly songs on car rides. Being "Parrot Heads" (Jimmy Buffett fans), my husband and I gave them no choice but to be indoctrinated into this world as "Parakeets". One of the best memories in our hearts is a scene of the boys, at ages two and four, at a sports bar karaoke stage, singing, "I don't know" over and over again as the only correct words that they knew to Buffett's hit, "Volcano". One of my husband's favorite bonding activities when the boys were toddlers was to sit with them in the car in the driveway with the radio on and the windows and sunroof open. The boys would crawl onto his lap and attempt to mimic daddy singing along to the car stereo(the musical instrument my husband claims that he know how to play!). Their innocent way of misinterpreting some of the lyrics was precious—the "fat man on the dock" was the "Batman on the dock" (Buffett's "Frankie & Lola"); "I like the night life baby", was "I like the night light baby" (The Cars' "Let's Go"). Kudos to my husband, Hugh for coming up with an inexpensive, healthy way to entertain our children!

We also enjoyed entertaining them with Jimmy Buffett's children's books, *Jolly Mon* and *Trouble Dolls*, co-written by his daughter, Savannah Jane, and *Swine Not*, co-written by family friend, Helen Bransford. We were thrilled to find *The Parakeet Album* by the W.O. Smith Music School Singers, a series of Jimmy Buffett songs sung by children. The poetic license they use to censor lyrics to assure it's all "G rated", is adorable (like beer becomes root beer)! Speaking of being G rated, we were thrilled to learn that Jack Johnson was doing the soundtrack for the kids' movie, *Curious George,* which made it a lot more palatable for us to go see with the boys! Additionally, two thumbs up to Jimmy Buffett for appearing on *Sesame Street* with his specially produced children's song, "Caribbean Amphibian", and to James Taylor for also joining the Muppets with his song, "Jelly Mon Kelly", and to The Spin Doctors for performing "Two Princes" on that show, as well as the numerous other acts who've shared their talent with our toddlers in this way. One of Jimmy Buffett's band members, Uncle Jim Mayer, has even become an award winning artist in the category of children's music.

Presently, our boys are teenagers, and anything that their parents like is treated with disdain. Just wait until they get to college and attend their first Buffett-themed party! Back in the eighties, I remember attending an outdoor Buffett concert at the stadium at The University of Florida which was reminiscent of Woodstock. It was a miracle that anybody in that crowd could stand up from their beach blanket and balance long enough to keep that beach ball bouncing through the crowd throughout the afternoon! Someday our kids will realize just how cool their parents really are (even though they'll never admit, "We Learned to be Cool From You" like Jimmy's song says.

Although my twenty-two year old nephew and a group of his friends from the University of North Florida, recently told me a funny story about their last Buffett party. Apparently when a neighbor called the cops complaining about the loud music, the police officer who responded to the call just laughed when they opened the door, sharing that he couldn't believe anyone would call the cops because of kids playing Buffett music!!

My older son, Hugh Mackay (named after his father and great grandfather) is presently doing his best to share the virtues of rap with me. To add a disclaimer, we only let him download the "clean versions" from I-Tunes. Hoping to bridge the generational gap, I'm giving it a try. However, I'm not a complete stranger to this genre as the classic hit, "Rapper's Delight" by The Sugar Hill Gang, is one of my all time favorites. In one of our past conversations, this (then thirteen year old) son was sharing with me how he admires these hip hop rappers for overcoming their circumstances and how some of their songs express the sadness of losing friends due to gang violence. Being a concerned parent, I delved further into the topic making sure that he understood how to separate his emulation of the music from the lifestyle. His quick witted response was, "Mom, when you and dad are out on date night tonight, make sure you don't get into any pirate sword fights since you like Jimmy Buffett music so much!" OK, to him I could only say, "touché!"

As children progress into the preteen and teenage years, the ways that they become more outspoken and independent can leave parents bewildered. Martina McBride has a song called "Teenage Daughters" that does a great job of empathizing with exasperated parents. The last couple of years have had my husband and me grateful for the popular video games, *Rockband*, *Guitar Hero* and *DJ Hero* for introducing our sons to the incredible classics of the eighties and giving us another way to share in their lives. It's amusing to see the look on their faces when mom and dad can sing along even to most of the heavy metal and hard rock hits inventoried in these collections. I cannot help but see the "me" of yesteryear as they are both beginning to memorize lines and become inseparable from their headphones. It's also funny to see retro-style large headphones alongside their collection of ear buds. Our boys are also growing up in a decade of a revival of superhero movies. One series that we've all enjoyed is *Transformers*. And through these movies' soundtracks, we've all been introduced to the music of Green Day and Linkin Park. This past fall, we were grateful for another opportunity to spend time together as Hugh and I accompanied our sons to their first concert when Linkin Park toured our area.

I've always felt that one of the most profound songs on the topic of parenting is Harry Chapin's "Cat's in the Cradle". This song so dramatically reminds parents to strive to prioritize and make time for their children. (Jumping forward in the chronology of the story I'm about to unfold here, I was delighted to hear a local church pastor, Fr. John Deary, quoting this song in one of his sermons). Phil Vassar's "Don't Miss Your Life" & "Just Another Day in Paradise" as well as Kenny Chesney's "The Good Stuff", re-emphasize this point too. Trace Adkins also does this with, "Just Fishing", his song telling the story of how a father spends some mellow quality time with his daughter. Similarly, "Butterfly Kisses" by Bob Carlisle, "Ready, Set, Don't Go", by Billy Ray Cyrus, and "There Goes My Life", by Kenny Chesney, are full of fathers' pledges of love for their daughters. And then there's Jimmy Buffett's playful ode to his second daughter, "Delaney Talks to Statues". In this one, he says, "She's growing up too fast for me and asking lots of questions, some I know the answers to, and some, I'm looking for suggestions". I say, "Aren't we all?" And this is just one more song line showing how this favorite artist of mine, has a way of just relating to the masses.

As far as those answers, I think we can find some of them in **Michael Tolcher's "Sooner or Later"**. I heard this song during a spin class and was so impressed by the lyrics that I regained enough breath from this cardio workout to yell out to the instructor asking who it was by. I then put it on my Ipod and played it aloud several times for my older son, telling him that I could really relate to the refrain, "Sooner or later you'll listen to what people have to say, but now you learn the hard way"! ( (& again, fast forwarding in time, I was blown away while sitting in a Ft. Myers beach bar one evening when they announced that next up to the mic. during this Island Hopper Songwriter's Festival was he! And *he* turned out to be a nice guy who shared with me that his mother had a lot to do with the lyrics of that song which made perfect sense to me!

Ironically Michael Tolcher's song also includes using sunscreen as one piece of advice to impart to your children, just like the Sunscreen song, quoting a famous graduation speech recorded by Baz Luhrmann. Rascal Flatts' "My Wish for You" and Rod Stewart's "Forever Young"(one of my all time favorites) also impart heart-felt wisdom from the perspective of parent speaking to young adult child.

**One note that I'd like to add regarding children, is that I believe in never giving up on them. I believe that it's a parent's life-long obligation to continue to strive to Love their children into the people they're capable of being.** I am learning though, as they reach the teenage years, that maybe instead of commanding unrealistic perfection, like Miranda Lambert laments about in "This Aint my Mama's Broken Heart" it is sometimes wise to pick your battles like Michael Franks as he sings, "I'd Rather Be Happy Than Right"!

Continuing with songs about family, when my friends and I were having babies, I put together some wonderful baby shower mixes *(RTA)*. But next time I do one, it will not be without, **the absolute tear jerker, "Mom"** recorded by Garth Brooks (and written by Don Sampson & Wynne Varble(another performer I got to meet during that Ft. Myers Bch. Festival) but something tells me that there must have been a woman in on the lyrics of this one too! Have your tissues ready before you search for Garth's performances with Ellen DeGeneres, Robin Roberts and the CMA audience all sobbing to this self described "mama's boy" singing this one! And I so appreciate that my younger son, Eric, being a deeper thinker like me, seemed to get it when I played it for him.

**So now you can see how much music has played into my work life, my love life and my family life. The next chapter will explain how it even found a way into my financial life and became a catalyst in my emotional recovery from an identity crisis brought on by economic distress.**

However, before I go there, prompted by my colleague's challenge, I feel compelled to further demonstrate the many ways that I believe music can move you. **Maybe it can't actually change you, but it can help you to *change your tune* and may often do so without your conscious participation.** In the movies, music is strategically placed in certain scenes to evoke sadness, fear, anger, joy or laughter. It is very capable of setting the mood. In their song, "More Than A Feeling", Boston says, "It's more than a feeling when I hear that old song they used to play; I lose myself in a familiar song; I close my eyes and I slip away". It's as if music can transcend time. I honestly cannot hear The Ohio Players' "Love Roller Coaster" and not feel motion sickness coming on from riding the Super Himalaya at the State Fair! Speaking of coasters and music, there are two that I know of with musical themes: Walt Disney World's *Rock n' Roller Coaster* featuring Aerosmith (present day has me associating their "Sweet Emotion" with the zero to sixty speed of that ride), and Universal Studios' *Hollywood Rip Ride Rockit*, where you get to choose from several musical genres to accompany you on your wild ride.

Some people may be more sensitive to music's effects than others depending on whether they address life more with their heads or with their hearts. Certain spiritual leaders dictate that all of life is determined by our feelings. A publication by Abraham Hicks says, "You can never have a happy ending at the end of an unhappy journey; it just doesn't work out that way. The way you're feeling, along the way, is the way you're continuing to pre-pave your journey, and it's the way it's going to continue to turn out until you do something about the way you are feeling". And I believe music just may be a source for changing feelings. Can you hear Enya's, "Only Time", and not sadly pause and think about how it was constantly played during the media coverage of the aftermath of 9/11? Can you hear "Linus and Lucy" (I'm familiar with the version recorded by David Benoit), and not see Snoopy from "The Peanuts" series, joyously dancing around in your head? Think about your favorite holiday song. Doesn't it do a good job of getting you in the spirit? These are just a few examples of how music transforms us.

As far as changing one's attitude, it is my observation that real change does not happen automatically. It comes gradually with subtle influences over time. In his book, *The Slight Edge*, Jeff Olsen, one of my business mentors, stresses the power of persistence as he explains that small continuous efforts over time eventually kick in, resulting in compounded effects. He also claims that most people are the average of the five people that they spend the most time with. In this way, associations are important; hence the term, "guilty by association".

**Many parents realize this as they advise their children to choose their friends wisely. Possibly though, these same parents should also advise their children to choose their music wisely.**

Especially in formative years, it is important to choose the correct musical mentors. We may all need to pay attention to the messages in the music we are listening to because it is my belief that these subtle influences permeate our personalities with compounded effects over time. It's like my high school computer teacher always said, (back when we all started with TRS80's), "garbage in, garbage out". And finally to this point, as a motivator for his company, Jeff Olsen has been known to direct his salespeople to be aware of their own music. He refers to this as their enthusiasm, the energy in their voice and all of the unspoken nuances present in body language.

An Italian woman I recently met told me her story about coming to this country, further demonstrating this point. She explained how within six months of her arrival here, with a new job and a nine year old son and no knowledge of the local language, her husband left her. She shared how her most important survival skill suddenly became her ability to keenly observe people and gravitate exclusively toward those with positive energy, a trait she could only perceive since she couldn't understand a word they were saying. She told me how she just became very *in tune* to others' vibes. Four years later, she is now working in her dream job, using her innate talent to produce one of a kind hand painted gowns for dance competitions and is in the process of purchasing her first home here. Its stories like hers that prompt me to have more musical awareness from the outside world and also from within myself.

So how can we continue to take it a step further and go from simple listening, to pausing and thinking, and possibly problem solving through music? **When in a quandary, I've made it a habit to call upon my collected inventory of lyrics to possibly shed light on a particular situation.** At this point, the lyrics to one of those seventies mellow rock classics comes to mind with the words of Don McLean in the song, "Bye, Bye Miss American Pie":

> **"Do you believe in rock and roll,**
> **can music save your mortal soul?"**

My answers to those questions are:

**"yes", and "quite possibly".**

In a recent countdown of Country's All-Time Top 40, Trace Adkins tells the story of how he got a letter from a listener thanking him for his inspirational song, "You're Gonna Miss This". He explains how he was astonished to read how on one fateful day while driving with the radio on, his song touched a man so deeply that he pulled his car off to the side of the road and began weeping as he reconsidered his plan to commit suicide.

I'd like to paraphrase a short story sent to me years ago by my Aunt Mary, from an article titled, <u>Encouraging words</u>, written by Mike Riley. Two frogs that have fallen into a pit are leaping for their lives to get out. Other frogs come and yell to them to give up because it's a hopeless situation so one of them does, and eventually falls to his death. The other frog, who apparently is deaf, thinks that they are all yelling for him with cheers of encouragement which is what causes him to persevere and eventually conquer this challenge. The morals printed at the end of this story say: "There is power of life and death in the tongue (Proverbs 18:21) & **An encouraging word to someone who is down can lift them up and help them make it through the day. A destructive word to someone who is down can be what it takes to kill them. Be careful what you say. Speak life to those who cross your path"**.

The only song I can think of about frogs is "Jeremiah Was a Bull Frog"(which is one of my favorite karaoke tunes) by Three Dog Night. It might be interesting to see a remake of this song with a new verse retelling this frog story. It would be even more interesting if the new version was done by the group, Crazy Frog!

To further convey the power of words, in an interview with Oprah, the late Maya Angelou, acclaimed actress, poet and orator, said, **"People will forget what you said; people will forget what you did; but people will never forget how you made them feel"**. At least on my part, **I think this goes for songs too.** I cannot seem to forget how certain songs have made me feel at certain times in my life. Another way I've heard it said is, "People don't care how much you know until they know how much you care"-Zig Ziglar. In an email I received a few years ago, this point was made emphatically. The Story of Mark Eklund, the former Catholic School Student Killed in Vietnam, was a true story written by a Franciscan nun named Sister Helen Mrosla of Saint Mary's School in Morris, Minnesota. I'd like to briefly retell it now:

While attending a funeral for one of her former students, a teacher was made aware of some of the ripple affects of her kindness. The parents of the deceased soldier approached her and thanked her for a lesson she implemented in her classroom over a decade before. They explained to her how grateful they were to her for making their son feel special and they produced an old piece of loose leaf paper with thirty-something lines scribbled in different handwritings, to show her. When this teacher saw the paper in their hands, she knew instantly what it was. It was this boy's list of all of his classmates' compliments. You see, that day in school, the assignment's instructions were to write something nice about everyone in the class and share it with them. This boy's parents then explained to her that this list was found in this soldier's pocket when he died and that he always carried it with him. Several other classmates were in attendance at this funeral and many of them overheard this conversation. One by one, they all started chiming in about how they each still had their list and as one of their most prized possessions, they knew exactly where it was. Apparently this story was originally published in the Topeka Capital Journal in 1998 and was later reprinted in Readers' Digest. I can hear this story being recorded by a country singer, put to some sentimental music and sung with a lot of feeling.

This soldier and his family were fortunate to have something positive to focus on in difficult times but what if sometimes all somebody may have is a song? There are some beautiful patriotic songs (RTA) about freedom that hopefully bring solace to the many military families having to make some supreme sacrifices. Lee Greenwood's "Proud to be an American" always gives me fleebuzz (a term my high schools friends & I came up with for what we identified as sentimental goose bumps). Zac Brown sings about being "free as we'll ever be" and Kenny Chesney sings about "Freedom, Sweet Freedom". But all too often we all take it for granted. My husband recently introduced me to a song by a country singer named JJ McCoy. The day he originally heard it (either on Gator Country or Cat Country, our local country stations) the DJ explained that this song was written by a soldier feeling home-sick for "The Sunshine State" **(And ironically, apparently while this young man is over there facing death all around him on a daily basis, he too wants to escape to "Margaritaville").** The song names a few popular Florida destinations where this guy would certainly rather be; and has him reminiscing about "walking Duval Street with a Margarita in his hand".

And while on the topic of not appreciating how precious life is, I'm guessing that the man who wrote to Trace Adkins was having contact with people in his life, but unfortunately probably mostly negative. However if there was anyone in his life who was aware of his suffering and trying to communicate concern, **why was it that the words of a stranger on the radio reached him more deeply? Could it be that in some of our darkest hours, when we feel most alone, music is more capable of reaching our souls?** -Maybe so. **Maybe sometimes music creeps in when we're not really even paying attention before we have a chance to block it out or put up defenses, like we may sometimes be in a habit of doing to people in our lives.** Like when we're driving and we sometimes slip into automatic pilot arriving at our destination and not remembering all of the turns or the roads we took to get there. Maybe the repetition of certain rhythms accompanied by certain lyrics being recited as song refrains, burn into our mind's eye subconsciously. Other times, maybe the power of a song can be so compelling that we are stopped in our tracks and forced to focus all of our attention to those ones that really get through to us. They say that singing is a higher form of praying so maybe good songs are a higher form of communication. At the very least, a good tune with simple lyrics seems to be much more capable of permeating our memories. In this world of constant overstimulation by computers, email, voicemail, texts, Facebook, Twitter, Instagram, Snapchat, etc. etc. along with traditional television and radio, we often can't even recall our own phone numbers but like I said, most of us can recite Jenny's!

In support of this theory, Bob Seger says, "I like that old time Rock & Roll; that kind of music just soothes my soul". In the seventies hit, "Drift Away", Brothers in Blues sing: "give me the beat boys and free my soul, I wanna get lost in your rock and roll and drift away...when I'm feeling blue, guitar's coming through to soothe me...thanks for the joy you've given me, **I want you to know that I believe in your song,** with rhythm and rhyme and harmony, you've helped me along, making me strong **& I'm counting on you to carry me through**".

We all have days that we'd prefer to get past, and when we need to sing the blues, like a best friend, music will quietly accompany us. I also find that songs can stir my soul, just like Triumph's "Magic Power" describes with the following lines: "She climbs into bed, she pulls the covers overhead & she turns her little radio on. She's had a rotten day, so she hopes the DJ's gonna play her favorite song. It makes her feel much better, brings her closer to her dreams. A little magic power makes it better than it seems...You're thinking it over, but you just can't sort it out. Do you want someone to tell you what they think it's all about, are you the one and only who's sad & lonely...**Then you hear the music and it all comes crystal clear. The music does the talking, says the things you want to hear**...I'm young, I'm wild & I'm free. I've got the magic power of the music in me. The world is full of compromise, the infinite red tape. But the music's got the magic, it's your one chance for escape...The music keeps you going & it's never gonna stop..." (Thank you to Sam Densler of Songwriters Island for reminding me about that one hit wonder!)

I cherish the memories of certain stages in my life but Adkins' "You're Gonna Miss This", has a way of humbling a person into appreciating those moments as they are happening, not wasting them away complaining. A few decades ago, Heinz ketchup immortalized Carly Simon's hit, "Anticipation". I appreciate how this song celebrates the excitement of looking forward, but I mostly love the line,

**"These are the good old days".**

Appreciating the here and now is a topic that I will revisit with the help of lots of songs, later. For now, let me just say that the above lyrical examples seem to support the idea **that songs can be like friends who remind us of what's important in good times and bad.** And I suspect that I'm not the only one to sense this. Sometimes all we want is a temporary escape; like the woman in the old bubble bath commercial who sinks into her tub at the end of a long, stressful day as she sighs, "Calgon, take me away". Certain songs can help us daydream of being on a serene island while in the middle of a traffic jam. This is a concept that Jimmy Buffett has built a career on. He has been known to explain that "Margaritaville" is not a place; it's a state of mind. Sometimes like Kenny Chesney says, **"leaning on some friends I know, The Road and the Radio"**, music is our partner on a long, lonely road trip.

Other times, all we want is to be understood. The empathy that exists through so many songs can be a real friend in times of need. Maybe that depressed Trace Adkins fan actually did not have anyone in his life. But maybe the kind father figure voice coming through the car speaker was enough to lighten his loneliness and remind him that it may be time for him to reach out again. As the song depicts, hopefully good memories from the past came rushing into his heart, reassuring him that good times can come again. It's likely that he received the message that from now on, he should make the most of them. This applies to all of us. And when these good times do finally come and we no longer need to drown out our sorrows, our friend, music will take our hand and lead us forward urging us to skip along with it and sing a happy tune!

At the very least, music can keep us company as we interact with the world around us. In *The Sound of Music*, Julie Andrews claimed that "the hills are alive with the sound of music". John Denver sang praises for nature in his hits, "Rocky Mountain High" "Sunshine" and "You Fill Up My Senses". James Taylor sang "Fire and Rain" in coping with human loss and Bob Dylan told us, "The Answer is Blowin' in the Wind". **Could it be our instinctive nature to relate to our world through song?** New born babies often require white noise to be able to sleep. While in utero, all sounds must seem like muffled humming. But like in Dr. Seuss' *Horton Hears a Who*, it must bring comfort to know that there is a world out there. In the hit, "Sir Duke", Stevie Wonder says, **"Music is a world**

**within itself, with a language we all understand**; with an equal opportunity for us to sing, dance and clap our hands, You can feel it all over". We are born with a need to know that we are not alone; so when no one else is around, the voices on the radio can fill a void. I admit, from the age of twelve, I could not walk into a room without turning the radio on. I remember hearing the broadcast first hand when Elvis died and when John Lennon was shot. When I think about it, that was around the time several of my siblings were leaving for college and my mom began working full time in order to compensate for the additional expenses of cars, insurance and tuition. I probably found solace in just having extra voices in the room. Maybe I began to lean on the radio as my imaginary friend. Even today, I always work with it (usually Radio Margaritaville or BeachFront Radio or Songwriters Island, w/ an occasional switch to jazz or classical stations) on in the background. Coming from such a big family, commotion feels more normal to me while complete silence makes me restless.

Then there are times when it seems there is no immediate answer to our problems but somehow knowing that somebody else has walked in our shoes, provides some comfort, like when recession hit home for my family. **For anyone facing downsizing, "Times are rough and I've got too much stuff", from Jimmy Buffett's "One Particular Harbour", seems so simple yet profound.** Songs that tell stories that we can relate to whatever we may be going through, can really put things into perspective. As my son points out, Eminem's award winning song, "Lose Yourself", delivers a convincing message to today's generation about making the most of opportunities. This song gets through to me because it always leaves me craving to hear it again. I put it on my iPod which I keep on shuffle mode for jogging, and lately I keep finding myself hoping that it's coming up next. It is so powerful because you just know that his message is coming from his experience, and he speaks of demons we all have inside: doubt, insecurity, hesitation, fear of failing, and fear of succeeding. This song lurches you from that point, to a point of getting out of your own way, to seize all that is available to you. **Sometimes a song can do this more simply than a lecture or a book.**

According to my brother Don, who attended a recent performance by Dennis DeYoung, originally of Styx, this musical genius is now addressing the crowd at his concerts, explaining how his current success is based on not giving up but giving it one more try and how he wrote the classic hit "Lady" on a Wurlitzer piano in his garage. I remember one of the first seasons of American Idol, when present-day megastar, Carrie Underwood confessed that she almost didn't even try out for this contest. It's hard to believe that someone with such a powerful voice and dynamic presence on camera, could have ever doubted herself but we've all been there. We all do this. **In "Someday I Will", Jimmy Buffett sings, "If it never worked before, try just once more, that's what your heart is for".** These artists, along with countless others, deliver compassion and motivation through their music. I'm proud to refer to them as "artists" as:

> **so much of my personal experience has added up to life imitating art in the form of song lyrics.**

So can music make a difference? I guess that's a personal question to be answered on a case by case basis depending on how much credence you give it. Let me just say, that if you are going to give it considerable credence, choose wisely and then let it serve you well. **There is a multitude of wisdom and lighthearted joy to be found in the world of music.** Should you attempt to turn to music for a higher purpose, plenty of inspiration can be found there too. In "Let it Be", The Beatles share a religious experience. In "Show Me the Way", Styx finds religion. In "I Can Only Imagine", Mercy Me can bring anyone with a soul to weep. In "Day by Day" from *Godspell*, Robin Lamont sings a prayer. There are songs about healing and healing our land. Jonathan Butler's song on that subject is mesmerizing. In "Work it Out", by Jurassic Five featuring Dave Matthews, we are challenged to "Live and learn, soul search and make it right". In my youth, a Coca-Cola commercial popularized a song by The New Seekers showing flower children standing in a field singing **"I'd Like to Teach the World to Sing in perfect harmony,** all standing hand in hand and hear them echo through the hills for peace throughout the land". I'm not saying that we can solve the world's problems with one happy all-inclusive song, but it could be a good start. And I can't think of a better time for someone to remake the 1965 song, "What the World Needs Now is Love Sweet Love" written by Hal David.

There have been countless benefit concerts in support of all kinds of good causes. There are multitudes of poems, quotes and stories, full of positive messages that would make great subject matter for songs, and I'll include several of my favorites throughout this book and many more in the online Appendix accompaniment. Kansas' hit, "Dust in the Wind" was inspired by the title line which was found in a book of Native American poetry.

**The thing is that song lyrics, whether put to symphony or reggae, are really just lines of poetry made to look cool. Rhyming stanzas become lyrical refrains which breathes new life into them. It is my belief that if we let them, they in turn can breathe new life into us too.**

In the next chapter, I'll explain more about this *new life*.

"When Life leaves you speechless,
Songs give you Lyrics to Find Meaning."

2

# A New Lease on Life
("Another Pleasant Valley Sunday" The Monkees)

Today I met Jerry, a middle aged scruffy looking man dressed in faded workman's clothes. Upon first glance at him, I wondered to myself if his similarities to The Grateful Dead's Jerry Garcia, stopped with his first name and appearance. He pulled up in his dusty F150 pick up, arriving twenty minutes early for our appointment. I suspect that he hoped to enter the rental house on his own before I arrived instead of waiting for me to accompany him for the showing, as is protocol. Since I live right around the corner from this particular property and as their real estate agent, the out of town owners had entrusted me with the job of finding a suitable tenant, something told me to go directly to check on this house instead of stopping by my own place first to unload my groceries and let the dogs out.

Once again, my instincts guided me correctly! As he put his truck in park, Jerry was surprised to see me pulling in right behind him. He confessed that he had hoped to go ahead and start getting a look around before I got there. I chose not to make an issue of the likely assumption that his agent had probably given him the combination to the lock which is a "no-no" in our business. Something in his voice during our earlier phone conversation spoke to me on a deeper level and reminded me to empathize with this man even though his tenant screening report revealed some unfavorable information. He was just so relieved to find a place to hang his hat. He wasn't going to complain about the extremely outdated house or the complete lack of privacy in the back yard. The energy in his voice only revealed his relief that this landlord did not reject his application based on his tarnished credit score. I smiled to myself knowing that I was partially responsible for that. Having seen so many decent hard working people recently displaced from their homes, I chose not to pass judgment on this guy and encouraged the homeowners to give him the benefit of the doubt as he attempted to make this new start. After all it was only a few years earlier that I was in his shoes. Besides, he had scraped together enough from his present pay to adequately cover the necessary deposit.

So as the ice cream in my back seat began to melt, we proceeded to take a brief tour of the house (a 3 bedroom, 2 bath 1980's canal front home that did not sell after 3 years on the market). Jerry nodded in approval as we walked through each room. But as we made our way back toward the front door, he paused and shared some of his thoughts as he reflected on better times before October 1st, 2007. He explained to me that this was the day that he received that devastating call from the city development department informing him that all new contracts for his services were being cancelled for budgetary reasons. While I was securing the key back in the lockbox, he hesitated and looked at me shaking his head. He sighed, "Before then everybody was so happy. I don't understand what happened". My immediate reaction to his words was pleasant surprise. I found it unusually refreshing to meet this guy, someone who didn't have a multitude of theories on what exactly went wrong causing this housing crisis and who was to blame!

**I offered him sympathy and words of encouragement, assuring him that he was not alone and shared that it was actually October of '05 which was a similarly fateful time for me. During that month, I experienced some of the most exciting (good and bad) times of my life.**

On October 17, 2005 I was dancing on air following a private concert by my lifelong idol, singer/songwriter, Jimmy Buffett at the grand opening of one of his new restaurants in my hometown of Fort Lauderdale, Florida. I was overjoyed to be chosen from the crowd to join him on stage for a rendition of one of his greatest hits, "Cheeseburger in Paradise"! For me, meeting this star, whom I had admired since the age of twelve and had grown up attempting to emulate his lifestyle, was a dream come true—

**Time seemed to stand still in that moment when Jimmy paused in the middle of a song and said, "It's time to call some 'Reeferettes' up here"**

(his band is called, The Coral Reefer Band). He followed by saying, "You can't come up here if you don't know the words, so on the count of three, everybody sing the chorus". My husband, Hugh was pushing me to the front of the crowd and cheering me on, yet commenting that I might be flirting a little excessively. I remember snapping back at him exclaiming, "It's Jimmy Buffet, of course I am"!

**I'm sure that I must have looked like one of those crazed Elvis or Beatles fans, grinning from ear to ear, batting my eyelashes and blowing kisses in his direction, but apparently it worked!** ...............

**Jimmy looked directly at me** as I flawlessly belted out, "I like mine with lettuce and tomato, Heinz 57 and French fried potato, big kosher pickle and cold draft beer, Good God Almighty, which way do I steer"? Then he pointed at me like one of those posters you see of Uncle Sam and said, "You"! I felt as if I were Courtney Cox when Bruce Springsteen chose her from the crowd to join him on stage in the MTV video that was commonly aired before her career had taken off (one of my present coworkers adores Bruce Springsteen as much as I adore Jimmy Buffett, so she loves imagining herself in this scenario every time I retell this story)!

This is when I froze in total disbelief.------------------

**All I could think to myself was that suddenly I wasn't sure I could remember the words to "Happy Birthday"!**

I hesitated because I didn't want to overstep my bounds and get in trouble with his intimidating body guard. Plus I didn't want to trip on all of the instruments' cords and ruin the whole show! It was such a tiny stage. I didn't know which way to turn. Then one of the security guards came over to me and held the rope up over my head in order for me to pass under. His expression flashed a scene in my head from the *Vacation* comedy movies when Christie Brinkley is skinny dipping in a hotel pool and she calls out to Chevy Chase who is gasping from the pool deck, "Well, are you going to go for it"? It seemed as if this was the question that the guard's facial expression was posing to me. As I realized that the other two women who had also been chosen were already in place on either side of my idol, and that this was a once in a lifetime opportunity, I finally snapped out of it and leapt onto the stage, wedging myself in between them. In the photo from that evening, there is no missing my starry-eyed grin during that brief encounter when I got to rub shoulders with this legend. And to this day, my husband teases me because I have not yet washed that blue sun dress!

That night I was able to slip an envelope to Jimmy's promoter who promised to give him the fan letter I had enclosed. The next day, unbeknownst to me, my husband, Hugh posted my letter on BuffettNews.com and encouraged me to read some of the responses it was getting from other Parrot Heads. One such entry, from a blogger named, "Mr. Twain", said, **"It's so cool how one Parrot Head's life experiences seem to mirror those of so many others.** Thanks for sharing that. We need more stuff like that". And in response to this one, another named, "Grams", said, "Isn't that the truth!! Great Letter!!"—these encouraging words from like minded individuals (that I still have yet to meet), are part of what prompted me to take on this writing project years later!

Then one year, for Hugh's birthday, I posted a message titled, "The Top Ten Reasons I'm Glad I Married You instead of that Buffett Guy!" And I'm not sure how much Hugh liked it, but someone named, "Tequilla Revenge" said, "Hebert, you made my summer. That's beautiful". Of course I'm always wondering if Jimmy visits that site and corresponds under an alias??? (If you'd like to see these letters you can refer to the section called "I've Got Letters to Send You" in this book's online appendix).

## "Did it Really Happen? Was I Really There?"
### Cheeseburger in Paradise-Plantation, FL 2005

*Anyway*, like so many Buffett related events, the proceeds from the tickets sales and Buffett memorabilia auctioned off that night, benefitted charity. This time it was the Make-A-Wish Foundation ®, established to bring hope, strength and joy to children with life-threatening medical conditions. However by attending and supporting this fund raiser, I in turn had one of my life long wishes granted! I remain ever so grateful to this organization for this, and now hope that the proceeds donated from the sale of this book at any of their future events, keeps "paying it forward".

This night came at a time when I was living in my dream home which my husband and I did our best to transform into our own "Margaritaville". With both of us being native Floridians who grew up on Buffett music, it was only fitting that we carried this tropical theme throughout our home featuring a tiki bar as a focal point. We had taken advantage of the real estate boom and upgraded our house and filled it with lots of toys. Our two boys were taken to school and their sports activities by golf cart. We enjoyed the nature preserve bordering our property and had the new boat in the marina down the street.

On the topic of boating, I'd like to share that for me this activity has always been thought of as a luxury that I've never taken for granted. The truth is that I was not raised near the water. We lived more affordably inland and my family did not have a boating budget. When I was growing up, as much as I loved going to the beach, it meant a 30 minute commute across town through traffic and a hassle to find a parking spot in the paid lot once there. Then all of our gear had to be dragged from the car to the shore. But I do remember being so excited when mom and Aunt Mary would plan these all day outings even though it required a lot of effort on their part, packing picnic supplies and piling our whole gang in their station wagons so all of us cousins could spend time together this way and I remember actually liking the feeling of having vertigo afterward from hours of playing in the waves.

However it wasn't until I transferred to college in Tampa as an adult that I was fortunate enough to befriend a girl whose father left his 15 ft. Boston Whaler at his vacation condo nearby in Englewood, for her to use. **It was during those weekends spent with her that my eyes were opened to all of the beauty of Florida's west coast in a way similar to what Jimmy Buffett sings about in "First Look"** where he says, "that's when I swallowed the hook, on my first look around". During those island escapades with my friend from Illinois, I was delighted to encounter dolphin playing in our boat wake and otters playing on the dock as we pulled up to some of our favorite dockside spots. The friendly people we met and the old Florida style sites we encountered, like one of the most quaint places in the world, Cabbage Key near Captiva Island (celebrated in Michael Franks' "Barefoot on the Beach" song and rumored to be where Jimmy wrote, "Cheeseburger in Paradise", although I've heard conflicting stories), really made an impression on me. I remember this friend commenting to me that I was the one from Florida, so I should be the one taking all of this for granted. But for me, these boating excursions made me feel like a kid in a candy store. And I remember thinking to myself, with all of this beauty so conveniently located within our state, why would it ever be necessary to travel to Hawaii or other exotic locations? I guess I should have been careful about what I wished for, because to this day, I have yet to venture there and actually hardly ever leave the state of Florida!

Then when I met my husband, he had friends with boats. When we were dating, one of our favorite outings was to join the crew of a sailboat and participate in a weekly race across Tampa Bay. But don't be fooled. It was more of a booze cruise and a reason to play songs like Buffett's "Boat Drinks" and strangely, we never won the race! Then when we moved to Ft. Lauderdale, Hugh talked my brother into letting us use his boat in exchange for Hugh's marine mechanic skills. I'm positive that in those years, we put ten times more hours on that old Glastron than my brother ever did. But that brother, appropriately named Jim, knew that we took better care of it than he did so he didn't mind. I can honestly say that close to a quarter of my sons' childhoods were spent aboard a boat. Don't get me wrong. We still worked very hard and put in lots of hours at the office but Hugh always made sure that we still had these family quality days as often as possible. We'd pack a picnic lunch and all of their favorite beach toys and spend hours building sand castles, going on nature walks and teaching them to throw frisbees and footballs. And it was Hugh's brainchild to hide "pirate treasure" (loose change, costume jewelry, fake dablooms from the beach shops, tied in a sack or tossed in a Ziploc) buried and marked with an "X"; when we went to island beach destinations. Our boys' eyes sparkled as they unearthed various shiny trinkets which they later added to their shoe box collections tucked under their beds; and we treasured the memories we were creating of these adventurous expeditions with our boys.

Babies love the water and the motion, and there is nothing like having a little one doze off in your arms at the end of a day spent in the sun, swimming and sight seeing. **Looking down at those contented, pink little cheeks kissed by the sun, and soothed by the twilight balmy breezes with mellow music like Jack Johnson or Dave Matthews playing in the background was time I'd never trade!!** When **Jimmy** sings about family boating time in **"Delaney Talks to Statues"**, he says, "Father, daughter, down by the water. Shells sink, dreams float...**Life's good on our boat"**. And Hugh and I too, look back on those times as some of the most sentimentally valuable hours of our lives.

Let me add here that we didn't even consider getting our dream home until Hugh was first able to get his dream boat. And I remember our conversation leading up to that purchase...It went something like this- Hugh could justify any expense by convincing me that such indulgences were actually business expenses because by either joining a country club where he could impress businessmen with his golf skills or by getting a boat so we could better relate to the waterfront lifestyle of the clients we hoped to attract, our business clientele would become elevated. Then I asked Hugh which one he liked better (golfing or boating); to which he answered, "that's like asking me which one of my children I like better!" Then I remember thinking that if I encouraged the golf option, I'd be a golf widow with two very young golf orphans (meaning that the boys & I would never see him) but if I encouraged the boating route, at least that could be something we all could enjoy together as a family and we surely did!...

So once we were able to increase our sales by the percentage needed to buy our own boat, Hugh proudly deemed this 1999 27 ft. World Cat that he was ready to take off the hands of a successful business man from Michigan, to be named the S.S. "Hebert Necessity" (pronounced, "A-Bear Necessity") and he had some guys with a booth at the boat show design a logo with a picture of Baloo, the Bear from the Disney movie by that name (fast forwarding, Jimmy's new album includes a song written by Jerry Jeff walker's son, that acknowledges, "Something About A Boat, gives a man hope!)

And since this new boat was good at handling deep waters, on one memorable Easter morning voyage, Hugh was determined to get through Port Everglades Inlet and out on the ocean before sunrise. He wanted the boys to experience the sun coming up over the horizon from this vantage point. So we got our forlorn guys up around 5:00 a.m., let them hunt for their Easter baskets, scurried them into the truck, and set out for the marina.

**The sunrise was glorious that day, but before the day was over, we all witnessed something even more profound.**

After fishing several miles off shore for a couple of hours with no bites, and watching the boys gobble down numerous jelly beans and melting chocolate bunnies, we decided to head in, because we were going to meet my dad for noon mass and an afternoon Marlins' Game. As we got about half way back, Hugh spotted something floating in the water. He explained that fish often congregate under floating debris because they like the shadows these objects create, giving them shade. When I asked where we were going, Hugh pointed to a grayish triangular large object floating on the surface about 100 yards in the distance. As he pointed, the boys and I squinted and fixated our eyes in the direction of the object. But as we got closer, we began expressing some hesitation. Eric said, "What is that?" Little Hugh said, "It's a fin!" To which his father and I said, "Oh no, no it couldn't be. Or if it is, it's somebody's idea of a joke" (I remember thinking that it looked like the wing of a small airplane or like part of the mechanical shark in the old *Jaws* ride at Universal Studios). Then Hugh proceeded to bring us right up to this gray triangular floating object......just as it began flapping and went under water!!! Then we all saw a 30 ft.(well, let's just say it **was** bigger than our boat anyway!) basking shark rolling over in the water's surface and then go under!- which left us all completely speechless! It must be similar to what whale watchers experience. We just couldn't believe our eyes. Then the protective mother in me, ordered Hugh to take us away from there before this enormous creature capsized us!-(the front deck of our boat had little railing and the surface was flat enough to become like a slide if we tipped too much). And as our boat turned and made a b-line for shore, we kept recapping the incident and questioning if it really happened. Yesterday I heard a commercial ask, "What is the most amazing thing you've ever seen?" That brought this story & the quote, **"Life is not about the number of breaths you take, but about the moments that your breath away"** to mind. I can't believe that I never even got a picture of that thing, but then again, since I'm sure it'll forever stay stamped in our minds, I guess it's neat to know that it'll be one of those special sights and memories shared only by the four of us.

Especially with this example, to say that boats can open up a whole new world for you is not an exaggeration. As we all know, Jimmy Buffett could not be the person he is today without all of his nautical experiences. Kenny Chesney's song "Boats", explains that the most important feature of a boat is **the way it can make you feel**, as he sings, "Old Joe's got a Boston Whaler, he bought in Key Biscayne. He swears since the day he got her, she's been nothing but a pain, When the suns at his back and the winds in his face, it's just him and the wheel. **He wouldn't take a million for the way it makes him feel**. Boats, vessels of freedom, harbors of healing, boats…" And in "Boats to Build", a duet with Alan Jackson, **Jimmy Buffett** says: "Sails are just like wings. The wind can make em sing, Songs of life, **songs of hope, Songs to keep your dreams afloat**". Musician and songwriter, Jack Mosley sums it up this way: "They dance to a rhythm that comes from the sea; they're not afraid to live out their dreams. Here's to Small Boats on Big Oceans & life lived at sea, to the few brave souls who dare to believe that there's more to this life than an office downtown. **Here's to Small boats on Big Oceans** and dreams you can't drown". This same artist also has a song called "Time on the Water" with the words: "When I've had enough of all of this stuff…I need Time on the Water; when you know in your soul that's the way it's supposed to be". Then there's Christopher Cross' timeless, "Sailing": "Well it's not far down to paradise; at least it's not for me. If the wind is right, you can sail away and find tranquility. Oh the canvas can do miracles, just you wait & see, believe me. It's not far to never, never land, reason to pretend. And if the wind is right, you can find the joy of innocence again...Fantasy, it gets the best of me when I'm sailing. All caught up in the reverie. **Every word is a symphony**, won't you believe me?

**These guys seem to be either on something, or *onto* something.** They seem to be describing a natural high, similar to John Denver's, "Rocky Mountain High". I believe they're trying to share with us how rejuvenating water can be. I think that even body surfing can simulate the rocking motion that most of us might subconsciously associate with being rocked to sleep as infants, just like Darius Rucker's remake of the "Wagon Wheel" song…"hey, mama rock me". Those who are fortunate enough to spend time out on the water seem to be living the dream. The fortunate thing about it though is that it doesn't seem to matter what type of boat you're on. The experience is not reserved for yacht owners. Kayakers and cruisers alike seem to benefit from time on the water. It doesn't seem to be about the way you get out there, it's just that you do get out there, away from it all, in touch with nature and in touch with yourself. I think that's the freedom that Kenny Chesney is referring to above.

Maybe it's because it's kinda hard to multi-task when you're under way (unless you're in a yacht) so you become a captive audience to the fresh air and the sun shining on the water. And when our boys joined us, unless they wanted to jump overboard, they had to sit and face us and talk to us (actions that aren't so easy to always get them to do these days now that they're teenagers!) and it usually turned out pretty well. We even once helped them with some of their required reading for school by taking turns reading aloud passages as we idled through shallow areas or anchored in some quiet spots (one book that lends itself well for doing this, is our town's local author, Wilson Hawthorne's "The Last Pirate" (w/ lots of seaside imagery).

Eric & Hugh Hebert-Singing a Boat Tune, 2002

In the interactive site connected to this book, I actually got a lot of help on the boating songs category. I found an edition of the Boat U.S. Magazine on my bathroom floor (which is where my husband usually leaves it) with a headline that caught my eye. It was an article titled, "The Boating Playlist". And some of the comments that the author, Tim Murphy shared were: "When I was 16 years old and living in the fo'c'sle (bow area that houses crew) of a 130-foot brigantine the first time, I heard "Song for the North Star" –**one of many times my life was incontestably steered by a song**". Mr. Murphy goes on to explain that the list he provides comes in two halves. The first part is a top-10 list, based on a survey of boaters conducted by Discover Boating, an arm of the National Marine Manufacturers Association. Then he says, **"The Starter Kit wouldn't be complete without highlights from the whole Jimmy Buffett oeuvre. In fact, it's no accident that our first playlist begins and ends with Buffett.** He's even hiding there in the middle. **Love him** or hate him, **JB's music has thoroughly infused the boating scene since his 1977 release, "Changes in Latitudes**, Changes in Attitudes". And (according to him) his better songs came before that: By the following year, when

54

"Cheeseburger in Paradise" hit the airwaves, **Buffett's Parrot Heads would evermore dominate the space where boats and music meet"**.

And jumping ahead, Zac Brown has a more recent release with the lines, "**You can find me where the music meets the ocean**...You Can Jump Right In". In Jimmy Buffett's song, "The Coast is Clear", he shares: "I come down to talk to me when the coast is clear". This song shares how he gets back in touch with himself in this therapeutic way. And for many people, going to the beach and at least being able to be present with this form of nature, has a similar affect.

**Maybe for me, I appreciate how a sailor has to consult his *navigational charts* in order to steer his course at sea, because I have made it a habit to consult the *song charts* for guidance and direction in my journey through life! Maybe like an anchor can keep a boat grounded, I rely on good lyrics to keep me grounded.**

One song that instructs us on taking action is Swing Out Sister's, "Break Out" with the words, "The time has come to make or break. Move on, don't hesitate. Break out". Jimmy Buffett is very convincing when he sings, "Come along and have some fun. The hard work has been done. We'll barrel roll into the sun just for starters"-"Barometer Soup". And many people choose to come to Florida for this type of retreat and sing along with Jimmy as he says, "taking time to escape the maze, blue skys and ultra violet rays,...Floridays".

When I think about Jimmy's mom's advice (printed from a t-shirt produced by his sister which I will share later) about living by the sea, I think about how many people tell me that we Floridians are living the dream. I am perceptive to their sincerity when they express how coming to the beach makes them feel like coming home because I know what they mean. They don't have to be a native Floridian like me to relate to this longing. When I briefly went to college in the mountains of North Carolina, as much as I enjoyed getting to see the seasons change, and the undulation of the rolling hills which was all new to me, ultimately I longed to get my toes back in the sand. And I think we all benefit from being near or in the water.

In its purest sense, water cleanses us and quenches our thirst. Obviously we use it to refresh and to bathe; but I'm talking about water in a deeper sense now. **I'm reinforcing the concept that water and being in it or near it, can possibly help to wash away our troubles, just like all of these guys are singing about.** Taking in the beauty of the sun shining on the water can soothe our souls. And isn't it handy that the Earth's surface is made up of ¾ water? And the human body is made up of similarly significant proportions of water. Without water, we cannot survive. But maybe this is truer in more than just the physical sense-? Whether driving or walking across a room, do you know anyone who can be near a water view and not glance in that direction? Have you witnessed others coming in contact with the sound of the surf and not tilting their heads to stop to take a brief listen? Haven't you seen people smelling the salt air and almost subconsciously joined them to take a whiff with satisfaction? I believe we all may be programmed or least compelled, to take water in with all of our senses. And the contentment this brings has led many to sing about it. To further demonstrate, I'd like to share a verse from Brad Paisley's "Water"- "Inflatable pool full of dad's hot air, I was three years old, splashing everywhere, and so began my love affair with water". **And of course, Jimmy Buffett has a whole album called, "Hot Water" (whether this is referring to a hot-tub or his boyish mischief, it's something he seems to like being in!).** In another of my favorites he says, "Take Another Road to a hiding place, disappear without a trace....Leave my cares behind. Take my own sweet time. Oceans on my mind!"

There are several commercials that remind us to make a point to get away from it all (just like JB sings, "we all deserve a happily ever after Every Now & Then") like the one from Royal Caribbean Cruise Lines telling us "the sea is calling, answer it royally" and the RV commercial saying, "Find your away" or the car commercial telling us to "release your inner Mustang". And then there are several by Mission.org (but it is funny how a large percentage of my seasonal neighbors are actually here from Michigan?). The beauty of childhood is that it is meant to be free of distractions. Most kids don't (and shouldn't have to) worry about daily responsibilities and pressures like we take on as adults, so they can more easily get in touch with their joyous side. But most of us adults need these commercials and songs to remind us to retrain ourselves to not succumb to the vastly overly stimulating world we live in. And usually getting away from it all is easier said than done. Just like Robbie Dupree sings, "Why Don't We Steal Away" because sometimes finding a way to make this happen, does feel like you're having to steal or escape from regular life in order to covet your own small piece of happiness. But when we do manage it; we always swear that we're going to do it more often because it does seem to allow us to return to daily life with fresher perspective.

Once while at a theme park with the boys, I asked my husband why he seemed so stressed. His answer unfortunately, did make a lot of sense. He said that he felt like he was supposed to be doing something else. What I didn't realize was that his voicemail was filling up with messages from clients and coworkers making requests of him. This made me so sad for him not being able to let go like we all need to. Then I thought about how in my dad's day, he could take a full two week period of time and drive out of state to a cabin in the woods (with no phone) and not have to bring along a cell phone to tie him down. In Michael Frank's song, "Barefoot on the Beach", he says, "safely out of reach from faxes and the telephone". Present times would require him to add: texts, email, ipad, etc., etc. (skipping right over the beepers era). So, while modern advances add conveniences, I think they also rob us of some of our freedom. And I guess until they perfect and reasonably price waterproof phones, so far water is one place, thank God, still safely out of reach!

In "Finer Things", Steve Winwood says, "While there is time, let's go out and feel everything. If you hold me, I will let you into my dreams. For time is a river, rolling into nowhere. We must live while we can and drink our cup of laughter". Kenny Chesney's song, "Reality" puts it this way: **"For me it's a beach bar, or on a boat underneath the stars,** Or with my band up on stage, for a while everything's okay. For some it's a fast car, moonshine in a mason jar. And everybody has their way somehow to escape Reality, yeah, sometimes life aint all that it's cracked up to be. So let's take a chance and live this fantasy cause everybody needs to break free from reality. Yeah some days it's a bitch, it's a bummer. **We need a rock and roll show in the summer to let the music take us away, take our minds to a better place where we feel that sense of freedom".**

These are examples of the importance of occasionally getting off of the treadmill of life and taking a different path, maybe even down a country road. John Denver and James Taylor each certainly found clarity on their "Country Roads". This method better suits my father and brother, who love the mountains. I recently gave them each a t-shirt that says, "The mountains are calling and I must go". Sometimes it's not possible to actually go right then and there so you may have to do like James Taylor when he sings, "I'm Going to Carolina in my Mind".

One year when Hugh and I attended a family reunion at a lake in the mountains of Georgia, my aunt Mary offered to watch our seven week old infant and his toddler brother so Hugh could give me a tour around the lake. During those brief moments on the back of his jet-ski, with a soft breeze on my face, cruising around taking in all of the scenery and gazing up at the blue sky, I did a little meditation. I told myself to take it all in, and store this freeing feeling so that I could conjure up this peaceful place in the future whenever I felt stressed. Similarly, once when having some minor surgery that required general anesthesia, as I counted backwards into unconsciousness, I remember telling myself to go to my happy place. After the procedure when the nurse tried to pull me up and help me regain consciousness, she said I was giggling which was unusual for most patients she encountered in this position. Then I told her that I was dreaming that we were at the beach and I was trying to get back on our boat from the shore (which was tough to do gracefully) & always required a helping hand from someone already on board in order to be hoisted up.

In Smash Mouth's, "Walking on the Sun" they remind us, "don't delay, act now, time is running out". Well, I'm not suggesting that we live in fear because our days are numbered, but the truth is, someday time will run out for each of us. As they say, "nothing is certain but death and taxes!" In *Dead Poet Society*, Robin Williams played the role of a high school teacher encouraging his students how to relate to the words of some of history's greatest poets and more importantly; he taught them about the power of acting on your instincts and standing up for what you believe in, reinforcing the concept of "Carpe Diem" **"Seize the Day"**. Which I have also seen posted as **"Seas the Day"**! (fast forwarding again here, I really do feel the world lost a great one in this talented actor).

Similarly, Kevin Bacon's character in *Footloose* (which included great music by Kenny Loggins), led his high school on a dance revolution even though he had to rebel against previous laws and closed minded elders in order to make it happen. Then there's the classic movie, *Ferris Beuhler's Day Off*, when Matthew Broderick has the time of his life indulging in a little (mostly harmless) rebellion from his regimented life. My son was so proud when his social studies teacher praised him for laughing when he called out "Beuhler (pause)...Beuhler" during roll call on the first day of school!-telling him, "finally! I've been doing this for years and you're the first one who's ever laughed!"

*Anyway,* returning to the time when the housing market was on the fast-track, many people we knew were investing in vacation homes in order to have their reality outlets but we always told ourselves that our boat was our vacation retreat. It was what Hugh called our "In Town/Outa Town" or our form of what many people refer to as a "Staycation". Hugh even really thoroughly enjoyed working on the boat in every capacity-changing the oil, tinkering with the engine, periodically bottom painting & polishing it, even emptying the head!). He really worked hard to get that vessel and he took a lot of pride in it. **So we worked hard and played hard and strived to achieve a balanced life. And Life Was Good.** Our real estate business was affording us a rewarding lifestyle in south Florida. We felt "we had it all just like Bogie & Bacall, sailing away to "Key Largo"-Bertie Higgins. The necessary monthly outlay to keep this up was astronomical, but money for the bills was always just the next transaction away - that was until the day that the transactions stopped coming...

**Well, I've heard it said, "Into each life,**

**a little rain must fall..."**

Apparently it was our turn for a downpour, because exactly one week after the *Cheeseburger in Paradise* Grand Opening, Hurricane Wilma hit our hometown of Ft. Lauderdale (yes, the song by The Scorpions that says, "Here I am, rock you like a hurricane", came to mind along with America's "Sandman" song, with it's hurricane reference refrain). But while we suffered very little compared to the devastation from Hurricane Katrina that year in Mississippi and New Orleans, **we didn't realize that this storm was part of a chain of events which would cause us to have to make some seriously uncomfortable lifestyle changes.** Several active hurricane seasons led up to this time. Numerous tropical disturbances continued threatening our coast throughout the years of 2004 and 2005. It seemed like we were making storm preparations every other weekend; putting up shutters, taking in patio furniture and plants, stocking up on water, ice, canned goods, flashlights, batteries and gasoline were only part of the necessary time consuming tasks. Making arrangements for pets and safeguarding sentimental valuables and important credentials, as well as testing out the portable generator in case we actually got hit, were also crucial steps. Each time we were "in the cone" (comedic musicians, Pete & Wayne, who are regulars @ Sloppy Joe's in KW, have a hilarious song called "In the Cone Again" with apropos lyrics describing the situation, even with a reference to weatherman, Jim Cantore, put to the tune of Willie Nelson's "On the Road Again!); *anyway*, it meant losing several days of work because everybody in town was preoccupied. If we had pending closings, homeowners insurance could not be granted as long as the storm was "in the box". And if a property did become damaged, transactions were further delayed awaiting new negotiations, insurance claims and repairs (especially if the damage required replacing roof tiles). For months after a serious storm, finding a match to each specific shade and shape of roof tile was now a challenging feat. People would drive across the state and form lines around city blocks at the mention of a new shipment of certain tiles.

As far as the damage to our own home after Wilma, we lost about a quarter of our roof and three quarters of our patio screening. The storm rolled in about six hours earlier than the projection we last heard when we went to bed the night before. From the onset of the howling 100+ mile per hour winds that woke us up in the wee hours of the morning, we could hear ceramic roof tiles bouncing above our heads. As curiosity got the better of us, we ran to the one window that we hadn't been able to get covered in time, to get a peak outside. Despite the fact that we thought that we had tied down all objects that we couldn't carry in, we saw our 80 lb. barbeque grill rolling into our pool. Against my protests, Hugh ran out to catch it just in time. Also fascinating to watch, were the four foot rolling whitecaps escalating in the neighborhood retention pond and then slamming through the back yard. Later we discovered that the rock climbing wall that had been attached to the boys' backyard swing-set, had become embedded high up in the trunk of the next door neighbor's front yard Oak tree. Our home was certainly still habitable, and none of us were hurt but conditions in town were not so conducive to daily living.

(NationalGeographic.com photo)

Prior to this storm, Broward County had not actually been directly hit by a hurricane in over 4 decades, and despite several false alarms, we were not prepared for all of the effects of this one. Most traffic lights were not operable so every intersection had to be treated as a four way stop. Trusting that other drivers would adhere to this instruction was unnerving. Driving at night was completely out of the question. Downed power lines dangled across roadways and you never knew if a puddle contained a live wire (actually at least one in a neighborhood near the Everglades unfortunately did, and resulted in the death of a toddler while on a walk to get some fresh air with his mother). Household supplies were scarce. Residents had to stand in line in the heat for hours if they were lucky enough to find stores that were open and stocked. Of course, looting was also a negative byproduct of this crisis. Without air conditioning in South Florida, it was necessary to sleep with the windows open. For safety reasons, if you were operating a generator, it had to be kept outside but the thick cord kept the door ajar. This was a very populated town and most of our neighbors were used to keeping their doors locked and the security alarms armed throughout the night. Now we were all on one big camp out! As food in our fridges began to spoil, we held campfires to make use of what we could preserve. There was an initial camaraderie in the cul-de-sac as we all celebrated our relief in our survival. But then as spoiled food, yard clippings, debris piles, sewers and body odor began to escalate; irritability and the reality of the situation began to settle in.

One day I went jogging to try to release some stress. Our neighborhood was surrounded by nature preserves containing many 60+ ft. high and 100+ year-old Pine and Oak trees. When I approached one part of the sidewalk that was covered in fallen branches, I tried to navigate my way through by hopping and skipping over the piles like I was running through an obstacle course. Unfortunately during this exercise, my calf must have brushed up against some disagreeable organisms on one of those branches which resulted in a rash across both of my legs and stomach (which persisted for 3 weeks & three doctors could not identify). Other lingering sites were tree roots now ripped out of the ground, turned on their sides and jutting up to 12+ ft. in the air. Several public parks were closed for over a year for clean up. Many neighborhoods did not have full trash pick-up for months. You know that feeling that you get after several hours of riding in a car when all you want is a hot shower and a healthy meal? We existed with that feeling for over a week, then like everybody else we knew, we decided to temporarily leave town. Besides, school had been cancelled, all of our closings had been cancelled, **and like the electricity, we were out of power to do anything else!**

Our first destination included a trip to Key West. There was an annual Parrot Head convention (described in greater detail in the next chapter) taking place on Duval Street that week even though so many of the bed and breakfasts had been flooded when the storm passed through that part of the state.

Next we visited family and friends in St. Petersburg. They got the weaker side of the storm causing very little disruption so all accommodations were in order for us there. We were having such a pleasant time avoiding the reality waiting for us at home. We took our time as we headed back in that direction meandering through Florida's west coast. Besides, we could only go so fast while towing our 10,000 pound boat which we used throughout the week to tour several new waterways with our boys and the family dog. **Hugh and I try to keep a mutual awareness for serendipity in life so we are always on the lookout for pleasant surprises.** During this return trip, we decided to take a detour from the highway to look for a good dinner spot and found ourselves feeling very at home when **we discovered the biggest tiki hut we had ever seen** at a place called, "Paradise Tiki Hut Bar & Grill". Of course the place was filled with Buffett style décor, easy going people and our type of dockside bill-o'fare. After dinner, we let the kids and our dog, Stitch (which our boys named after their favorite Hawaiian cartoon character), stretch their legs with a run at the nearby beach as we continued to enjoy the sites of Florida's west coast **within this small town atmosphere known as Cape Coral.**

Eventually, as we returned home, order began to be restored in Ft. Lauderdale. As we unpacked from our trip, we began to pick up the pieces of our little corner of the world and resume our daily lives. **However unlike the storm, our real estate business remained stalled.** Even so, we optimistically reassured ourselves that this was just a temporary slump which is a common tendency for those in our field. We were sure that it would bounce back any day, so for the next several months **we continued to pour our hearts, energy and life savings into what we thought was our future.**

My mother who had been a real estate broker since the 70's assured us that throughout her career she had fallen into a few ruts, but that "when the going got tough, the tough got going". Some of her other frequent quotes were: "God helps those who help themselves" and as every small business owner would attest, "it takes money to make money". So keeping all of this in mind, we consequently spent many hours and dollars distributing marketing material.

One night after sweating all day in the sun delivering our business literature on foot to surrounding neighborhood homes, we planned to spend the evening relaxing by the pool and barbequing by the lake. After soaking for a few minutes in the hot tub, Hugh realized that he had forgotten to bring out a towel so he jumped up and quickly ran back into the house to retrieve one. As he rounded the corner leading to the hallway bathroom, he slipped in his own puddle, slamming his shoulder into the ceramic tile with a powerful blow. Hugh is a broad shouldered guy with plenty of upper body weight and with the right amount of speed upon impact, tile can be bone crushing. This fall completely dislocated his shoulder and tore his rotator cuff resulting in the need for major surgery, followed by a lengthy and painful recovery period and mounting medical bills.

Being independent agents, we did not have comprehensive medical benefits with affordable group rates like those provided by large organizations. And there certainly would be no disability or unemployment checks coming! Most of our medical expenses had to be paid out of pocket since we had a plan with a *ginormous* deductible that even Hugh's surgery did not fully meet!! (and luxuries like the dentist or eye doctors were completely out of the question!) This was to say the least, another setback in our productivity.

When we bought our house two years earlier, we laid out a substantial down payment and now we had no choice but to take out an equity line on it in order to cover daily expenses. We had every intention of getting out of this debt once we could regain our footing. Simultaneously, it seemed that many local residents had gotten fed up with the repetitive active storm seasons and untouchably rising housing prices in south Florida at that time and decided to head for higher ground. Since our county, near Miami on Florida's east coast, was running out of vacant land, the builders started taking their business elsewhere and enticed these buyers to follow them. Suddenly, it seemed that everybody was talking about "heading for the hills" of the Carolinas, Tennessee and other neighboring states in search of less volatile climates and housing markets.

At this point, we yearned for the days when our biggest challenge was getting a contract written for our clients before some other buyers beat them out in a bidding war. We'd gladly take just one more sale, even if it was a difficult one. In our business, bringing buyers and sellers together often meant getting involved with all kinds of personalities and opposing goals usually creating friction among the involved parties, requiring a variety of life skills to successfully get to property closings. We like to think of ourselves as problem solvers. But now our biggest problem became trying to find a way to continue earning a living with these skills. As time went on, that probability became less and less viable. **Lots of people made predictions, but nobody knew when the housing bubble was going to burst. We all now only wish we *had* had a crystal ball! Everybody's got a story to tell about the day they were offered "X" amount for their home (which seems exponentially higher than today's market value)- And everybody follows up with what they coulda, woulda, shoulda done!**

Since our entire livelihood and that of most of my relatives was directly tied to the housing industry, we all just couldn't give up. Most of us took out new loans and took on extra jobs, convinced that this was all just a temporary situation. Hugh and I did both. I sought out jobs that would allow me to bring money in, but would not result in additional child care expense for my own kids and ones that would still also allow me the flexibility to drive my husband to and from his post surgery therapy appointments several times a week. I did telemarketing for an insurance company, made gift baskets for another company's marketing department and babysat other people's kids whenever possible. Hugh completed loan applications over the phone and tried to concentrate on his physical and our financial recovery. **When fall rolled around again, Hugh and I were watching for signs that we were on the right path to that recovery-**

Then an interesting DVD was dropped in our laps. Like in most sales industries, personal development and motivational programs were constantly being presented to us. *The Secret*, produced by Rhonda Byrne, is a presentation explaining *The Law of Attraction*. My Basic understanding of the idea is: "what you most focus on will manifest in your life". The scenes from this DVD demonstrated this concept in ways big and small and challenged us to give it a try. I do not recall what music if any, is played in this film, but I think it would be neat to have a collection of personal stories which support this concept, told in a song by someone like Jonathan Butler, who seems to convey wisdom when he sings, or maybe by Enya, whose music seems to carry a celestial or metaphysical vibe, or by Sting, whose voice seems to exude confidence, making any message more convincing.

*Anyway*, like the program suggested, Hugh and I agreed to pick a dollar amount that we would like to manifest into our lives. **We chose the amount of $20,000 of unexpected income to wish for and focus on.** We agreed to conduct normal daily activities, yet make sure each day to conduct brief meditations simply on that exact dollar amount. This was not a formal process. We'd just picture a check in that amount written to us while in the shower or while driving (you get the idea). We stuck to this routine for a couple of weeks not discussing this experiment with anyone else. **Now if this were a mystery novel, I'd tell you to pay attention to this point of foreshadowing!!!......**

As December arrived and it was time for the annual neighborhood holiday parade, we sponsored a nautical themed float. Our boat on the trailer was made to look like a sleigh pulled by our pick-up truck, which was made to look like Rudolph, followed by our neighbor's Jet Ski and golf cart - all in a "Christmas in the Caribbean" (Jimmy Buffett's Christmas album) theme. We organized a decorating party for our block the night before the event. While I was leading a group of children in our driveway in a painting activity to create the scene with Santa's packages, I got an interesting call from my younger sister, Anne. Anne's exact words were:

**"I did something that you're either going to be upset about or you're going to think is the neatest thing ever!"**

My confused response was to ask her to repeat that statement. As she began, I decided to remove myself from the group of busy elves and settle into my favorite Adirondack chair away from the noise. **I wanted to be able to give my full attention to what she was about to say. It certainly was not anything I could have predicted-** She proceeded to explain to me that she entered me and my family as contestants for the reality show, "Wife Swap"! In my impression, this is a show that addresses dysfunction in families and challenges two very different mothers to switch places for a week in order for all involved to learn tolerance and gain perspective on how the other half lives and to ideally maybe take away a few pearls of insight on how they may or may not want to incorporate some of what they learned in their households after the experience. But thinking that we already had the perfect life, my first response to my sister was to say,

**"What were you thinking?" But she quickly blurted out, "Wait, it's related to Jimmy Buffett!"**

Now she really had my attention! She went on to report that while driving to work that morning, she heard a casting call on the radio for "the best Parrot Head family". When she got to her office and submitted an online response describing us, the casting director immediately got in touch with her saying, "your sister sounds perfect for this" and she urged Anne to convince us to apply. Not thinking of myself as a confrontational person, and actually being a little shy, I was hesitant.

**Then she mentioned the fee that would be granted to the participants:…..$20,000!!** (*"things that make you go hmmm"…*)

So we spent the next several weeks filling out questionnaires, answering phone interviews (even our boys were interviewed), and creating our own demo tape, as the show's casting director instructed us to do (we even submitted one scene showing me grocery shopping for the family with a cart full of beer and Margaritaville brand Margarita Mix, while I said, "Only the essentials", like the scene in Jim Carrey's movie, *Dumb & Dumber)*! We got along great with the lady from the show, being a Parrot Head herself, but she kept warning us that all final decisions would be up to the producers.

And as much as this seemed like fate, it turned out that we weren't chosen for the program and to my knowledge; no such episode ever came to fruition. After the in-depth interview process (while it is the show's policy to not ever tell anybody a final "no" and certainly not with a reason),

**we were privately told that we were "too functional"!**

It seemed that the producers were hoping to find parents who indulge their children in all of the "Margarita Madness" at Buffett tailgate parties and maybe even regularly carry on like actual pirates, instead of **those of us who just incorporate a little escapism into our daily lives through this fun-loving music.** The irony of the situation was that without this additional funding, we became quite dysfunctional ☹ since we went on to lose our business and our house and ended up starting all over again just like my new client, Jerry. But as you will see**,** I eventually got through it all, **due in no small part to the help of some empowering song lyrics!**

3

# Af-*fin*-ity
## (why Buffett?)

This is a snapshot of the mysterious cloud that formed in the sky immediately following one of the shuttle launches at Cape Canaveral, an event Jimmy Buffett has been known to show up for -possibly to come see his friend, Desdemona? -& years later, actually ended up sharing about (what I suspect was this same day) in his song "The Rocket that Grandpa Rode"!

I'm so glad we didn't miss seeing this pre-dawn launch, from our friends', Mike & Zoe Grant's (parents to champion surfer kids) favorite spot on the beach in Melbourne. As we'll all never forget, the shuttle looked like the sun in a fiery orange ball as it appeared in the horizon and within seconds, zoomed out of sight. Like our space program, you never know when certain opportunities may be gone for good.

*Anyhow*, after the reality show escapade (described in the previous chapter), what left me shaking my head was-

**How could the producers of that show have had such a low impression of Parrot Heads to start with?**

This brought my attention to the realization that our group as a whole may be getting a bad rap. Sure, we're a bunch of free-spirited, coconut bra wearing, tequila chugging, in your face obnoxious song screaming nuts, but that's just on the weekends!—just kidding! That behavior is usually reserved for tailgate parties, concerts and conventions.

**The rest of the time, Jimmy Buffett fans, especially those who are members of the hundreds of fan clubs worldwide, are usually high functioning professional people who make fine contributions to society as well as to many charities. So please allow me to elaborate on the many virtues of Parrot Heads and attempt to explain our af-fin-ity for Jimmy Buffett and for one another........**

Of the more than 40 albums that Jimmy Buffett has produced, it's next to impossible to pick one favorite song. There are so many on so many different subjects. As I've been known to say, **Buffett music can be a sedative or a stimulant.** When we need to relax, he's given us a "License to Chill" and when we want to party, he'll join us for "A Livingston Saturday Night"!-But **I think it's the Calypso poetry that makes him a musical genius.**

To paraphrase a thought provoking comment in the book, *Jimmy Buffett and Philosophy*, published by Popular Culture and Philosophy, Jimmy Buffett has become a mastermind at creating his own niche. As I recall, in the song "We are the People our Parents Warned us About" he says, "I was supposed to have been a Jesuit priest or a Naval Academy grad. That's the way that my parents perceived me, those were the plans that they had. But I couldn't fit the part; too dumb or too smart-aint it funny how we all turned out?" and in "A Pirate Looks at Forty"(which he claims is not necessarily autobiographical, but I wonder?-) he states, "My occupation's just not around", so it seems that he went on to invent it– brilliant! In "If it all Falls Down", he sings, "Guidance counselor said, 'Your scores are anti-heroic, computer recommends hard-drinking calypso poet.'...Studied life at sea, studied life in bars; never passed my SAT so I thought I'd study extra hard!...We had plenty of lawyers, we had plenty of doctors, we had people to make us things, we had people to sell us those things,

**Didn't have enough room for those things,**

(as I would soon learn the hard way! ☹)

we build lots of self storage...**Calypso Poet shortage!**" And in the next chapter, hopefully you will join me in seeing how I feel this guy was ahead of his time in knowing the skill of how to reinvent oneself & also in recognizing society's tendency toward collecting clutter. Good for him and good for us. **I for one, find a great deal of direction in a great many of his songs.** For instance, I invite you to listen to some of the words to a song that I find to be full of hope, faith and inspiration:     "Someday I Will"

"Big or small, if you have a passion at all,

say someday I will.

Whatever thrills you, anything you love to do

say someday I will.

**You don't have to know who, may help you**

**make it come true,**

**Just say someday I will.**

**You don't have to work it all out;**

**you don't have to tear it all apart,**

**You just need a place to start..."**

**Also before this story is over, you will see how I relied on these words** to get me through some hard times. And this is one example of how this mogul of the Margaritaville empire, can just speak so plainly and reach so many of us eager to learn from his success.

**And I think I speak for most of us when I say it's not just his financial success we admire. It's more like we admire**
his **Happiness Quotient**
and the example he sets for us to reach for our dreams

and follow our instincts like despite discouragement, he found a way to do.

To further support this point, I'll share a quote by the late entrepreneur & inventor, Steve Jobs:

"**Have the Courage To Follow Your Heart & Intuition** They Somehow Already Know What you TRULY WANT TO BECOME"

And I am learning that when I follow this instruction and follow my first instinct in making choices, it **always** turn out better. Of course, I'd like to think that my instincts are relying upon prior knowledge and previous lessons learned, but more often what pops in my head seems to be unpredictable yet eerily accurate.

In his songs and in any interview that I've ever seen or heard, Mr. Buffett genuinely seems happy. Like Frank Sinatra's, "I Did it My Way", **Jimmy Buffet's songs share his steadfast ability to be true to himself. Ironically, that characteristic**

**could be a large part of what makes him a better person for everyone else.** I watch closely when he is performing. When you think about it, some performers just go through the motions. Can you imagine having to muster up enthusiasm to sing Margaritaville for the gazillionth time? I personally get impatient during his most common playlist because I'm so anxious to hear some of my other favorites. I find it interesting when these songs are all someone knows, yet they claim to be a big Buffett fan. I call these people, "Parrot Head Posers" and I get frustrated for them because I think they could be *missing the boat!*

In his early work, Jimmy produced a song discussing his insistence in writing and singing for personal reasons, not for what his agent wanted of him in order to make him more marketable; similar to a concept explained as a battle between the ego and the spirit in the book, "The War of Art" by Steven Pressfield. I guess Jimmy has showed that former agent! **By remaining true to his art, and surrounding himself with multi-talented musicians,** I'm sure he's made more money than either of them ever dreamed! He used to claim that he had never won an award for his music, but he said, "with fans like Parrot Heads, that is reward enough!" However in June of 2011, Jimmy won the Country Music Channel's Performance of the Year Award for his "CMT Crossroads" episode featuring himself with The Zac Brown Band. If I'm not mistaken, during this performance, Jimmy gave Zac a significant nod of approval as he handed off the proverbial "tiki torch" (a guitar pick) to this protégé, with words of praise and encouragement for his future in this business.

I find further demonstration of my point in the feel good movie, *Cityslickers*, where Billy Crystal portrays a frustrated advertising executive in a mid-life crisis. As a result, he and his two best friends decide to partake in a cross-country adventure with a group of ranchers. During this expedition, Billy's character meets an older & wiser cowboy who claims to know the secret to life (I once saw a decorative sign in a house I was showing to a perspective buyer, that said,

**"What if the hokey pokey really is what it's all about?"**

which is also the name of another Buffett song!) *Anyway*, in the movie, this guy dies before they reach the end of the trail but fortunately that is not before he has a chance to share this secret with Billy. He tells him, "It's all in your little finger". Then he explains that it's something different for everyone and each of us has to figure out for ourselves exactly what is most important to us in life and then focus on it & let that be enough to make us happy. Billy's character has an epiphany and realizes that he already has all he's ever wanted waiting for him back home. Like Dorothy in the *Wizard of Oz*, he realizes, "there's no place like home". And in the movie, *The Bucket List*, the bittersweet ending has two elderly gentlemen who are facing terminal illnesses, discussing how it is the belief in some religions that when we encounter God, He will instruct us to sum up our life on Earth with only two questions. The following lines are delivered by the calm, omniscient-like voice of Morgan Freeman:

**"Did you find joy? Did you bring joy to others?"**

Well, if you ever make a point to attend a Jimmy Buffet tailgate party and concert, apply this question to this performer. From the looks of all of the beaming, smiling faces that I encounter at every concert I've attended, my idol will pass this test with flying colors! And just maybe all of us Parrot Heads are not so crazy to repeat the phrase,

**"WWJBD= What Would Jimmy Buffett Do?!"** (this line can also be found in Alan Jackson's, "Five O'Clock Somewhere" & in The Boat Drunks', "This Aint Duval St"). Still, being raised Christian, and striving to raise moralistic children, I do not mean any disrespect. I did not come up with this quote. I realize that in its original form, "WWJCD="What Would Jesus Christ Do?"; this phrase challenges us all to be virtuous, compassionate humans. But it is comforting to think that maybe we can do this and still enjoy ourselves. When the

"Wife Swap" producers were interviewing me, they asked me what kind of people I did not like. I didn't have to ponder that one very long at all. As a very young person, I realized that self-righteous hypocrites rubbed me the wrong way. I'd like to think that I have nothing in common with people who go around judging others and thinking that they're better than anyone else. My husband's answer was, "I am only intolerant of intolerant people!" He read a comment from a blogger on Buffettnews.com that had this to say about the idea of a Buffett-themed "Wife Swap" episode: "They are probably going to pair you with a Mormon family or the like. Hopefully by the end of the week, Linda will have all of the kids skillfully operating a blender and asking, 'Why is Jimmy always skipping Provo?!!'"

But as far as having a right to enjoy ourselves, if Jeremiah, the bull frog can claim, "Joy to the World", shouldn't we join in? Shouldn't we figure out what we get *jazzed* about? Maybe Jimmy Buffett isn't such a hedonist after all. Maybe we've been right all along to follow in his ways of worshiping nature and seeking all of the joy that this world has to offer. So, like Morgan Freeman tells Jack Nicholson (in the movie mentioned above) right before he dies, "Go find your joy" or according to businessman and author, Jeff Olsen, "Go find your music"...

**Well for us Parrot Heads, we know its Buffett music & the lifestyle he portrays and we don't hold back about it!** The leaders among us have even created a whole Trop Rock genre (which a while back, I heard DJ Jeff of BeachFront Radio, claim that this genre now apparently has its own sub-genre, "Conch Rock"). This culture has its own award ceremonies and events year round run by The Trop Rock Music Association and newsletters and timely articles about living this coastal lifestyle shared in blogs and online magazines such as**, http://phlockersmagazine.com/.** To get a visual on what it's all about, I suggest checking out the video on Don Middlebrook's song, "Wagon Wheel Gone Trop Rock"! Some fans even turn their own backyards into venues for house concerts (like the ones we've been invited to @ the "Sandbox" & "Higgins' Mostly Bar & Grill" & "The Laughing Parrot" & The Bat Cave" BTW, Hugh & I reserve the name "Someday Isle" for the one we're dreaming of creating someday in the near future!).

*Anyway*, if it's true that Jimmy Buffett put Key West on the map, then he certainly paved the way for other performers to follow in his footsteps and play his cover songs nightly in the many venues that keep that town as a popular tourist destination. **However evolving from there, so many of these guys (&gals) have so much talent that they've taken it a step further and written & recorded much of their own well received material.** There are now popular Trop Rock bands/artists in towns across the country and fortunately, we get to hear them on a variety of independent stations & even some on Radio Margaritaville. And for a complete guide to the "Who's Who of the Trop Rock world", we can turn to Andy Forsyth's book, "Trop Rock Songs/Stories and Tales from the Singers/Songwriters". We also get to see most of them, all in one place, once a year in a larger than life 5 day "Woodstock style" music love fest **Phamily Reunion** (parrot Heads prefer to use the "ph" for the "f") called, **"The Meeting of the Minds"**, held annually in Key West at the end of October (and NO, it is not "Fantasy Fest"---its our own event!!).

Upon our first time attending the annual "MOTM" convention, Hugh and I had the pleasure of meeting a band called **"The Boatdrunks"** and their vast following from the Chicago area. As we got to town late into the evening on the first night, it seemed everybody else had a healthy head-start as far as being in party-mode. And as we rushed into the original Margaritaville on Duval Street to get caught up, we encountered a huge crowd practically hanging on the edge of the stage, as these guys announced the next song. I'll never forget feeling confused as the floor suddenly seemed to clear and some guy bumped into me saying, "We get in a circle for this one mam". What happened next had me even more perplexed since I thought I knew "all things Buffett". Then this group of adoring fans linked arm in arm in a huge circle, and began swaying back and forth as they all sang along to the Boat Drunks' anthem, **"Hollow Man"**. It was quite a "Kumbaya" moment for all of those present. Several hours later, Hugh and I sat at a bar across the street and bought this group's lead singer, Mike Miller a drink as we shared compliments of the powerfulness of his song. I remember Hugh telling him that if he could just once again channel the state of mind that he was in when he wrote that song, he undoubtedly would have another hit on his hands!

As far as us Trop Rock fans, I'll share a conversation I had with my friend, Sam Densler of Songwriters Island. His station features only original music, written & performed by the songwriters and his events showcase their work.

As Sam and his wife, Gina and Hugh and I and our friend Laurie (who is membership director of the Trop Rock Music Association) sat at the Lazy Dog in Key West listening to Wes Loper last year, I asked, what do you think it is about this whole scene that makes us all feel like we're on a natural high? It's not that we're just a bunch of bar flies. Promoting this music is a hobby we're passionate about and take seriously. We usually are so caught up in the performances that we don't tend to drink much at all. I think these events are kind of like our grown up version of an amusement park **(BTW, are we the only ones whose favorite part about going to Universal Studios in Orlando is knowing that we're going to end the day with happy hour @ Margaritavuille?)**

But back to pinpointing what it is that makes us so keenly in tune with these musicians- **I suggested that maybe its because we know we are in the presence of people who are following their dreams.** I relate to this idea like Jimmy's line in "I Wish Lunch Could Last Forever" when he says

"Carnival's in the Air". It's similar to the concept of "oneness". As I mentioned in this book's intro, one thing I've noticed is that when many people are focused on one thing, like holiday spirit on Christmas Eve or patriotism (especially when our country is being threatened), or even a flash mob formed to make an impression for a special event, it is the collective energy that raises all of our spirits. And also like I previously mentioned, I suspect that this oneness is what Bob Marley was referring to in his "One Love, One Heart, let's get together and feel alright" song (this concept also became the theme that Lucy Buffett called upon to bring unity to the gulf recovery process).

I think another reason we're so excited for these guys is because most of them are just so delighted to have a chance to have an audience that they beam contentment. They're up there doing their thing and that makes most of them happier than the large percentage of the population who never go for it. But many of these guys & gals have other full time jobs & this is something they may never have thought they could pursue. Later I'll share a poem called Someday Isle, that addresses procrastinating happiness but for now, if I had to identify a song that delivers the same theme, it would no doubt be Trop Rocker, Jack Mosley's "The Sand". In this one he restates, "happiness is a state of mind…**Live your life like it's a Jimmy Buffett song"**!

A conversation I had with one of my local favorites, Scott Novello of our area's "High Tide" band, told me that people ask him all of the time if he is going to try to make it big; to which he replies, "I am very happy being booked around town regularly and visiting with local folks and making them feel good with my music. I'm not looking for anything more". Scott's 6 yr. old daughter though, may prove to be a different story--when he hands her the mic. & she belts out every word of Jason Mraz's "I Won't Give Up" not missing a beat or a syllable of those tricky lyrics, she usually gets a standing ovation! High Tide has a refreshing eclectic playlist with somewhat of a reggae vibe. And in my opinion, they do exactly what they're supposed to: provide relaxing yet fun background music so you can still have a conversation or a mellow dance with those you came there to enjoy it with. High Tide has the gig at some of our favorite waterside spots like Nervous Nellies, overlooking the bridge into Ft. Myers Bch. & Miceli's, just over the bridge in the nearby fishing town of Matlacha, & Low Key Tiki, just past there into rustic St. James City toward Pine Island). Just before sunset is my favorite time to take in this whole scene.

One of the things I love that Scott's band also does so well is what I like to call a (& I'd like to coin this phrase)-

## "Song Smoothie" (a blending of a couple different songs that starts with one, leads to another, borrows the refrain from one that fits well & then returns back to the original, for example, Van Morrisson's "Into the Mystic" to Zac Brown's "Free" & back, -kinda like a lot of great foods blended together, only this kind (like Buffett's "Juicy Fruit" is good for your soul!).

So now back to the "Why Buffett" issue? And maybe the reason I feel so compelled to explain myself is because my teenage boys give me such a hard time about this. My older one tells me that to him, **Buffett is like Broccoli**…it's something that he was so forced fed when he was young that he can't stomach the sight/sound of it now (although like the vegetable, he acknowledges that most likely someday, he will concede that he knows it is good for him!-just wait til he gets to college & attends a pool party where the girls are all in bikinis- then he'll boast how he knows all of the words to all of the Buffett songs!!). And this leads me to another of his comical comments: One day he called me into his room & shared with me an episode of the satirical show "South Park". He had cued it up to play a scene where they were doing a Buffett parody (which I like to think of as a "parroty"!) *Anyway*, the main character was attending an aides benefit when the scheduled act backed out (I think it was supposed to be Elton John according to the show's script)and Jimmy

Buffett was substituting for him. Then Eric Cartman blurts out, "Oh no, nobody likes Jimmy Buffet except Frat boys (& I jumped in w/ "that's not true") but then he finished that statement with "and alcoholic women from the south!" (to which I said, "oh"… ☹ in a low voice as I looked down feeling quite guilty!) Then they show Jimmy's character singing "wasting away cuz of aides & stuff".

Well, I'm sure that the writers of that show will admit to being equal opportunity offenders! And my younger son, Eric says that back in the days when we used to take them boating through Port Everglades and out to the point where there was no land in sight, **there was more Buffett music than water!!** But in my defense, I still think of this guy as a family man **who, if nothing else, focuses on appreciating nature and certainly knows how to tell stories about making friends,** which I still think are good lessons for my kids!

And speaking of friends who pave the way for one another, at that first MOTM we attended, one of the scheduled performers was a guy we had never heard of at the time. Nonetheless, while we were holding our breath hoping that Jimmy would show up (BTW, Trop Rockers have produced some funny songs about us naïve MOTM newcomers like Rob Mehl's "Waiting for Jimmy" & Kelly McGuire's "Blame it on Jimmy" & The Boat Drunks' "The Girls all Want to See Jimmy" & Matt Hoggatt's "Dear Mr. Buffett" (who was lucky enough to finally get some support from Jimmy!) *Anyway,* as I was saying, it seemed everybody else was willing to stand in the rain for hours to make sure that they didn't miss one minute of Jerry Jeff Walker's performance. It seems to be common knowledge that he was one of Buffett's mentors during his early days in Key West. But this rough and tumble former Key West carouser, sings one of my favorite love songs, a beautiful devotion to his wife called, **"Lady in Texas"** that speaks from the heart so honestly and comes across so genuinely. I also find myself occasionally repeating his line, "It's not like I got a bunch of bodies in my trunk…I'm an Alright Guy"(from a song by that title);

especially on days when I feel I might be being too hard on myself! To my knowledge, the only hit this artist ever had played on the radio was "Mr. Bo Jangles". But this guy has a vast loyal following just the same. So when all of us Parrot Heads are singing along with **Jimmy** to his song, **"We Learned To Be Cool From You"**, we're thinking of Jimmy, but Jimmy just may be thinking of his old friend, Jerry Jeff?- (along with the other greats he sites in the song).

As far as Jimmy Buffett showing up at these conventions, let's just say that he's never officially on the schedule--But we will always envy those people who share their real life "close encounters of the Buffett kind" or a rare "Buffett sighting" as fate landed them in the right place at the right time. We hear how they were grabbing a quick cheeseburger and a cold Landshark at Margaritaville and suddenly a hush fell over the crowd. As they looked around, they saw the staff rushing to lock the doors to keep the place from becoming mobbed and realized that the expressions of sheer exhilaration, similar to someone who just realized that they had won the lottery, on everybody's faces, was due to the sudden presence of the ever famous and infamous legend of Key West getting ready to treat them to an impromptu performance! Then there's the legend that the "Balcony Girls" tell of how they got to meet Jimmy during a concert back in the 80's; or how our friend, Tom got the casting call to be an extra in the shooting of the "Fruitcakes" video-or skipping ahead a few years, those that were fortunate enough to be in the crowd when Jimmy surprised them at the street fest (the part of the MOTM that is open to the public, held smack in the middle of Duval Street). I wore black all that week that year because I was in mourning about the fact that we weren't going to be able to get away for it then and my "Jimmysense" (like Spiderman's Spidysense), just told me that this was going to be one of those years that he would show up! I think I must have heard the cries of exhilaration from the crowd, all the way across the state because I woke up in the middle of the night with a strong feeling that we had missed something special and sure enough when we got up and checked the computer, the whole incident was reported with the headline, "Key West's Favorite Son appears for crowd...."! Uugghh ☹ Jimmy's got a song called, "I heard I Was in Town", which describes his own surprise at how his fate starting with his days arriving in Key West as a struggling musician, has ironically played out. **In his own words, "a great song is more than just words and music. It's like a thumb pressing against the pulse of living that relates a simple truth about a complicated process"**. In my opinion, this singer/songwriter has mastered the art of simple truths of our time.

I did warn you in this book's introduction, that **"I Hear Voices"**, like the song of that name by Randy Orton. And the more research I've done on this topic, the more I find others who feel the same way. I was recently delighted when my husband and I sat down to watch the Kenny Chesney DVD and heard some of this artist's comments. In this film, he reflected on his journey as a performer on tour and shared background information on some of his songs. When he stated,

**"You hope somebody sees their life in your song"**, I wanted to reach through the TV screen and reassure him that we do! He acknowledges, **"We all have a song that somehow stamped our lives, Takes us to another place & time**...And I go back to the loss of a real good friend and the sixteen summers I shared with him. Now "Only the Good Die Young"(Billy Joel), stops me in my tracks; Every time I hear that song, I go back..."

And Eric Church appeals to Bruce Springsteen fans while reminiscing about growing up to so many of this star's hits. He says, "To this day when I hear that song, I see you standin' there on that lawn, discount shades and store bought tan, flip-flops and cut-off jeans. Somewhere between that setting sun, 'I'm on Fire' & 'Born to Run'...When I think about you, I think about 17, I think about my old jeep. I think about the stars in the sky. **Funny how a melody sounds like a memory. Like the soundtrack to a July Saturday night"**.

Just like BJ Thomas announced his thoughts on the subject back in the 70's, **"I Believe in Music**...Music is Love & Love is Music if you know what I mean". (The thing is, I do know what he means!) **People who believe in music are the happiest people I've ever seen**. So clap your hands & stomp your feet & shake those tambourines. Lift your voices to the sky & tell me what you see. I believe in music. I believe in Love. **Music is the universal language**, and Love is the key to peace, hope and understanding and living in **harmony**".

Another local trop rock performer in our area, named John Frinzi is growing in popularity as he is consistently booked at Margaritaville while continuing to produce his original work. One of his CD's, "Shoreline", has seven songs co-written by Tom Corcoran. Tom also wrote two of Jimmy Buffett's classics, "Fins" & "Cuban Crime of Passion" along with several books, including one titled, "Jimmy Buffett, the Key West Years". Upon our first encounter with John Frinzi, my husband and I found his voice so close to the sound of Jimmy's, that we quickened our pace down Duval Street when we heard him singing to see if we might be among those in attendance during one of those surprise sightings of Jimmy!---which of course, was not the case but the talent & the energy at that Street Fest **did not disappoint!**

Hugh and I were very excited though, when we did see ourselves on the Jumbotron at Margaritaville in Orlando as they showed various concert footage and we were some of the lucky ones filmed at one of those tailgate parties. At the concert in Tampa that year, I wore a shirt that I had made with a photo from the night I got on stage with Jimmy, with the words, "Did it really happen, was I really there?"-"Stars Fell on Alabama". Hugh wore one with the same picture, only his said, "My own darling *Linda* & some pretty boy with *no* hair!"-"Blonde Stranger". It was so much fun answering other fans' questions about how we got a photo with Jimmy or if we had photo-shopped it, etc. That is one story that I'll never get tired of telling! **I just wish I could have gotten to at least shake his hand or talk with him for a few moments but still, it is an awesome memory!**

We have also been fortunate enough to have a picture of our family doing the fins salute, posted on the bulletin board at the original Margaritaville in Key West. And one Miami Dolphins game during the year when their stadium was called, the "Landshark Stadium", proved to be profitable for us as Hugh joined me in wearing a grass skirt and bikini top. The Parrot Head Club was invited to participate in the half time show and be treated to a pre-game concert, where Hugh actually got a nod and a smirk from Jimmy! The monetary profit though, came from all of the dollar bills that strangers kept stuffing in his string bikini top!!

As for Jimmy's fans, by being the best he can be, I think he treats us right too. I have heard him refer to himself as "a shameless entrepreneurial entertainer". As to how functional we fans may be, Jimmy has said, "Parrot Heads are like Deadheads with credit cards". Well, in this economy, I'm not so sure that is so true anymore but nonetheless, **we are determined to keep the *fun* in *fun*ctional!** When we have our heads in the clouds looking for Jimmy's plane, "The Hemisphere Dancer", we still have our flip flops planted firmly in the sand.

A comment that comes to mind is another quote from the movie, *"Ferris Beuller's Day Off"*. That movie became one of the top grossing films of its year, I feel for several reasons. First, the overall *life is short message*, so divinely expressed by a young Matthew Broderick, as he was among the first to break the fourth wall, and step out of character to speak directly to the camera, (and was the first in my memory to include an after the credits clip). This theme was expressed in the movie's promo poster with the tagline, "Leisure Rules" (pretty Buffettesque if you ask me!). Then there was the inclusion of so many landmarks of Chicago, the writer, John Hughes' (good name!) hometown. He said the film was his love letter to this city. Also, someone had the foresight to cast young Charlie Sheen as a very convincing drug addict-(who knew?? LOL!...sorry Charlie, still lov ya!) Lastly, there was the unforgettable music played during one of the final scenes, the song called "Oh Yeah"(which I love to jog to) made famous by Yello, sung in a super low voice. *Anyway*, in one scene, someone is polling students throughout the school about what they think of Ferris. One guy says, "He's a righteous dude". Well, I guess that's how I feel about Parrot Heads. I for one, want to set the record straight and stick up for our honor. We are not raucous home-wreckers; at least not on weekdays! Seriously, the misconception that we're all about irresponsible Margarita Madness is way off. We just remember how to party like teenagers even as we approach our later sixties like our fearless leader! Even in this recession, **we're not ready to "throw in the *beach* towel" on the sunny side of life!**

In "Nautical Wheelers" Jimmy sings about "living & dying in ¾ time" and while most of his material is not so much about such serious subject matter, it is interesting how sometimes his fans treat it with reverence. For example, I'd like to share a Facebook entry posted a few years ago by DJ Jeff of **BeachFront Radio:** "Last song on our 2-4-1's dedicated to **Bry Harris** from **Parrot Island Band** who fulfilled a dying man's request earlier today and sat by his bedside singing Jimmy Buffett songs to him while strumming gently on the guitar. Bry, you are what the TropRock world is all about. Thank you, **DJ Jeff Allen and The Amish Beach Party Radio Show".**

I of course clicked, "like," on this entry and then commented, "Great story, Buffett ballads do make a great sedative; when it's time to *rest in peace*, what better way to make the transition---Good for you for delivering such, *last rights*, Bry. And ironically, I had Buffett ballads playing on my portable CD player, in the delivery room, when my children were brought into this world"-

The following popularly circulating email depicts most Parrot Heads' perspective on life, if you ask me-

"I Love This Doctor" by Hunter S. Thompson

"**Life should NOT** be a journey to the grave with the intention of arriving safely in an attractive and well-preserved body, but rather to skid in sideways- Bible in one hand- chocolate in the other- body thoroughly used up, totally worn out and screaming 'WOO-HOO, what a ride!!'"

One guy, who apparently lived by this philosophy, was the infamous Captain Tony, whom Jimmy immortalizes in a song called, "Last Mango in Paris". During one trip to Key West, Hugh and I met 'ol Captain Tony, who according to legend, was once elected Mayor of the city because of his impressive resume as everybody's favorite bartender! On the night that we discovered this place, we encountered the man himself propped up at the bar, signing ladies t-shirts (while they were wearing them) and not missing a chance to sneak in a little flirty smile or kiss as he posed for pictures, oxygen mask and all!

**The only thing that a Parrot Head might want to add to the above statement about life, is that we need a pitcher of margaritas in our hands too!** With an ever optimistic liaise-faire attitude, we follow the policy that **when life gives you limes, make margaritas!**-an attitude that can be very helpful these days!

We are also happy to bring others along for the ride as Parrot Heads (the official international organization being called, Parrot Heads in Paradise, Inc.) are known to happily share their time and good attitudes. As I said, Parrot Head Club events categorically benefit charities. Since their inception, over 200+ Parrot Head Clubs around the U.S. and a few international ones, have donated over $30 million to local and national charities and accumulated over 4,000,000 volunteer member hours. The purpose of this Parrot Head Nation, founded by Scott Nickerson in Atlanta, is "to promote the international network of Parrot Head Clubs as humanitarian group sharing information and social activities for mutual benefit. With the general welfare of the community in mind, their purpose is to assist in community and environmental concerns and provide a variety of social activities for people who are interested in the music of Jimmy Buffett and the tropical lifestyle he personifies". **In other words, we party with a purpose!**

Through our moves around the state of Florida, my husband and I have been card carrying members of three such fine organizations. Through this venue, we continue to form life-long friendships with like minded kindred spirits. The Charlotte Harbor Parrot Head Club has strong membership and frequent events in "Buffettesque" places like "The Navigator", a rustic fish camp style waterfront establishment, complete with gator on the menu and an airstrip in the parking lot. This place has been voted best Trop Rock Venue several years in a row. Owners, Dennis & Nancy never charge a cover. They regularly host entertainment and only ask for a non-perishable food item to be collected & donated to charity (or a specific item that the artist of the day is passionate about sharing). To follow is a picture of Dennis showing off his vintage Buffett collection (including one of my all time favorites, "Ridles in the Sand" especially because this one contains our wedding song). Also in the background of the photo is singer/songwriter, Paul Roush, performing his originals including the very endearing song, "God Watches over Fools, Drunks & Children, & We've Been All Three".

Most of their events, as well as most of what's going on around town, are regularly promoted in this area's South West Florida Parrot Magazine. And if you're lucky, the staff for this entertainment magazine will treat you to a ride on their custom stretch golf cart, which they can be seen driving through Buffett tailgate parties and local events. Just like Buffet concerts, at these events, we're all phamily!

Robert & Kristen-arriving in style!

**At the last concert, I contemplated what specifically it was that I appreciated so much about Jimmy Buffett as a performer. Then I realized that oddly enough, every time I see him up there skipping around with the enthusiasm of a child, I am proud of him.** After the last encore, once we've all leapt to our feet and clapped until the lights have come up, I mentally applaud him once again. As much as I've had a great show, and my husband and I have gotten every penny's worth, because Buffett concerts are truly all-day events, it's more like I am happy for him. It's like I want to say, "Good job! You did it again!"

Jumping ahead again, at a concert in Australia, he fainted and fell off the stage. There was a brief blip about it on the news. Apparently it was just a mis-step coupled with exhaustion and probably some dehydration. From the video clip that I watched, it just looked like he had poured out every ounce of energy for the crowd that night (which is not uncommon for him) and was finally ready to exhale. Up to that point, his concerts normally did not include opening acts or breaks. I think that as a performer, Jimmy Buffett gets caught up in the act himself and doesn't ever want to short change his fans. As much as he has a reputation as a beach bum, it is evident that his present empire has been built on a strong work ethic. That year his tour was called the "Finland Tour", referencing the commonly known fan salute derived from the ever popular song, "Fins". A few years back, the name of the tour referenced the Circus. In a song called, "Big Time under the Big Top", he describes how his act is like a circus rolling into town. It's an annual event with a well established theme where everybody partakes in the celebration with festive costumes and traditional party behavior. It is so true. He has shared that he grew up watching his parents enjoying Mardi gras, and I think that he does his best to recreate that aura of indulgence for us. I'll repeat again, that as he says in "Changes in Latitudes", "if we weren't all crazy, we would go insane". **I have also heard him describe his perceived job as being the responsibility of keeping summer around as long as possible.** And we can't deny that certainly, if anybody deserves the title of being the son/sun of summer, he has earned it! However, I do know of a certain Trop Rock fan that moved back to Florida by being motivated to do so solely by Howard Livingston's "I'm living on Key West Time" anthem! Welcome back where you belong, my friend, Laurie! (wish I could sing it to you in the "Welcome Back Kotter" tune!) Howard also hosts a show that is pretty convincing on this theme!

One of Jimmy's concerts was actually broadcast live on CMT. It was his "One Love-One Ocean" (slogan created by his sister, LuLu) event, a free concert benefitting the Gulf Coast after the oil spill crisis. This upbeat show brought a realization to the area that all was not lost. And the word is that those who were lucky enough to be in attendance still swap stories about what the day meant to them. One such fan, who apparently had to travel to get there, wrote: **"When all seems bad, partying with Jimmy B sounds like medicine worth the price of any plane ticket"**. I say, "Amen to this"! As I surely relate to the medicinal purposes of it! At the Florida state Fair Grounds in Tampa, the gates open first thing in the morning for a 7:00 p.m. show so that all of the die-hard fans can start setting up for an all day tailgate party. Often before we all get there, we even start with pre-parties the night before. And if you're in the Tampa area, there is no better venue for these parties than Skipper's Smokehouse. The outdoor courtyard is shaded by a canopy of tall trees and the benches, barstools and bandstand are what you might expect at a rustic Jamaican camp ground. But they serve up plenty of oysters and beer and homemade music which is the perfect warm-up for a Buffett concert.

At the tailgate party, people transform their cars into sharks, beaches, swimming pools, tiki bars, variations of famous places like Margaritaville, Captain Tony's, and The Southern Most Point/Portable Bar (just to name a few that we stopped by that day)! And people dress in costume as everything under the sun including sharks, parrots, pirates, cheeseburgers, blenders, mermaids, hula girls and certain song characters like the exotic dancer, Carmen Miranda. It's not just the women either-there's nothing like the men in their coconut braziers! People partake in activities such as: Buffett trivia contests, paddle board demonstrations, hula hoop contests, giant games of *Twister*, S*lip-N-Slide*, Spin-the Wheel style games of chance, Shot-ski Tequila shots & Jello-shot consumption, dancing and plenty of exhibitionism! My favorite is just to people watch because there's always plenty of interesting sights! We've watched people go by on horse-back, motorized coolers, giant bicycles, on top of taxis, on double-decker buses with fully stocked convenience-store style refrigerators, golf carts of varying sizes and themes, RVs and scooters.

For many groups, this is a reunion where they bond with old friends and for a day, they get to act like kids again. It's an escape where the world does not exist beyond their booth. For others, it's a day for making new friends. Within the boundaries of these events, I have yet to meet an unfriendly, unhappy person. Everybody shares whatever they brought to the party and a jovial camaraderie abounds. **Some people say if you miss the tailgate party before a Buffett concert, you've missed half of the show!**

And when the actual concert starts, you will not see theatrics on stage. There will be no flashy stage costumes or pyrotechnics show. Jimmy is usually bare foot in shorts and a t-shirt. The rest of the crew dresses in whatever they're comfortable in. That way, everybody can concentrate on the music. In one of his all time biggest hits, and one of my favorite ballads, "Come Monday", Jimmy stated a long time ago; "I guess I never was meant for glitter rock and roll". **We the fans however, take the role of dressing in costume, and let the band do what they do best-deliver one hell of a show!** Even Jimmy admits that he has "the unique vantage point of watching all of us from up on stage". I suspect that his expression of always looking like he's laughing to himself is due more to his watching the audience with all of our animated costumes, dance moves and acting out of his songs! And from what I can make out on the Jumbo-tron(since I have yet to get a close seat, other than the Cheeseburger in Paradise party), this guy actually seems to still be enjoying himself up there after all of these years. During these events, it seems like he really appreciates his fans. No doubt, he prefers his private life on a daily basis, but to keep it up for all of this time, I think it stopped being about the money a long time ago.

Jimmy has another song where he refers to his style as "Homemade Music". And he's become a master at making so many others feel at home with it. I just don't see how anybody can argue the message of **live life to the fullest and always stay spontaneous and sentimental**. At least that's what I get out of it. In another song acknowledging his fan base, "Here We Are", Jimmy refers to his concerts as "family reunion costume barbeques". With humble gratitude, he claims, "not even I with my head in the sky, could ever guessed it". And to share the credit, he acknowledges his loyal band members, saying, "Not even we on our bended knee could have ever blessed it". Maybe he really is just a good actor. Maybe I'm just fooled by a haze of feathers and fins, but I don't think so. I think that this guy is genuine. In "Only Time Will Tell", he asks, **"Is there a message in my song?"** I say, can usually find one! 

All of the artists who make up the Coral Reefers could probably make it big solo; yet most of this band has stayed together for several decades. Jimmy must be treating them right and they all must be truly enjoying themselves. It's another satisfying bi-product of a Buffett concert to witness a well matched team performing together. I think Jimmy does a pretty good job of living by what he sings. I think most of his messages do come from his life experiences or those of some like-minded song writers.

For example, **Mac McAnally,** who refers to their work as "semi-true stories". I like to call him Jimmy's right hand man, because I cannot remember a performance when I haven't seen him standing right there, and he has written so many of my favorites. Mac has won the CMA Musician of the year multiple times and is called a songwriting hero by Kenny Chesney! And with songs like, "You First" on Mac's own, "Down by the River" CD, which includes a powerful tribute to war heroes, it's easy to see why. Mac claims that, "Jimmy has a unique ability to go into a crowd and make it personal". There is plenty of truth there but I couldn't have been more thrilled to have had the pleasure of telling him that I acknowledge what a strong contributing breeze he has no doubt always been to that wind beneath Jimmy's wings! And during that show, I loved how he called his job **"a rolling ball of goodwill"**!

**Peter Mayer** brings a background as a college jazz guitar teacher but his lyrics seem to be full of lessons too. He spent years as the opening act for some top 70's & 80's touring bands but My husband, Hugh was delighted to recognize influences of some of his other favorite artists (The Rippingtons, Jonathon Butler and Paul Simon) in Peter's work. I got to see him and his son, Brendan deliver their rendition of Simon & Garfunkel's "The Boxer" at the Smokin Tuna Saloon in Key West (a premiere spot for songwriter festivals). Let's just say it was memorably moving! And Peter's "Faith in Angels" song is nothing less than spellbinding! I had the pleasure of passing a commemorative bracelet to a security guard who threw it to Peter on stage as he was dedicating this song to DJ Jeff, a friend to most in the crowd, who chose this place and time to have his ashes spread. When you watch Peter perform, you understand the quote posted on his website: **"And when the show is over, I'll sing to the stars cause I know they will listen if you tell them who you are"**.

Not to be shown up by his brother, **Jim Mayer**, who plays bass for The Coral Reefers, is on the fast track to stardom as an award winner in his own category, children's music. This "Uncle Jim" to twenty nieces and nephews has reached #1 on XM Kids Radio twice and is the recipient of an iParenting Hot Product Media Award and a Children's Music Web Award. In 2005, he was voted Best New XM Kids Artist in the XM Nation Awards. **I dare those producers of "Wife Swap" to find any dysfunction here!**

On the Coral Reefers' vocals, referred to as "Referrettes", there is **Tina Gullickson** who refers to her position with them as **"the best job in the world"** and **Nadirah Shakoor** who joined the band in 1995. She's become known for singing the bridge in "Son Of A Son of a Sailor". In one of the recordings of it, Jimmy refers to her as "a new set of sails". She in turn acknowledges him with her recorded album, "Nod to the Storyteller". She's been nominated for a Grammy Award for her part in the hip-hop Group, Arrested Development's album, *Zingalamaduni*. She's toured with Madonna and other megastars and released several additional albums including some with her brother, drummer, Rasheed Shakoor. Concerts of recent years spotlight Nadirah when Jimmy takes his brief breaks. When Nadirah takes center stage, it seems she is truly in her element. She is one of the most effervescent performers I've ever seen. Her angelic voice is powerful and her delivery truly reveals her passion for sharing her talent. The unspoken energy and vibe that seems to accompany her is rare. One of the only other performers I've seen sing with such reverence is Jonathan Butler who I once saw in a very memorable Christmas concert (described in chapter 5). **I've heard it said that creativity is a form of prayer; and to me, when Nadirah sings it seems so**.

So I say to anyone who may dismiss a Jimmy Buffett and The Coral Reefers performance as trivial bubble gum music, (and I've met a few who've tried) you don't know what you're talking about!! A run-down of the talent on that stage (see RTA for adt'l info on all members) **sounds more like a masterpiece from the Renaissance era to me!**

The following picture **is what Jimmy says he has 'the unique opportunity to see"** during his performances, as the crowd waves their "fins"!

When we can't get to the actual Margaritaville, Jimmy has even provided a virtual world of such for us to indulge in online. According to Ben Silverman's blog, discussing the best & worst celebrity Facebook games, "this buffet of Buffett lets Parrot Heads chill out on a tropical island, virtually boozing it up at a beachfront bar while spending fake money on fake Hawaiian shirts. Yeah, sounds kind of irritating. But believe it or not, Margaritaville Online is actually a lot of fun, earning high praise from critics and even snagging 'Best Social Game' honors at the recent Canadian Video Game Awards. Designed by legit game developer types at THQ, it's one of the best celeb efforts you'll find on Facebook." I have had phellow phriends inviting me to play, which I really want to do, once I finish this book! I love the quote I recently saw that said,

**"Facebook is the new Hotel California…You can check out anytime you like but you can never leave!!"**

And apparently Mike Miller knows what they're talking about as he shares in his hilarious song, "Dear Facebook'! (On a side *note*, if any of you entrepreneurial types out there want to help me launch my idea of marketing shirts or a whole line of stuff w/ the theme, "Don't be a Phony"! (ie. get off your devices & actually live in the real world instead of cyperspace, pls. call me!—don't text or email, or FB msg., please just call! ☺)- Just like the theme of Jimmy's "Everybody's on the Phone" and Miranda Lambert's "Automatic" songs. And now there is also Margaritaville TV……Buffett World, Several Facebook pages, and possibly a movie in the works, dedicated to this icon. But if it's **still** not Buffett music that makes your heart sing, I guess that's okay-although I've been known to threaten to "defriend" those who refuse to give it a try. For example, once when I was having a conversation with a rocker friend from a popular local band, he admitted to me that he was **not a Buffett fan,** although he did not put it so nicely. Anyway, at that point, I turned to him, gave him a gentle pat on the back and said**, "Well, it's been nice knowing ya!"** Maybe nobody gives a *hoot* about my personal opinion, as I'm no certified music critic. I do feel qualified however to earn the title of a life-long music fan. In his book, *Tales from Margaitaville*, Mr. Buffett quotes Mark Twain in saying, "write about what you know". I've chosen to write about meaningful music. I feel much of it is found in Buffett-related songs.

And since I admit that Margaritaville is just a fantasy land for most of us and that we do have to function in the real world, I'll return back to the real issue that prompted me to write this book: the frustrations of our downsizing dilemma—At the time **when our "stuff" started hitting the fan**, the only song I could recall being familiar with on the topic of money from Buffett's collection, was "Carnival World". That one says, **"Spend it while you can; money's contraband. You can't take it with you when you go"**. I admit that following that line of advice has not always served me well. The song goes on to say, "There's no free ride in this carnival world". That part I've been learning the hard way.

In the upcoming chapter, I'll further discuss **our stress over our distressed property** and how my life seemed to be playing out like a sad country song! For now let me just say that since our displacement, I have encountered many other good people also having to start all over.

One of the main reasons
for this book
is to hopefully help
all of us gain some
closure on foreclosures!

# 4
# The "F Word"!

("Money, so they say is the root of all evil today" Pink Floyd)

The title of this chapter may have you concerned that I'm about to spout obscenities like some of those explicit songs that we try to shield our kids from but are nonetheless downloadable on iTunes. But unlike the four letter word that most commonly would come to mind here, the last several years have had me cursing more with three syllable words like: foreclosure, Fannie Mae, Freddie Mac, recession, depression, downsizing and bankruptcy! Now if that doesn't sound like the makings of a country song, I don't know what does! These and many other "*F*" words have become all too commonly painful for many of us who are *facing* them especially in and beyond our *forties* and *fifties*! After I was well on my way through writing this chapter, one of my clients shared with me that her sister, Carlene Thompson, also a realtor, has recently published a book called, *Fannie Mae is not A Slut*. I haven't read it yet but I suspect that there might be a fair amount of derogatory irony in that title!

To indulge in a bit of *folly*, I can't resist sharing David Allen Coe's, "You Never Even Called Me by My Name". In the version that my husband downloaded, this singer takes a mid-song segue to explain that when the songwriter, Steve Goodwin, sent him the lyrics claiming that it was the perfect country song, Mr. Coe corrected him saying that it couldn't possibly be such without any mention of the classic necessary elements: "mama, trains, trucks, prison or getting drunk". So as he tells it, Mr. Goodwin followed up with the following verse: "Well, I was drunk the day my mama got out of prison and I went to pick her up in the rain. But before I could get to the station in my pickup truck, she got runned over by a damned old train". David Allen Coe's delivery with that song is so good that it's become one of my favorite sing-alongs and before I finish my story, mine may contain most of those elements too!

**Previously, "mid life crisis" usually referred to the lack of *fun* in one's life. Now its often related to the lack of *funds*** and the need for *frugality* in our lives! Losing your job or losing your home or both, can literally make you *feel* like a real loser! *Furthermore*, having to start all over in a time when jobs are scarce can *flabbergast* you and make you *feel* even more like a *failure*! This can also be *frustrating* for the senior citizens who've had to give up their *freedom* and come out of retirement as they've seen their investment *fortunes fizzle*! **One of my husband's friends recently commented to him that she never imagined herself in her sixties having to say, "Would you like *fries* with that?'** But all too often taking any form of income that you can get, is becoming the reality for many senior citizens, and members of the general public alike. *Fending* off creditors while trying to *fend* for yourself and your family can make you *fret*. It can bring about a *flood* of emotions often resulting in *feeling fragile* and *feeble*, maybe even like a *fugitive* or *felon*. But don't curl up in the *fetal* position; this does not have to be *fatal*. Read on, *forge* ahead, *find* out how some of us have *figured* it out so you too can get through this *faze* of life.

I am intentionally using the sandwich technique, a method of hiding bad news in between two more positive points. I learned this approach during my years as an elementary school teacher. When I had to meet parents of students and report on their child's progress, I would always start with a compliment first, then slip in the area of concern and end with a reassuring comment. So the above paragraphs were meant to approach this subject with a lighter *flair*.

But the truth is *foreclosure* is not *fun*! Just take a look at the *facts* as reported by Fox News in an article titled,

**US Homes Lost to Foreclosure Up 25%,** (Sept. 16, 2010): "More than 2.3 million homes have been repossessed by lenders since the recession began in December 2007, according to *RealtyTrac*. The firm estimates more than 1 million American households are likely to lose their homes to foreclosure this year. In all, 338,836 properties received a foreclosure-related warning in August, up 4 percent from July, but down 5 percent from the same month last year, *RealtyTrac* said. That translates to one in 381 U.S. homes".

An article by Daniel Indiviglio of The Atlantic, titled,

**2010 Set a New Record for Foreclosure Activity**, (1/13/11), reinforces such facts: "High unemployment helped to drive a new record number of 2.8 million foreclosure filings in 2010, according to foreclosure tracker *RealtyTrac*. Despite another monthly decline in foreclosure activity in December due to the delays banks have been experiencing since October after being forced to rework their processes, total filings for the year were up nearly 2% compared to 2009's old record. By looking at how states most severely affected by the housing bubble fared, it's pretty clear that the problem last year was more tied to joblessness than to subprime mortgages". 2010 set a new record for foreclosure activity". From *RealtyTrac*, to follow is a chart depicting annual foreclosure activity by type from 2006 through 2010.

The previous facts do not even take into account properties being sold via short sales. In the 2010 <u>Florida Realtors Short Sale Report</u>, the following comments were made:

"Florida's foreclosure crisis continues to fuel a growing number of short sales. The result is a market saturated by "distressed" properties, including bank-owned homes, foreclosure sales (REO), and short sales".

**If you ask people who've gone through a short sale, they'll probably agree with Randy Newman's song that says, "Short people got no reason to live"!**

That may be a bit extreme but if you ask anyone involved, they're sure to tell you, **there's nothing short about short sales and you usually don't *sail* through them**! It's categorically a long arduous process that supposedly is the lesser of the evils in this situation, but it's no day of "Sailing" like Christopher Cross sings about! To clarify, a short sale takes place when a homeowner owes more than the present fair market value of a house. In this situation, the bank agrees to allow the property to be marketed at the fair market value and accepts a reasonable offer from a new qualified buyer. At closing, the place is transferred to the new owner once the previous owner proves that they are in a position of hardship and conforms to all other bank demands, which usually involves volumes of paperwork, several months of uncertainty waiting for the bank to respond with final terms and often continued future payments as they are not necessarily fully released from their deficiency. The benefit to this process is that as of the present, short sales have less of an adverse affect on a seller's credit and for a shorter period of time than a foreclosure. The aggravating part is that new qualified buyers often drop out of the waiting game in the interim time it takes to get an answer from the banks and the seller has to repeatedly start the process over and over in hopes of not running out of time before foreclosure is activated. There is a national company that has been designed to take some of the mental anguish off the home owners and realtors involved, called **Nationwide Short Sale Solutions/Blue Anchor Advisors**, which proved to be very helpful in our experience.

I'll bet that the popular 70's & 80's band,

**REO Speedwagon, never would have predicted that part of their name would later be related to such an unpopular term- (REO= Real Estate Owned, or foreclosed upon property).**

One night at one of my favorite happy hour spots, the middle aged female bartender shared with me that she received her first kiss from that band's lead singer-(I'll leave the names out to protect the not-so-innocent)!

And speaking of REO's, "highest and best" has become a term that bankers use when a foreclosed property has attracted several bidders and the bank has to ask for all interested parties' highest and best offer with in a narrow window of opportunity. It is good that this process usually drives the home value back up in this auction-like procedure. But it's unfortunate that some of those behind the scenes who may be in the position of power, have let fraud creep into the system, giving those in the industry a bad name and not at all bringing out the highest and best in themselves. Those who've seen this as an opportunity for personal gain at the expense of others have only muddied the waters and delayed this nation's cleansing of this crisis which is very far apart from the "highest and best" I referred to upon the part of songwriters in the forward of this book. Fortunately, new guidelines continue to be enforced as this phase in our economy evolves.

The following paragraphs taken from the <u>Florida Realtors Foreclosure Report</u>, take a closer look, describing it through the words of individuals throughout our state:

>Foreclosure Date: 6/06/2008, Kathy
>
>• 60% of monthly income going towards housing costs
>• Experienced divorce - "I have found this entire experience to be devastating. I'm behind in income tax and every other obligation and can't file bankruptcy as

I'd lose my car. I'm in total financial ruin due to the on-going crisis of the Florida real estate market. Prior to the shift in our market area, I had savings, no revolving debt and a very comfortable income. I am now living in a friend's home, am in fear of losing my car and get approximately 30 calls from creditors and/or attorneys on a daily basis. Life is not fun and I am frustrated beyond words. Every day I continue to be thankful that it's just me, not a family, not my children, that are faced with this horrid situation and I am humbled when I work with families who have lost everything and still need to feed their children".

Foreclosure Date: October 20, 2008, John

• 55% of monthly income going towards housing costs • one child and three dependents living in home • Experienced job loss and divorce - "They refused to work with me because my loan was FHA insured and they were going to get paid by the government so they were not interested in helping me. My wife and I both worked in the construction field. We both lost our jobs. Because of the financial problems my wife left me with my new baby girl and we are getting a divorce. I have been living with my brother and his wife and 2 kids for over a year because I cannot afford to get my own apartment and pay for transportation & child support. This problem has destroyed my life and I feel that of my baby girl".

Foreclosure Date: 7/1/2009, Barbara

• 60% of monthly income going towards housing costs • Experienced job loss and unexpected medical bills - "Lenders would not talk to me or negotiate. Take it or lose it. I lost my income due to the decline in clients as I am a realtor. My health took a dive and I had a kidney operation. This took my income and I didn't feel well either. When the company loss mitigator sent me a schedule for payments, and I asked for the breakdown of costs. They would not give me details or speak to me at all. They never kept me informed. Another realtor tried to do a short-sale, I think they were too late!"

Foreclosure Date: Pending, Deb

• 50% of monthly income going towards housing costs
• Three children and one dependent living in home •
Experienced job loss, unexpected medical bills, and divorce - "This home has been for sale for 2 yrs....the bank says it is waiting on? ... buyer may walk....divorce, hospitalization, loss of income, and family medical emergency. **I was a top-producer. Then I became ill**, my fiancé was injured in a motorcycle accident, he spent 3 months in a hospital 60 miles away. Loss of wages combined with a decline in market values, renters not paying rent I was unable to make my payments. **My income went from 200K a yr to 30K a year".**

Foreclosure Date: 6/17/2009, Wayne

• one dependent living at home • Experienced job loss
– **"There are no local offices, so a face to face with a rep. was not an option.** I had started a business with two other people. One died suddenly and the other person took all the assets of the business and literally left town. I can't pursue legal action at the moment for lack of funds. I am 62 years old and I think that has a lot to do with the employment situation. Were I a younger person, I may have a better chance of employment in my trade. **The job market in Florida is shrinking and I am not afraid to try something else but there are no opportunities".**

Foreclosure Date: Pending, Maria

• 75% of monthly income going towards housing costs

• Two dependents living in home • Experienced job loss and unexpected medical bills - **"The lender only**

**wanted to work based on what he wanted, & didn't take into consideration any of my suggestions.** We cashed out all our annuities, pension funds & life insurance in order to pay. **During the short sale process, we got an incredibly good offer, but the lenders didn't want to negotiate, both their expectations were completely unrealistic.** I don't understand it. They will both lose at the foreclosure court steps come November 2009". The house needs repairs, the values in the neighborhood keep coming down, so... I don't understand their rationale."

I hope these *facts*, *figures* and hearing other people's *frustrations*, will reassure you that if you are going through or have had to go through this, "You are not Alone", just like Michael Jackson sang. The above bolded parts were what we were experiencing first hand.

On the days when it felt like my *faith* was *fading*, this experience had me wanting to "*fade* away" like the girl in the previous illustration. At one time, this was to be this book's cover (design by Danette DeRouin). The caption is a phrase I developed from a reference in Buffett's book, *Tales From Margaritaville*. That picture reminds me of a very charismatic Van Morrison song called, "Into the Mystic". While enjoying a few drinks at that same happy hour spot, Hugh and I heard the band, High Tide (mentioned in the previous chapter) for the first time. That night we sat off in the distance from the bandstand, down by the water, but my ears perked up the minute they broke into this melody. I knew I had heard it before but couldn't identify more than a couple vague lines. However, the entire way home, I became obsessed with having to identify the rest of the lyrics. I felt strongly that it was a Van Morrison song and that I had heard it in a movie. When Hugh and I googled it on the computer, knowing the artist and a few correct words was helpful. Although identifying which movie I had seen it in, since it was apparently used in several, took a bit longer. Then when I came across the title, *Patch Adams*, I knew that had to be the one. So Hugh and I proceeded to watch a clip of that movie on Utube. We never even got to the part including the song, but I became overcome with emotion just replaying a glimpse of this film. I actually have a hard time putting into words how profoundly convincing Robin Williams played the part of an unconventional doctor who strived to bring joy to a place so typically filled with gloom and ultimately suffered personal loss on several levels (and I believe this was based on a true story). I guess what still surprises me is that from the instant I heard the first couple of notes playing, everything around me seemed to fade away and focusing on this song became my dominant thought. I sensed that this song was somehow connected to an important message. At that point, I honestly don't think I'd heard it in over a couple of decades, but instantaneously, I was drawn to it as if I had seen that melancholy movie the day before. Then for several days following, I felt compelled to keep replaying this song over and over. The song's words are mysterious and the perfectly mellow way Van Morrison (& Scott Novello of High Tide) deliver them, makes it effectively charismatic.

But back to "the *fog* of '07" (which is what that period in our life felt like), like one of those people quoted earlier explained, without local offices where you can go and discuss the situation face to face, people do end up feeling alone and lost. Trying to get a bank representative on the phone, who is so inundated with the onslaught of surmounting files requiring their time and attention, results in people feeling like just another insignificant number and often makes them just want to give up. While the years have helped my memories of this agonizing process *fade*,

Sooner or later we all have to *face* the music & *face* it with music, I did.

**Like Jimmy Buffett explains about the "Hula Girl at Heart", "she knows how to face the music" and if nothing else, I wanted to be like her!**

In the July 11th edition of Ladies Home Journal, an article titled, What Does it Take For a Woman to Feel Happy & Fulfilled?- it says, "As women get older, the pressures they feel from society change. Young women (age 19 to mid 20's) feel the most pressure to look beautiful. From their mid 20's to mid 40's, women feel the most pressure to **have a nice home.** As they move into their 50's, they feel the most pressure to **have a certain amount of money".** So I guess there's a reason why I seemed to take this all so personally. I grew up being serenaded with songs like the Beatles', "Penny Lane" and **I still wanted to be, "There beneath the blue suburban skies"!** One day I saw a broadcast claiming that one third of this nation's homeless are in Florida which explains why so much of the anguish resulting from this housing crisis seemed to be right out my back door. Throughout this dilemma, not wanting to whine to everybody around me and consequently feeling like there was nowhere else to turn,

**I found myself reaching out for song lyrics to bring me comfort.**

## Around this time, I also started wondering what Jimmy Buffett & the housing crisis (2 reoccurring themes in my life) might have to do with each other??

I thought maybe the answer was-**both have a record number of recordings, both are especially well known in the state of Florida, & both have a common tie-in to water:** Jimmy often sings about being *on the water* and distressed property owners are referred to as having a house *under water*--!!??

Recently I saw someone comment on Facebook that they were **considering starting to take more financial cues from Jimmy Buffett than from Warren Buffett.** And my internet login page today prompted me to read an article about how you can now buy a plot of land on the moon. Jimmy has an album named, *Beach House On The Moon*, and beautiful songs like, "Come to the Moon" and "Everlasting Moon", so maybe he has known something all along...?

At one point, I wondered if I should consider calling this book **"The Buffett Rule,"** or even just, **"Buffett Rules"** because **Parrot Heads like me, do think that Jimmy Buffett Rules! & we think that many of his song lyrics give us good rules to live by!**

*Anyway*, not being able to escape to the moon, the *fateful* day arrived when my husband and I had exhausted all our resources and we could no longer scrape together enough to make one more house payment. Before significant increases in taxes and insurance, we were carrying the payment and even though we may have been within $1000 of being able to continue to do so, we were told by our bank that they did not offer any type of loan modifications. **We even had a buyer, who was willing to pay close to what we owed, and we offered to take on the difference in future payments, but the bank would not agree to work with us.**

Then I thought about Candi Staton's "Young Hearts" song with the words, "Self preservation is what's really going on today". And since Hugh and I were beginning to see that we now had to focus on self preservation and look for a long term solution, **we went into damage control mode.** We took inventory of our household and placed all unnecessary items online for immediate sale. Away went the boat, tiki bar, golf cart, trampoline, guest room furniture (where we were going there probably wouldn't be room for guests) and all other items of excess. Fortunately this effort yielded us some money toward moving expenses because Hugh took the first job he could find which was an entry level position with a company across the state. He'd be working in his previous line of work, which was the field of medical sales. **This meant that we had a week and a half to pack up, clean up, place our home on the market and pray for this new thing called a "short sale" before the *foreclosure* process activated.**

Now, this was 2007 and foreclosures were not yet common in our area. So when we left town in what seemed like the middle of the night, it was tough not to *feel* like the *freaks* of the neighborhood.

**This becomes a time when you *find* out who you real *friends* are.**

While everybody else was still busy keeping up with the Jones's (some were even still *flipping* houses), **our ignorant bliss had come to a screeching halt.** It was so easy for others to point out all of the ways that we had gone wrong in order to assure themselves that this could never happen to them. **Even though nationally, the housing bubble had not yet officially burst, those of us whose sole income** was most directly tied to this industry, were the *first* to *fall*. And the more success we had up until then, the *further* we had to *fall*. Then I thought about Jimmy's "If it all Falls Down" song and tried to make light of the situation. Without *foresight* to do otherwise, we had reinvested much of our income back into the housing market. As I've mentioned, my mother has been a real estate broker since 1972 and most of my six siblings worked in related fields. We had a mortgage broker, an insurance agent and a title company owner as well as several sales associates in the family. Our family get-togethers felt more like a day at the office, especially as we all began to feel the pinch in the early stages of the housing slump.

Hugh and I were the first in the family to have to move on. Hugh's new job required him to have to go immediately into training at his new company's home office up state in Gainesville. He would now be selling medical equipment that required intricate knowledge of the product, so that meant that the entire move was up to me. **My eighty year old mother became my roommate that week as we packed around the clock leading up to moving day.** I only took breaks to produce marketing material for this home or conduct online job searches for myself or investigate rental properties on the west coast of Florida. Hugh's sales territory would include most of southwest Florida spanning from Naples to Venice. Keeping rising gas prices in mind, we tried to focus on the middle region of his territory in which to relocate. **Consequently, this would land us in that small town of Cape Coral** which we had recently passed through.

Our main priority then became finding a place to rent with a good school nearby hopefully in a family neighborhood for the boys' sake. Before that could happen though, we had to prepare for this relocation. My mom and I started the monumental task of boxing up the contents of my household with idealistic goals. We were determined to keep it all labeled and organized. Since we would be moving just a few days before the new school year started, I made an effort to set aside the boys' school clothes so they would be handy for their big first day. I also set out an interviewing suit for myself and an iron in case any of these items became mangled during the trip. In addition to the iron, I was careful to equip the hands-on box with phone chargers, scissors, important paperwork and anything else that I deemed potentially helpful during the hectic-ness of a move.

Next, I had to take on the job of sorting "the keepers" from the items that could be cast aside. **Since we were going to be downsizing, much had to be eliminated and in a hurry. In most cases, the only decision to be made was, is the item garage sale worthy or should it be dropped off at Goodwill, or as a last resort, should it just be dragged to the curb? Mom thought most of my stuff was "curb worthy"!** After raising seven children, she had learned how to run a tight ship and couldn't stand the sight of clutter. I have to admit that after a short while, the pain of facing the clutter also overtook my sense of attachment to most of my worldly possessions and Jimmy's line,

## "times are rough and I've got too much stuff"
### blared in my head!

Years earlier Hugh and I had attended a seminar conducted by a financial expert where he described American greed as follows: "We buy houses and stuff them with things: furniture, appliances, electronics, decorations and numerous other 'must-haves' and this is what drives our economy". His observation could not be argued, but now many of us were realizing that we had to change our ways and we had to do it fast!

My mom and I worked our fingers to the bone in that summer heat. While out retrieving the day's fast food rations, we would raid dumpsters behind stores for more boxes. Other family members would occasionally drop by to lend a hand or an additional roll of tape or to check out my discarded items in between running their own households. **But it has always been my mother who is the best "*foul*-weather friend"** anyone could ever wish for. I am referring to foul as the opposite of fair but not fowl like birds, although her loyalty certainly qualifies her as a Parrot Head in my heart! When you are down, she is in your corner. And that week, she spent every waking moment by my side. She also has a silly side to her and sometimes late at night, we would even get punchy. Every time we thought we were making some real progress, we would open another closet door and stand in bewilderment at the avalanche of items that was descending upon us!

One afternoon, mom needed to nap. I knew I had to keep moving because I was afraid that if I sat still, I wouldn't be able to get back up. Moving day was fast approaching. While she rested, I decided to direct my attention to one of my favorite spots in the house. This would be the nook that we had built into a corner of the kitchen with windows that overlooked the tiki bar, pool and lake. It had comfy bench seating like in a restaurant booth, with underneath cabinets for all our liquor bottles and party platters. I remembered how excited Hugh was when he picked out the wood used in its creation and stained it to match the family room furniture. This was the main hub of the house. It was where our family always gathered. I remember how I was filled with gratitude and pride when we were moving in. As I was unpacking and loading items into the spacious pantry, I cried tears of joy in disbelief that we got to live in such a special place. But now it was time to "push that pride aside", like Chaka Khan sings in "Tell Me Something Good".

**Then, as I piled the contents of that cabinet into a cardboard box, it felt like the contents of my heart were being tossed in there with it!**

In the quiet stillness, the seriousness of the situation hit me.

**I wanted to drop and weep. I did.**

All I could think was, "How could we have let this happen?" **We once had healthy equity in this house.** It was bigger than we needed but we were fortunate enough to get into it because the previous owners called us to help them sell it and through negotiations with them, our discounted commission helped as a down payment. At that time we had lived for several years in the same development in a smaller floor plan on a lot that did not have room for a pool and we were being harassed by the association because when friends dropped by, their cars blocked the sidewalk because that house was on a short corner lot. However this was a very popular neighborhood in suburbia and once we put that place on the market, we were able to sell it within a week for a substantial profit. So why wouldn't we make the leap?

As realtors, we know that location is everything and as soon as we saw the lot where this place was built, we fell in love with it. It was located in the back of a cul-de-sac overlooking a lake which bordered a state park. The front of the house had a view of the only natural hills in the county. Every weekend, from our front window, we watched people horseback riding through the trails that revealed Indian artifacts when the development was being built. We excitedly paid the previous owners their asking price and convinced ourselves that this was our last home-ha! This was where we were going to retire (ha-ha)! This was the community where we took the kids trick-or-treating. The forest right outside our front door was where we took many nature walks and conducted scavenger hunts. Those hills were where we sat to watch the fireworks. The surrounding paths were perfect for Easter egg hunts. The front window was ideal for displaying our Christmas Tree. The boys could now have swimming parties for their birthdays. This was the neighborhood where the boys' friends lived and because we purposely made it so inviting, most of the time they were all hanging out at our house. This was the place that we could envision them bringing their college girlfriends home to. It had everything, and **it had all of our hearts wrapped up in it.** After all, Neil Diamond in his

"Heartlight" song which was written about *ET* in the movie of that name, said, "Home's the most excellent place of all and I'll be right here if you should call". And **I wanted to give my boys this kind of security. I strongly believe in establishing family traditions and it sure seemed like this was the perfect place to put down our roots.** Now I wasn't ready to be transplanted!

**While it lasted, we were giddy to actually be living in our dream home!-So now, exactly how did this turn into such a nightmare?**

How was it all so quickly being ripped out from under us? **I was envisioning all of us being scooped up by a garbage truck and being forced to slide into a dumpster as we tried to hang on scratching and clawing. To me, whatever was waiting for us on the other side of the state stunk!** Especially because I knew that **every aspect of this move was about** *the take away.*

## Downsizing is usually not uplifting!

It is harder to let go of something you've had, than to have never had it at all. Now was the time to pay the piper for all of our overly ambitious mistakes. **In our defense, they were mistakes of ignorance. We always had the best intentions. No one saw this coming.** Many homeowners still have not fully accepted just how much their home values have actually readjusted.

Most disturbing to me was the thought that we were messing up our kids' lives. When you spend two years sharing what you think is Utopia with them, **how do you believably convince them that now leaving it all is for the best? Deep down, I knew that Hugh and I could find happiness and nice people anywhere as long as we were together. But looking your ten year old in the eyes and being firm as he pleads to not be taken away from his** friends and extended family is a challenge that I wasn't prepared for.

Up until then, I was the kind of parent who could fix any upsetting situation in my kids' lives. The little research that I had been able to conduct about our new city was discouraging as far as the home front and the school system.

**So I was afraid that I was now delivering my children to the 7$^{th}$ *Circle of Hades*, and for their sake, I had to do it with a smile!** For the kids sake, I could not continue to wallow in self pity and stammer around whining, "Why is this happening?!" I had to drag myself out of that dark place and put on a brave face. However I am usually pretty guilty of wearing my heart on my sleeve. **It was especially tough to reassure the boys when I was full of unanswered questions.** The biggest challenge I could handle at the time was just to get through each day.

# I clung to any encouragement I could find & I found the first bit of it in the words to a song.

The refrain kept repeating in my head as I tried to follow its instruction: "Don't try to explain it, just nod your head

## Breathe in, Breathe Out, Move On".

I actually dug out the boys' boom box and centered it on that breakfast nook and put that Buffett CD on automatic repeat to become my mantra for the rest of the move.

**To make it clear, it was not the loss of any of the material items that I was mourning. My disturbance came from a deeper level. It was like I was sensing a loss of myself.** All that I had believed in and had been working towards was slipping through my hands in an instant. There are many charming plaques boasting the phrase, "Home is where the heart is". **My heartbreak was not tangible. There is a song that relates this message so well. It's called, "The House That Built Me" by Miranda Lambert.** In it, she sings about revisiting the house with all of the rooms where she and her family carried out all of their daily routines as she was growing up. In my appreciation of it, I relate to how this song relays a feeling almost as if the walls could talk and if they did, they would tell the story of her life. And as far as the story of that song, from what I've heard, it was actually written by her husband, Blake Shelton. The story goes that he wrote it & offered to let her record it if she'd marry him—and it seems that worked out pretty well for both of them! **Even though a house is an inanimate object, for many people it can represent so much more.** Many people make a practice of returning to the place where they were raised to catch a glimpse of their childhoods and memories shared with their loved ones there. **In this way, homes can symbolically carry on the spirit of those that lived there.**

People in the real estate industry often recognize that **every house has a story to tell.** I regularly watch buyers and sellers acknowledge the passage of ownership with much more reverence than just signing on the dotted line. They hug as the buyers reassure the sellers that they are leaving their place in good hands and that they will continue to take care of it, like it is a pet or something. When I was growing up, I was fortunate enough to remain in my childhood home for twelve years. After that, we moved just down the street to the home where my parents still are. I believe having this place to return to has replenished my spirit each time I visit. There is something comforting about the familiarity of staying in my old room and walking the same hallways and neighborhood streets that I did while I was growing up. As a parent, I desperately wanted to provide this kind of security for my own children. **They say that moving is among the top most stressful events in life.** Even before the most joyous closings, Hugh and I usually witness somebody involved in the process hitting a wall and having a breakdown of one kind or another. But moving under those circumstances for us in 2007 was bewildering to me.

**However gleaning meaning in those few lines from that "Breathe in/out…" song** (which was actually written for the Hurricane Katrina victims), **did help put it all in perspective.** I had no choice but to "breathe in, breathe out, move on". As I summoned some inner strength, I consciously decided that **from that moment forward, I would think of this house as just four walls. I convinced myself that it was what was inside (the four of us), that made it a home.** I reminded myself that wherever we were to end up, together we would make that place a home. **The thought of relieving the daily pressure of how we were going to make ends meet would be worth it in the end.**

So now it was time to close the doors to this place for the final time and wave a kiss goodbye to our dreams there. At least temporarily, it was time to downsize our home and our expectations. As moving day abruptly arrived, we reluctantly got in the pick-up truck, trailer in tow, to set out across Alligator Alley, the 84 mile roadway connecting southeast and southwest Florida. Hugh got a weekend reprieve from his training so he arrived in time to remind me that we had a deadline to meet across the state. As time ran out, he declared that if we didn't leave that moment, we wouldn't be able to get the key to the place we had arranged to spend the night. I could not stall anymore. We had to finish the final load and go. To come to our aide, my good ol' dad who had spent the day helping us load-up, offered to pack the remaining items into his van and deliver them to us once we got settled.

**So with our two boys in the back seat gripping their full goldfish bowls, a parrot in a cage, a bearded dragon in a very smelly box and our bewildered Wheaten Terrier, we prepared to depart from Ft. Lauderdale, the place I was born, where all of my family still lived and the only hometown our boys had ever known.**

At the last minute, unbeknownst to me, my hands-on moving kit was cast back into the garage due to lack of room in the truck cab and all of my efforts to keep everything under control were proven *futile! Feeling* defeated, I jumped out to give my parents one last quick hug goodbye while trying to stifle my sobs, and off we went.

**It *felt* like even all of the rain that we hit going across the alley, couldn't match the tears that I shed throughout that trip.**

This was not the way it was supposed to go. Whatever plan God had in store for us had not yet revealed itself, so **like the surrounding swamp, to me, it just felt like the future was one big *fog*.**

And then we were there. But where was there? This all happened so fast. We knew next to nothing about our new surroundings. There was still so much to *figure* out and next to no time to do it. Rental properties were scarce and our first choice *fell* through leaving us very *few* options. It was still our main goal to rent a house near a good school and settle in before the school year began. Then we learned about **"school choice"**. This was the system this local school board put in place where residents were to submit 3 choices anywhere in the county where they'd like for their children to go. Apparently, where you lived did not necessarily dictate which school you were appointed to at all. **As one other parent that I met explained to me, "It doesn't matter where you live. Your kids could still be bussed two hours across town, especially because everybody else submitted their choices last spring and all of the good schools now have a waiting list".** I didn't consider this very *choice* at all!

Kelly Clarkson sings, "What Doesn't Kill You Makes You Stronger" but at that time, I was feeling week. I was feeling very defeated and the only thing that seemed to be getting stronger was all of my frustration. I've heard it said that, **"if you don't make a choice, life will make it for you"**. This *felt* like one of those times. I *felt* like everything was out of my control and I seriously began to doubt my ability to make any decisions. **Failing my children was not an option.** Their well being and successful adjustment to the changes we had thrust upon them was of upmost priority. For obvious reasons, private school was not an option. I considered home schooling but making new friends was equally important as their academia. *Finally* we settled on what we thought was a good compromise. It was not until the night before open house, that I realized that we might have made a mistake. According to the several parents that I met while acquiring the boys' school supplies, we were enrolled in one of the county's less desirable schools and of course, the place that was most recommended had an impenetrable waiting list.

The protective mother in me decided to show up an hour early for open-house and see what further information I could gather before I would subject the boys to this environment. It was my luck as I arrived, to encounter the PTO President in the parking lot. I introduced myself and shared some of the information that I had been told. He assured me that all of my concerns were unfounded and that any weaknesses of the previous year had now been addressed. So I went back and retrieved the boys and dragged them and all of their necessary supplies in to start their new life. Their teachers seemed pleasant enough although this was not the small school they had come from. My youngest was to share a community bathroom with several classes of students up to five years older than him. And because most teachers were female, supervision in there would be a concern. The commercial vehicle in the parking lot that I later learned would pass through the car line everyday displaying a giant billboard of a scantily clad woman advertising tattoos was also not an image I wanted reinforced in my kids' heads. **Although one incredible Buffett related encounter that we had in the hallway that first day gave me hope…**

As we went back and forth through the halls pushing the dolly carrying the boys' multitude of required school supplies (seriously, several reams of copy paper were only a small part of the lengthy lists!), we seemed to keep crossing paths with a man in his classroom doorway. After several nods and niceties, I finally decided to talk to him. He was an older gentleman with a big smile who happened to be wearing a brightly colored tie filled with tropical parrots. The first thing that flew out of my mouth was, "Hello, are you a Parrot Head?" He said, "A what?" Then admitting that he was only joking, he said "Yes, of course I am". So I immediately proceeded to pull out my wallet and show him the picture of me on stage with Jimmy from the Cheeseburger in Paradise grand opening in Ft. Lauderdale, as I said, "Well, look at this!" At that point, he acted dumbfounded. So I followed up by saying, "O.K., this is me, and you should know who that is next to me". **Then he said,**..."Yeah, but do you know who that is on the other side of Jimmy in the photo with you? **That's my wife!"** So as fate would have it, this couple from across the state was there that night in Ft. Lauderdale to share the spotlight with me on stage with Jimmy and his wife was chosen as one of my fellow "Reeferettes"! Then I said to him, "You mean I have been carrying around a picture of your wife in my wallet for two years?!" He then explained to me that he was one of the school's social studies teachers.

This Buffett related encounter brought back such pleasant memories and it got me thinking that maybe this wasn't going to be such a bad place after all. I was beginning to let myself hope that

## Finding common ground brought about by mutual music appreciation between this stranger and me

was a serendipitous sign of light at the end of my tunnel...or was it just the calm before another storm?

# IF YOU CAN'T HANDLE ME BLURTING OUT SONG LYRICS THAT RELATE TO WHAT YOU JUST SAID, WE CAN'T BE FRIENDS

(Real Country Ladies)

"Lately I been, I been losing sleep, dreaming 'bout the things that we could be. Baby I been, I been prayin' hard-said no more counting dollars, we'll be counting stars. Take that money and watch it burn, sink in the river the lessons I learned"

(One Republic)

# 5

# False *Cents* of Security

("you had a bad day…you sing a sad song just to turn it around" Daniel Powter)

In "Breathe In, Breathe Out, Move On," Jimmy Buffett says, "If a hurricane doesn't leave you dead, it will make you strong". We survived that hurricane. Now I was anxious to survive this move and find some silver lining in these gloomy clouds that I hoped would soon be lifted. However it actually seemed to get worse before **the song gods eventually stepped in to save me.**

After the pleasant Parrot Head encounter at the school, I redirected my attention to the task of finding a place to live. Since the day we made the decision to relocate across the state, we seemed to be hitting lots of road blocks. Rental properties were scarce and there was an ever increasing risk that if we were able to get in a place, we could get a knock on the door at any unforeseen point, from the sheriff informing us that the place was being foreclosed upon and we'd have to vacate. In this area, the real estate crash was taking a profound toll and many home owners were starting to take desperate measures. It was not uncommon for people who had invested in multiple properties during the boom to now occupy the one that they could still afford and rent out the rest until they got foreclosed upon. The thought of getting the kids settled and uprooting them again was unnerving.

The situation left us out of time and very few options so we had to choose among the lesser of the evils. It was narrowed down to two houses. We had to act fast on either the brand new house that had never been lived in, which made it very attractive to us but it was in a questionable neighborhood, or the older smaller 1960's place on a quieter street. The latter of the two had a cat being boarded in a bathroom that along with the odor of its litter box, attempted to leap out as we peeked in. At that stage of things with all that was overwhelming us, we decided to name each house we looked at to better lock them into our mutual memories. This one was to be called "the cat house". And while my poor husband has had 4 sinus surgeries and is highly allergic to cats, for lack of a better option, we chose "the cat house" as our new home. **We took it as a good sign that the front door was encased with beautiful stained glass parrots.**

As we began our new routine, Hugh continued attending meetings throughout the state and putting in more overnighters or 12+ hour work days. Since his work required so much driving (without a company car or gas allowance), we both knew that it was best for me to trade vehicles with him. Now my 5'2 height made it necessary for me to hoist myself into his full size pick-up truck each morning and maneuver it through this new town to make the twenty minute commute to the boys' new school. This city has 400 miles of canals and consequently, roads that are full of dead ends or only one-way traffic. Let's just say that I **did not** enjoy having to do quick U-turns in that rig! So this was one more source of contention. I was determined to hate that hand me down vehicle, which was even easier when it over-heated, stalled out and needed to be towed on the first day of school as I waited in the car dismissal line for over an hour!

But like the song by Eddie Kendricks, I needed to "Keep On Trucking". And while his song was a hit, this idea was not a hit with me! However with a roof now over our heads and the boys in school, I could direct my attention to finding a job. Easier said than done! I had a college degree and years of varied experience, but at this point **I felt like "an over forty victim of fate". Now these daunting lyrics from Jimmy Buffett's, "A Pirate Looks at Forty", had me too feeling that "it seems my occupation's just not around"**! I was not afraid of hard work. It's just that now I had to find a new career that allowed me to keep my children as my main priority. With Hugh's schedule so unpredictable (he needed to be present for the procedures that his equipment was being used for), I had to ensure that any job that I took allowed me to remain the one on call for all unpredictable situations that might arise in the household. If school was out or one of the boys had to be picked up and taken to the doctor, I was the one who had to be able to rearrange my schedule. And when you're new in a position, this is frowned upon. Without a network of other parents or friendly neighbors or family close by, I didn't yet have a support system in place to call on in a pinch. Also I learned that apparently when we left Broward County we had thrown ourselves from *the frying pan into the fire*. One day I heard it announced on the radio that Lee County was now among the top in the nation in unemployment. And apparently, according to many sources, it was also the foreclosure capital of the world. Companies here were not hiring; they were laying people off or going out of business. I couldn't help but notice all of the vacant storefronts while driving through downtown. Downtrodden was the word that came to mind.

The daily commute to the school took me through another part of the city that revealed a multitude of empty builder models and empty houses. We needed to be in this area for Hugh's work, but I couldn't help but wonder, "what, if anything, was in it for the rest of us?" A closer look revealed even more about the plight of some local people.

**Occasionally when curiosity got the better of us, Hugh and I would hike through the overgrown weeds and turn the handle to the door of an abandoned house. Surprisingly, more often than not, doors were left unlocked. But as we peeked inside, we were never quite prepared for the sights or smells we encountered...**

Like the sad scenes of a post nuclear war movie, or the unsettling lyrics to Nena's "Ninety Nine Red Balloons", it was sadly eerie to observe first-hand what remained in what was once likely a happy household or in Nena's words, "in this dust that was a city"- A random piece of furniture oddly left here and there, dishes stacked on counters with garage sale stickers, refrigerators with children's drawings on the front and rotting food (and sometimes maggots) inside, scuffed up murals on dented walls, the evidence of years of children's growth in height charts marked on doors, empty hangers dangling on closet racks, an occasional mismatched shoe in a corner, pet supplies, half used cleaning products, swimming pools that looked more like cesspools and various odds and ends were often chaotically strewn about.

As we crept from room to room avoiding the onslaught of invading insects, **we couldn't help but empathize with the people who left their homes so abruptly.** As this seemed to be becoming a compelling distraction for us, we were dumbfounded time and again; to **witness the chaos that remained as so many people, who most likely started with better intentions, undoubtedly ran out of time, money & options.** But they didn't just disappear. In the still silence, I often wondered, **"where did they go? Did they find work and move to another area of the country? Did they have a generous friend or relative to lean on?** (Like Bill Withers' "Lean on Me" song). **What other problems did they face? Was this the result of a divorce? A layoff? - both? Was it surmounting medical bills because of illness or injury?** Was life for them before this entire crisis, too grandiose? How did they explain it to the kids? **Were they like me, feeling powerless & heart broken to (against their better wishes) leave their home?"**

Like kids will, our boys took it all in stride but they missed having their dad around regularly and they missed home. To add to my guilt, my mother in law kept telling me, "The kids will be happy when you're happy". Maybe that was true but in the form of unsolicited advice, it just made me feel more inadequate. **Also what felt like a slap in the face to me was the complete inability of financially secure people to empathize.**

While trying to express my gratitude about the fact that Hugh had been able to find new work to one such person, I got a harsh taste of judgment which felt painfully like criticism. I explained that the rest of my family had not yet secured work outside of the housing industry so they were feeling the strain more than ever. With a sincerely baffled expression, this person then asked me why we all did not have savings to fall back on. The thing was that we had already gone through our savings.

**The length of this recession was indefinite but the money in the bank was very finite!**

If companies in our area did have vacancies, they were being flooded with hundreds of applicants for each position, most of which were younger and much more electronically savvy than me. And in retrospect, now I have had department heads tell me that they usually went with someone that they knew instead of plowing through the stack of resumes. It seemed that the school board's policy was to hire recent college grads who'd better fit into the budget rather than experienced higher salary requiring ones like me (& because of union laws, I couldn't even offer to take a pay cut). Besides, updating my teaching certificate after all of the years of being out of this field, would require classes with tuition and time I didn't have.

**I felt like Steve Miller and his band singing: "Well I'm looking real hard and I'm trying to find a job but it just keeps getting tougher everyday** but I know in my heart that I've got to do my part...".

So then I thought maybe I should try to possibly break into something new. I was feeling like an old dog but I was hoping to still be able to learn some new tricks. I wanted to believe that there was a chance that all of this upheaval would result in some new founded possibilities. Or was I bound to remain a "*has-been*" for the rest of my years? Taking a waitressing or bartending job wouldn't even make sense if I had to pay a babysitter for the hours I'd be away from home since Hugh still had plenty of business dinners with doctor clients, etc. And after a decade of running a successful business from home, the idea of starting all over for minimal hourly wage was a tough pill to swallow (but even those positions didn't necessarily fit into school hrs. only). At that point in time, this dilemma was becoming the reality for more and more Americans. To demonstrate the reality of how the gravity of the situation took so many of us by surprise, once again I will turn to a song but I'll need to skip ahead a few years to prove this point-

In an article from, Country Music is Love, Ronnie Dunn (formerly of Brooks and Dunn) had the following story to share: "There is a very unique story about 'Cost of Living'. That song came to me in 2008. Phillip Coleman had written almost the entire song, all the verses and stuff. It didn't have a title. It didn't have a hook line or a chorus. I asked when I first heard it if I could have a shot at it, saying, 'Could you just give me two days? I won't hold it up or anything'. Then I came up with the lines, 'two dollars and change at the pump, cost of living's high and going up,' and the song quickly finished itself. But while the country was reeling from financial losses all across America at that time, some of the label chiefs felt the song wouldn't be relatable in the future. I had one of the record guys saying, 'The economy will be turned around by the time you can get this song out'. Ironically, I had to go back into the studio to make the lyrics say 'three dollars and change at the pump' instead of two dollars".---And as I complete this chapter, we're getting even closer to $4.00!! ☹ Well, back then, I guess it was a blessing in disguise when we had to get rid of our pick up truck and trade down for a more fuel efficient and carpool worthy vehicle, a trusty minivan.

But returning to our early transitional days, thinking that we were now making more practical decisions, we felt that we deserved some time to kick back. So **when Hugh finally got his first paycheck, he surprised me with an evening out at the local Cheeseburger in Paradise in Ft. Myers. He sensed that I still needed to drown my sorrows and get some comfort food.** He was excited and enthusiastic about his new position. I still felt bamboozled, not yet through the after-shock of it all. The live music in the restaurant that night was the musical stylings of "Tequila Tom". Hugh kept requesting all of my favorite Buffett songs and repeatedly dragged me out onto the dance floor. I've never been a good dancer but that night I was glad for this opportunity to literally lean on him. With our enthusiastic support of the band throughout the evening, we befriended Tequila Tom and he encouraged us to join the local Parrot Head club. When we made our way back to our table, I remembered that the boys' household information questionnaires were due back in the school office the first thing the next morning, so I grabbed them out of my purse and began scribbling in order to fill in the blanks. But that was the problem. There still were so many blanks. We did not yet have a local phone number or any local emergency contacts. Then I paused to look up at Hugh and said in a slurred voice,

**"Since he's the only guy we know in town, do you think that Tequila Tom would be willing to be our kids' emergency contact?"**

Then Hugh had to leave town again and the first weekend in our new neighborhood had me unpacking a decade's worth of belongings in the August heat in a garage that would NEVER be able to fit a car in it! As I looked around at the chaotic mess, a very appropriate **song lyric again** blared in my head:

**"Times are rough and I've got too much stuff".**

Somehow these words could always bring a bittersweet smile to my face. When times really are rough, whatever the circumstance, there is enormous comfort in thinking that you're not alone; in knowing that somebody else out there has gone through a similar situation and has walked in your shoes. I guess it's true that misery loves company. Relating to song lyrics has become a life-long coping mechanism for me, but I never really realized how much I relied on that technique until that day.

Fortunately, that song, Jimmy Buffett's, "One Particular Harbour", goes on to joyfully sing about happier days and really gets you caught up in the crescendo. **But as Buffett music will do to most of us, I started feeling sentimental and nostalgic** and the ambition I had for getting through those boxes went right out that garage window!

So I decided to take a bike ride through the neighborhood and attempt to stake out some possible new playmates for the boys instead. I was delighted to spot several burrowing owls throughout the surrounding streets, but no signs of any male youths. I took it as a good sign to discover that this was a region highly inhabited by these owls which were the main subject matter in the movie that Jimmy Buffett co-produced & did a cameo appearance in, *Hoot*. And I learned that apparently many of the scenes were shot here! I do remember scenes when the police car had "CCPD" on the back (the name of the fictional town in the movie was "Coconut Cove") but now I figured out that this must have actually been a Cape Coral police car! We had read the entire book by Carl Hiaasen aloud to the boys prior to the movie's release a few years earlier. Of course we went to see the movie and bought the soundtrack on opening day and proudly have the video in our collection. We also met the people who were the owl handlers for the movie at a boating regatta in Miami! But now, those big eyed adorable little creatures could only entertain our energetic ten and eight year olds for so long and unfortunately, they would not be suitable substitutes for actual playmates. They needed some real peers to get them outside and help distract them from our new cramped living quarters. Unfortunately after combing the whole neighborhood, I only found three old men and they would not do!

It seemed that this neighborhood too had its share of abandoned houses. And unfortunately most of those that had inhabitants were usually filled with senior citizens. I was beginning to believe that this was an unofficial convalescent community. Each morning as I attempted to back the car out of the driveway, I had to watch extra carefully in the rear view mirror for the walking brigade of gray heads (especially the slowest ones with walkers) passing behind us.Fortunately though, most of these elderly folks were pleasant enough and many of them would most likely be candidates for the artificial joint replacements that Hugh was now selling!

So we needed to turn elsewhere to find all of those new lifelong companions that everyone back home insisted that our boys would find in no time. But where were the children in this town hiding? Most of the kids that they met at school were being bussed in from North Fort Myers and the boys were still too timid to invite anyone over. In our new dining room, I insisted we erect a ping pong table that I had found at a garage sale. This was another quick fix which initially led to some new bonding time among the four of us, but eventually we all needed to branch out. We found a local church and looked forward to attending our first Sunday service. Everyone there was very nice. Attending that first mass however further convinced me that living here was going to have us feeling like spring chickens for decades to come!

**While heading toward our car in the parking lot, a one sided conversation between me and Hugh went something like this: "Okay honey, I guess you're right. I've been totally bias about the people in this town. I was way off when I guessed that the median age was around 60. After being in that crowd, I think it's much more like 80!"** So sadly, there were no signs of families for us to associate with there, just a sea of gray heads as far as we could see from our pew at the back of the congregation. ☹

Without new distractions, the boys really missed their friends and cousins back home and their trampoline and I was getting concerned that they were spending way too much time indoors playing video games. For their sake, I was anxious for the local Parks and Recreation sports season to begin. I knew that exercise was another crucial key for me keeping my own sanity. I made a point to attempt to jog at least two miles daily and I depended on the resulting endorphins from those runs to get me through each day. One weekend when the four of us attempted to take a family bike ride, we realized that our neighborhood had no sidewalks and beyond our three surrounding streets, was only a busy highway. I asked people I met for recommendations for area parks that might have some paved trails, but no one could think of any.

It worried me that Hugh and I were not seeing eye-to-eye throughout this time period. He could not allow himself to get down, so he repeatedly accused me of being negative when I pointed out how hopeless this whole place seemed to be. He had a big job to accomplish and it was understandable that he couldn't reach for future success if he acknowledged and focused on our past failures. Besides, he was the one who found this town and with four hundred miles of waterfront property, in his opinion, what was not to like? He was enjoying his new career and didn't expect more from home life except to have me and the boys there. It may have been a smoother transition for the three of us if we had remained behind initially until I could work through all of the minutia, but Hugh and I didn't want the family to be apart any more than necessary and we wanted the boys to start the school year in our new city. He worked hard to establish his new business and in his down time, he just wanted to find a place to sit by one of those waterfront spots.

**He didn't see all of the empty areas of life that needed rebuilding for me and the boys.**

### It was my job to figure all of that out.

But I too, was embracing my own form of denial. Like I said, I could lose myself in a song or make it through the day on the high of exercise endorphins. But my third coping mechanism came every afternoon as it was, "Five O'clock Somewhere" (Alan Jackson). In order to calm my nerves at night,

### I would reach for the antidote to what was *ailing* me: hops and *ale!*

I'd like to think that there are much worse addictions. I suppose we would have been better off without having to make allowances for my beer budget, but other than that, this seemed like a harmless part of my daily routine. With recent events, and the continued lack of improvement in so many areas of my life, I decided to cut myself some slack. I'd shamelessly reach for any justification to carry on in this way. One such regression brought to mind the silly 80's slap stick comedy, *Airplane*, which depicted the scene of an impending plane crash. In that movie, one of the main characters in the airport control tower is repeatedly panned to as he says, "I guess I picked the wrong week to quit… smoking, drinking, sniffing glue, amphetamines, etc." Each scene progressively had him admitting to a more severe addiction. The thought of his statements was justification enough for me! This crashing in of my world around me which I was still trying to come to grips with, had me knowing for certain that this was not the time for further sabotaging myself with an unrealistic attempt at giving up such a crutch. Besides, in my case, being of Irish decent, it was in my blood to have a high tolerance for alcohol so this was more of a habit with very mild effects for me.

Life is full of compromise and I am convinced that learning to pick your battles is essential. When improvement is necessary, it rarely occurs all at once. You don't want to "cut off your nose to spite your face". If drinking in moderation in the safety of my own home kept me from having a nervous breakdown, I wasn't ready to force the issue. I'd have to save those challenges for another day. I had bigger "fish to fry" and

I didn't have to look too far to find lyrics to support this theory. **If Zac Brown could sing the praises of "a little bit of Chicken Fry and cold beer on a Friday night", it was good enough for me!** So each evening, this beverage along with a warm bath and the sedative-like effects of my favorite music usually helped me sleep at night (at least initially at this stage of the game). And as mentioned before, another recurring theme song for this period of my life became "Young Hearts Run Free" by Candi Staton, singing, **"Self-preservation is what's really going on today"**.

But while I was not ready to stop this habit, I was also not doing anything to improve my attitude. I used to be quite optimistic. I honestly try to look at most challenges as learning opportunities. I do like the phrase, **"when you lose, don't lose the lesson"**. I just couldn't figure out what all of this was supposed to be teaching me. At this point, it seemed like every which way I turned had me wanting to bang my head up against a wall. It was like I was stuck in a maze and a phase of hopelessness! Hugh could have peace of mind knowing that he was doing all in his power to provide for the family, but disappointingly, his initial salary was not making ends meet. I was climbing the walls with frustration.

Money was still tight and it was imperative that we continue to cut back wherever possible. **Like the self proclaimed, "Material Girl", Madonna sings, "Experience has made me rich", I was getting a wealth of first hand knowledge in life lessons!** One such lesson was being provided by The Rolling Stones when I heard them singing, **"You Can't Always Get What You Want, but if you try sometimes you just might find, you get what you need"**. Since our current situation was largely due to previously having too much access to credit, learning to live on a cash-only basis was absolutely necessary but that practice does require a learning curve of adjustments.

Michele & Jim Bob Duggar, parents of nineteen children and authors of *A Love that Multiplies*, say, "Buy used, save the dues"(this logic is likely why it looks like consignment shops, like described in Macklemore's "Thrift Shop" and Craigslist are here to stay). As far as Craigslist, **there were some advantages to living in the foreclosure capitol of the world.** We were constantly hearing about people getting a good deal on items they needed from people who were vacating their homes and needing some fast cash. The Duggars also buy all items (even cars) on a cash only basis. If they don't have the cash, they wait.

At that time in our lives, I have to admit that there were days when putting a healthy meal on the table was an after thought. If dinner hour crept up while I was caught up in an online job search and the boys were turning to me with grumbly tummies, I was determined to remain frugal with whatever quick fix I could come up with (like the Allstate commercial when the announcer shares how one of his customers is on a Ramen Noodle every night budget!). So pediatricians and protective parents may cringe here, but our kids got real good at ordering only from the $1.00 menu at the drive thru! I will say that for me, whether it's morning sickness, a hang-over or heart ache, there is no comfort food like McDonalds! And if we did ever indulge in dine-in restaurants, it was only if somebody was eating for free! Fortunately many restaurants started responding to the economy with all kinds of "kids eat free" or "bogo" (buy one, get one) or happy hour menu specials, (like @ Fletchers, on the corner of our street, thanks to our favorite bartenders, Joe & Jassen ). And we found out that the local Mexican restaurant, Iguana Mia offered free food on birthdays & free entrees (w/coupon) weekly. Hugh and I discovered this place upon our first house hunting trip here. We stopped in for a late night snack but had to ask if they were still open because the place was so empty (this was on a Thursday night around 9:00 p.m.). I remember the waiter laughing at us & saying, "where are you from?", when we asked where everyone was. He then proceeded to inform us that this is how Cape Coral is in the summer, which became my first realization that this is a very seasonal town. As we sat and enjoyed their free home made chips & salsa and sipped our margaritas, I thought of Jimmy Buffett's song, "When the coast is Clear" & jazz artist, Steve Oliver's, "Chips and Salsa!"

As far as collecting coupons, it was worth a few minutes to check the flyers that came in the mailbox but it went without saying, that if any catalogs came in the mail, I automatically did the planet a favor and transferred them directly from the mailbox to the recycle bin! I got a tip from Jack Johnson here since one his songs for the *Curious George* movie soundtrack says, "reduce, reuse, recycle". And I began to realize that **if I didn't see it, I didn't want it** (besides I reminded myself that those clothes never look as good as they do on those supermodels!). And I let U2 remind me in their "Beautiful Day" song, **"What you don't have, you don't need it now"**. And since this small town did not have a mall, I took a cue from my brother Don, who always says, "If Wal-Mart doesn't have it, I don't need it"! And if there was a specialty item that the boys needed for school or something, the fact that it required a little extra planning on our part to make the commute over the bridge into the mall in Ft. Myers, kept impulse shopping at bay. We were also becoming better at adopting the "if it's not broken, don't fix it" philosophy when being tempted to upgrade or replace items. As a matter of fact, this entire manuscript is being typed on a 12 yr. old computer!! The benefit here is that the longer we wait to replace it (& instead just keep cleaning it out & propping it up, even though there are constant issues), the more advanced and the more reasonable newer models seem to be becoming! And learning to fix things instead of promoting such a disposable society will no doubt be a necessary skill in the future. Teaching today's youth to be resourceful and know how to take something apart & put it back together instead of hiring out, could really pay off for them.

**However during those first several months, all of the adjustments and sacrifices we were making were not even beginning to result in the relief that we were desperately seeking.**

Knowing that I was capable of being a productive citizen, but not being able to figure out where to begin, made me feel like I was in a vice. **I kept thinking of Jimmy's song, "feel like I'm stranded on a Sandbar, stuck in my tracks like a street car".** Another song that played in the back of my mind was Maccoll Kirsty's "You Just Haven't Earned It Yet". The line in particular which seemed to keep replaying for me says, "You must suffer and cry for a longer time". I felt like Judy Collins as she sang decades ago, **"Isn't it rich? Isn't it queer, losing my timing this late in my career?** Where are the clowns? My dad used to love that song too. I always thought it seemed so depressing but unfortunately, I was relating to it now. Each 30 day period between Hugh's paychecks required a balancing act. As **we usually had too much month left at the end of our money**, but the thought of the holidays approaching and nothing under the tree for the boys was unthinkable.

You have to understand that Christmas was always taken very seriously in my family. Having a mom whose birthday is on Christmas (just like Jimmy Buffett along with Eminem's daughter, so my son tells me) ensured that my childhood Christmas memories were nothing less than glowing. Mom took her role as an elf to heart (& appropriately her maiden name was "Hart"). Every December when I was growing up, our household in Ft. Lauderdale was transformed into Santa's workshop.

(The Sullivan Family, 1996- by our favorite party spot-mom's tiki hut!)

Mom actually took down and boxed away all of her regular household decorations and knick knacks to make room for her Christmas collection. We not only had every tabletop decked out in splendor but we had many musical and moving characters throughout every room of the house, which can actually be kind of scary when that includes the bathroom! Then dad made sure that our home's outside was not neglected. Like Clark Griswold, of the Chevy Chase *Christmas Vacation* movie, dad also knew much about exterior illumination! For decades, we were a popular stop on onlookers' routes. We were in the paper and on the news. We were included in many clubs' tour of homes over the years. I want to add that one of the best presents I ever gave my mom was a framed print with an illustration of Santa Clause and the Easter Bunny conversing with the caption,

### "I'll believe in you, if you'll believe in me".

And the best term of endearment that my boys and I have been able to come up with for her is a fitting play on words- "Grantaclause", because nobody enjoys giving more than she does on Christmas Day. Her generous nature has also really rubbed off on my sister, Jan who's to be commended for remaining as mom's best shopping sidekick during the duration of hours spent picking out the perfect thing for each and every one of the forty-something of us in this extended family! This love of music all started for me on Christmas morning of 1972, when my best gift was my own table-top Victrola style, turn table. I still remember the plastic gold case that it came in. It was accompanied by a couple of 45's (picked out by my sister Jan) including **"Cherokee People"** by Paul

Revere and the Raiders, and Mac Davis' **"Baby, Baby don't Get Hooked on Me"**. I did take Mac's advice and I didn't get hooked on him, although I think Jan may have! However I guess it goes without saying that I certainly did get hooked on music. One of the other best gifts that mom ever gave me & each of my 4 sisters, was a charm saying, "Live, Love, Laugh". Back in the 70's, being among the first to own anything displaying this message, we like to think that we were partially responsible for helping to popularize this saying.

And recently, several decades later, upon returning from a business trip, my husband brought home a bumper sticker saying, "Live-Laugh-Love", that he found at LuLu's, Jimmy Buffett's sister's place (which Hugh describes as "Margaritaville" on steroids) in Gulf Shores, Alabama (the history of this place is rumored to be described in Jimmy's song, "Bama Breeze"). LuLu describes it as a place people come for good food and a good experience. There's no cover charge and plenty of free entertainment for the whole family including a sand filled play area/dance floor and a rope course with swinging bridges and teetering tightropes. It is said that every seat at LuLu's is the best seat in the house because the inviting atmosphere makes this a place people remember and come back to. Additional tidbits that I enjoyed finding in LuLu's magazine are the following: **"I like to live my life in Technicolor with a bright sassy soundtrack...I was taught at an early age to live out loud-and I do."** She was also quoted to say, "If I was to describe the boquet garni that gives the LuLu lifestyle its flavor, it would include a pound each of sand and positivity; a cup each of fun, laughter, integrity and curiosity; a heaping tablespoon of adventure, equal amounts of compassion, second chances and service; a dash of gratitude and a big pinch of yes". And in her giving spirit, Lucy explained, "Since my coastal roots include a little Cajun voodoo, I will leave you with a little Lagnianiappe...(for those of you who don't know, a lagniappe, pronounced, "LAN-yap", is a little something extra given to a customer by a merchant at the time of purchase, such as a 13th shrimp when you order a dozen)". Then she goes on to discuss **her important "f word",** *flexibility,* **saying that, "This goes back to that Buffett "making it up as you go" theme song.** It's okay to change your mind. It's okay to be wrong. It's okay to quit when something's not working and start again. It's okay to make a 180-degree turn in the opposite direction. It's okay for other people to have better ideas than you do. Sure, there is need for structure, planning, order, and organization. But if there is too much rigidity, you could very well miss a great opportunity when presented. Life is an organic and changing entity. You have no idea what may be in store for you, no matter how well you have planned. Sometimes life tends to add a little flavor here or stir up a little zest there-much like a cosmic pot of gumbo, flavored lovingly with what I call the 'mystery'. And there are two life rules that I am devoted to: always save room for dessert…and always save room for the 'mystery'."

**I'd like to thank Jimmy's sister (with a master chef background) for giving us all of that great food for thought**! And I'd like to share that she invites us all into her kitchen in her book, "Crazy Sista Cooking, Cuisine & Conversation with Lucy Anne Buffett, including a foreword written by Jimmy, & a whole section devoted to "Cocktail Hour" with the secrets of LuLu's specialty drinks among numerous recipes & stories. To see LuLu's playlist sampler, referred to as "Two degrees from Jimmy Buffett" RTA

Speaking of family members, I've got to believe that Jimmy and this sister were raised by a very wise, very caring woman, as I was. My mom had her share of tried and true statements that she repeated over the years to try and help us recognize life's lessons, but she never wrote them down, like Jimmy's and Lucy's mom, "Peets" apparently did. On his recent stop at LuLu's, Hugh also picked up a shirt for me with "Peets' Philosophy" printed on the back. Once you see this list, you'll most likely agree with me that this sure sheds some light on where Jimmy must have gotten so many ideas for his work and for how he lives his life. **I'm glad to think that I've pretty well mastered no. 4 on Peet's list, at least when it comes to listening to songs!**-(I've observed that the tricky thing about listening to people, is remembering that usually they just want to share or vent, & are not necessarily asking for advice). And I'm now working on no. 6.-

## "Peets' Philosophy"

(**Words of wisdom and inspiration** by Lucy's mom, Peets)

1. Read often, including the classics.
2. Accept everyone for who they are, not what they do.
3. Be well-traveled.
4. **Learn to be a listener.**
5. Live by the sea.
6. **Listen to your spirit and find joy.**
7. Education, like money, doesn't make you happy-but it sure helps.
8. Love and family are the best things we have."

This input from Jimmy's mom, brings me back to thoughts of my mom my and her holiday spirit. She always preferred traditional Christmas Carols, but Hugh and I have always begun the season with Jimmy's "Christmas Island" CD. And Since we've usually overplayed this one by Thanksgiving, we then turn to our collection of Jazz Christmas CD's including artists like GRP, Dave Koz, David Benoit, Peter White,

Jonathan Butler, Mindi Abair and many other noteworthy performers who have been part of the annual Cool Jazz concert tours throughout the country. Years ago, Hugh & I attended one of these at the Broward Performing Arts Center, which is a formal, old fashioned theatre house. That night, when Jonathan Butler approached the front of the stage and all of the house lights went down, he stood and sang, "Oh Holy Night" looking up in the direction of one lone spot light above. As if the scene didn't appear celestial enough, this performer's facial expressions and bellowing voice, that came from deep inside him, sincerely conveyed a genuine magical moment. To say we were all moved would be an understatement. I suspect that there was not a dry eye in the house; and **we all felt so blessed** to have this gifted gentleman put us in true Christmas spirit.

But now, as I struggle to complete this writing project and possibly forward a copy to Jimmy Buffett as a birthday present (although I feel like the Little Drummer Boy as I think, what could I ever offer to this king of Margaritaville?), I listen to his Christmas album and wonder if it might be Christmas magic that has also motivated him to remain young at heart and make a life long career of spreading joy to others throughout the land the way he does on his concert tours. After all, it was the sound of the Whos down in Whoville singing with joy on Christmas morning that made the Grinch's heart grow to 3 times its size that day. And like I said, my mom, who is also blessed with a Christmas birthday, sure has a big heart, **so I suspect that not all of Jimmy's cheer comes from margaritas and beer!**

And if you're still asking why I relate so well to Jimmy Buffett & his music, I can sight a few more possibilities. In "Wino and I Know" Jimmy refers to himself as "just trying to get by being quiet and shy in a world full of pushing and shove". Like this performer, I come from a large Catholic family and being the sixth of seven, I actually was a shy child. This was most likely due to the fact that somebody else was always talking & somewhere along the way, I must have gotten discouraged waiting for my turn to speak (now in this book, I must be making up for lost time!). As far as what it might be for Hugh, first of all, he proudly boasts that he shares the same birthday, June 1st, with Jimmy's daughter, Savannah. Then there's all of the sentimental substance in Jimmy's song, "Creola" where he describes growing up on the bayou. Since I married a man with roots in Lafayette, Lousiana, I dedicated that song to my father in law on his 80 birthday. The video I put together for his party consisted of several other Buffett songs too, like "Son of a Son of a Sailor" & "I'll play for Gumbo", along with a terrific tribute to life called "Don't Blink" by Kenny Chesney. This grandfather is a graduate of LSU and like Mr. Buffett, is a life long fan of the New Orleans Saints football team, ( I absolutely LOVE the live recording of U2 joined by Green Day, singing a tribute to this team & this town, starting with, "There is a house in New Orleans, they call the Super Dome, it's been the ruin of many a poor boy, in God I know I've won…" & they go on to make the words to the song fit this theme as they cheer on the Saints and REALLY get the crowd going!) and now in our household, we all have also adopted them as our team, even though I grew up in a Miami Dolphins rooting family.

This is a treasured photo that this family I married into, the Heberts (as previously explained, pronounced "A-bear(s)" but you would already know that if you're from New Orleans!) have shared with me-- It's a snapshot of patrons sitting at my husband's grandfather's place, the first air conditioned bar in Abbeville, Louisiana. So apparently he has this drinking thing in his blood too!

But returning to my first holiday season in Cape Coral, I was feeling self induced pressure to keep up the tradition of making magical Christmas memories in our household and since **there were not even lumps of coal in our Christmas fund,** I was determined to do something about it. That's when the following article headline caught my eye--"Job Jugglers on the Tightrope". This New York Times article claimed that the idea of being self employed even if it means struggling to make ends meet and juggling a hectic schedule seems to be a current trend driven by necessity. It stated, "Some portions of the population-especially the young, creative types like actors, artists and **musicians**-have always held multiple jobs to pay the bills. But people from all kinds of fields are now drawing income from several streams". One of those interviewed for this article, Mr. Fierro, has 4 jobs and a long term goal of developing his own merchandise line. The article reports that he is optimistic that he is more likely to achieve his goal by working on many projects than if he held a traditional job. Another individual sited in the article, Ms. Bronco, who graduated magna cum laude with a degree in musical theatre, who also works multiple part-time jobs, says she feels lucky to be employed at all. "The majority of the jobs I have right now are because people were laid off and they didn't want to hire back full-time employees," she said. "My willingness to have a hodgepodge schedule makes me more marketable". The article points out that, "when or if these job jugglers get on a career path, they may offer an attractive skill set because they are expert multi-taskers, hyper-organized and often very knowledgeable in technology. Having multiple jobs is an exercise in mental dexterity," the author claims.

Then it came to my attention that several people I knew or heard about were suddenly having to reinvent themselves too like:

Darla-when her territory and commissions were cut back in her lucrative telemarketing position, she used her best asset, her voice, and is now replacing that income with a collection agency that is trying to take a more non-threatening approach with her more pleasant, yet authoritative voice.

Jeff and Paula- when their real estate investments turned on them and they had to learn the hard way about the short sale process, they turned that newly acquired knowledge into a nationwide business helping others short sell their properties. They also started riding their bikes to work.

Fran and Fred-when their real estate transactions dramatically declined, they signed on with the banks to conduct broker price opinions for foreclosures, a move that has led to steady work and occasional listings for those bank owned properties.

Tami and Joe-when their plan to retire from the Police Department up north and develop new homes in Florida turned out to be bad timing, they moved into one of those inventory homes and used their security background to start a watch service for the many out of town homeowners who could not spend as much time being snowbirds as they'd hoped.

Rick & Rae-these two had the foresight to take an early retirement from his job (literally as a rocket scientist) in the land locked city of Orlando, & downsize from their family dream home there, in order to take a chance on following a dream of opening up and running a family owned beach town Inn. They had the vision to invest in a place that would allow their personalized renovations to transform this small set of suites into a very popular, yet affordable "Margaritaville" like destination in the middle of Fort Myers Beach called Sundeck Suites, which they and their three home-schooled children run (reminds me of Kenny Chesney's "Boats" song-he says, "Twenty years of a land locked job was all that Tom could take. Sitting at his desk alone and depressed, says this just can't be my fate. Went home that night and told his wife you can tell all your friends, it's been real but it aint been fun, gonna get us one of them…boats, vessels of freedom"). I would not say that Rick & Rae are free from work these days, but at least now they enjoy what they do-& knowing every restaurant & bar owner on the strip is quite a perk!

Valerie & Wayne-Having been in the mortgage business, when the housing market turned, they decided to take advantage of the rock bottom prices in the Cape and invest in a duplex that was also zoned for commercial use. They pursued a life-long dream of combining their fishing, cooking, decorating and music skills, and turned both places into a very popular bistro (serving the fresh catch of the day), connected by a charming courtyard which surrounds the band stand for the live entertainment that they regularly provide and participate in! It's the kind of place I imagine JB is singing about in his song, "I Wish Lunch Could Last Forever". They named it, Brewbabies, & while the popularity of this place is really growing, they still treat it like their baby!

Jerry-when the city laid him off from the big expansion project he was counting on, he took any construction work he could find. Many of his jobs involved rehabbing homes with Chinese drywall problems (a common occurrence resulting from the accelerated expansion during the real estate boom when materials had to be shipped in from overseas and unfortunately carried an unhealthy byproduct). He learned early on, how to detect this defect and took this experience further by developing a much in demand home inspection and Chinese drywall remediation company.

So after observing how these individuals rose to the challenge when their circumstances changed, I thought about past holiday seasons when I was able to make extra money by designing & selling gift baskets. Then I thought about Bachman Turner Overdrive's song, "Taking Care of Business; If you take your time, you can get to work by nine & start your slaving job and get your pay; but if you ever get annoyed, look at me, I'm self employed…". So I decided to give it a try in our new town. As illogical as it sounds, I thought to myself, "If companies here are not hiring, I'll go into business for myself". So I set about to acquire minimal supplies, gather some tasty and thoughtful treats, & produce a handful of sparkling samples. Then apron clad, with flyers in hand, I visited 55 local businesses. Everybody was delighted with my samples. So I sat back & waited for the orders to roll in.

During the next few weeks, several calls did come, but unfortunately they were all from debt collectors, not order placers. One by one, we were falling behind on credit card payments. Again at this stage, creditors were not making any allowances. They aggressively hunted you down through the mail and incessant phone calls. We were trying to do the right thing. We tried to keep up with minimum payments. We did not want to claim bankruptcy on top of losing our home. On a side note, I want to make it clear that I believe in making good on your debts. I do not condone irresponsibly avoiding your obligations or backing out of your promises. Throughout my teaching career, I put approximately twenty percent of my own earnings back into my classrooms, so I am not some kind of hoarder of funds. But at that stage of the game, banks were not bargaining with us or even discussing the possibility of renegotiating any terms so I had to follow the advice of a credit counselor who could relate to how fragile I was becoming. I remember the empathetic look on her face as she told me to write all of the banks a letter explaining our situation and expressing our good intention for the future, once we could get back on our feet. Then when the letters came in, I put them all in the "dwald" (deal with at a later date) bin & periodically when I could, I'd face the stack, assess what if anything could be tackled and send in a manageable amount. **But then the day came when** a car stopped in front of the house and **I could no longer hide.**

Out came a nice enough guy who was just the deliverer of more bad news. The mortgage company for our Ft. Lauderdale house absolutely would not consider a loan modification. We were being served that infamous *Lis Pendens*, which activates foreclosure proceedings. Time was running out to sell that house via short sale. There were bidders in place for that most desirable property, but at that point, the bank would not negotiate. I knew this day would come but now I knew for sure that no act of God (like us winning the lottery) was going to reverse all of the motions put in place that year. My lack of ability to bring in any extra money and the constant reminders of our compounding debt had me distraught. At this point I wish I had heeded the wisdom of Crosby, Stills Nash & Young, & also Madness' songs, both titled, "Our House" because the themes of each focus on the people & not the place that make a home; but as Thanksgiving came and went with no relief in sight, I worried that by next year, we could end up being one of those families that the school was collecting for in order to deliver a turkey dinner! Once again with my tail between my legs and my head hanging low, I decided to admit defeat and cut my losses. I was going to return all unused basket supplies in hopes to recoup some of my outlay. Now without a more productive task at hand, I could devote my time to the multitude of paperwork that the short sale company suggested we fill out & turn in, in hopes of still avoiding a foreclosure. A complete financial history was required. As if having to give detailed information exposing all of our delinquencies wasn't humiliating enough, listing my lack of income was even more shameful. The situation was disturbing me more than I realized by the time November rolled around. This pathetic feeling was constantly staring me in the face but the rest of the family was depending on me to be my happy-go-lucky self. After all, I prided myself on being a dependably stable, pleasant mom & wife. Sometimes I think that everyone would have preferred if I had remained in this comfortable denial, but the day came when an incident jolted me into acknowledging that my decreasing self worth had me in the middle of an identity crisis and **I became literally panicked-**

# 6

# The Perfect Storm

("I pushed the fool button"-JB)

It was a Saturday approaching Christmas. All I wanted to do was to get Hugh to sit down with me and review our life on paper. We desperately had to take an inventory of all of our accounts and formulate some plan of attack. We probably needed to go see a credit counselor. Maybe we did need an appointment with a bankruptcy attorney. Hugh however, was looking forward to some lighter leisure time. He had worked a long hard week and he was excited about the idea of taking the boys fishing.

Appreciating the idea of quality time for the three guys, I conceded. This however, left me with a sinking feeling that the whole weekend would come and go and I would never be able to get him to address the situation with me. I think I must have been on automatic-pilot driving through town that day and **every road seemed like the Beatles' "Long and Winding Road"**. That song was meaningful for me as it came to mind on the day years ago when my best friend, Diane left town. It goes, "You left me standing here a long, long time ago.... Many times I've been alone and many times I've cried...Anyway you'll never know the many ways I've tried...But still they lead me back to the long winding road". **Just like back then, I really needed a friend now.**

But instead of looking forward to finding a familiar friendly voice on the other end of the phone in those days, **I was afraid to pick up the phone. It might as well have weighed fifty pounds because every time it rang, it really weighed me down!** I was the one taking all of the calls and reading all of the threatening letters. I was the one communicating with the short sale company. I was the one

151

listening to the boys' disappointments day after day. When Hugh finally was around, there was an enormous *honey-do list* awaiting his attention. Thankfully he is a very handy guy and while I never wanted to interrupt his helpful tasks, at some point I had to make him acknowledge the magnitude of the hole we were slipping into. **This is the stuff that was on my mind that day.**

When he left to take the boys fishing, I drove across town to make my basket supply returns. Being holiday season, the stores were now more crowded and traffic was tedious. As I completed my errands and was almost home, Hugh called and asked me to pick up something for him. He was back at the house now and needed some particular cell type batteries for one of his tools. I made a quick turn into the closest grocery store parking lot in order to grab them and hopefully get home quickly. I walked up to the customer service desk and explained to the teenage clerk what I needed. He left the register and went to the far end of the counter motioning for me to follow him. After some deliberation, we found the matching size and returned to his station to check out. Only a line had formed there in our brief absence. I glanced at the lady standing in front who anxiously shoved her items across the counter to be rung up. I attempted to explain the situation but her response was, "Well, when I got here, nobody was here". I was furious because I just wanted to get home and calmly discuss all that was on my mind with my husband. I was hoping that the clerk would do the right thing and put her in her place but instead he cowered and proceeded to ring her up. She gave me the cold shoulder and turned her back to me in satisfaction. I slunk back hanging my head. Finally she finished and started walking away. As I stepped back up, the clerk realized his mistake and said, "I'm sorry." I calmly responded, "It's not your fault". Then before she reached the exit, that "witch" stopped in her tracks and turned around and screamed at me from across the store, "Bitch!" I couldn't believe it. Instantly every negative emotion wallowing up inside me was ready to explode and it did. I got my bag of batteries and stomped after her to give her a piece of my mind! I screamed to her, "How can you call me a bitch when you're the one who cut in front of me?" I don't remember what she said after that but we exchanged dirty looks & unpleasant gestures and got into our cars.

What I didn't realize until I was turning onto my own street was that she was following me! Literally thank God, my husband and one of the neighbors was out front because now I was shaking as my anger was turning to terror! I quickly explained to Hugh to prepare for the worst. I didn't know if this was going to turn into a drive by shooting or road rage or what. Fortunately, seeing that there would be witnesses, she drove past the house but didn't realize that our street was a dead end. She turned around in a neighbor's driveway and accosted me with more insults as she came back down the street and finally drove out of sight. I told everyone to help me get the license plate number in case she decided to return. Now I'd live in fear wondering if this maniac would come back and try to get further revenge on me or the kids when we might be more vulnerable.

With this incident fresh in my mind, I now had even more to worry about. Then the weekend ended and it was back to all of the creditors' calls and some misguided relatives even more incessant inquiries about my job search. When I picked up the phone, if it wasn't an automated attendant instructing me to contact their company or else, it was my mother in law saying "Hello Linda, did you get a job yet?" She might as well have been using her fingernails to scratch a chalk board into the receiver! And now she was coming to visit in person. As the time approached for her visit, I guess I was becoming more anxious about how to address all of the questions. The Saturday day before her arrival, I intended to scurry around cleaning and buying groceries. **I ended up with a trip to the ER instead.**

While changing the linens on our bed since she would be taking our bedroom during her stay, I started feeling nauseous. Maybe it was the fumes from the bathroom cleaning products.

The master bathroom was barely big enough to turn around in and maybe there was not enough ventilation while I scrubbed in there with strong chemicals. I decided to sit down as I was now also becoming dizzy. I detest vomiting & was becoming increasingly panicked with the thought of those involuntary convulsions. The more nauseous I got, the more I became convinced that I had a full blown case of the flu and those horrible stomach contractions were inevitable. "No good deed goes unpunished," I thought to myself. I had recently spent a few days back in Ft. Lauderdale at my older sister, Barb's bedside. She had previously completed a year's treatment of chemotherapy and had surgery. She was week and susceptible to viruses. She had a terrible case of the flu while I was there (However she has since fully recovered and her's is a shining success story of someone who faced this battle with unyielding courage and beat it!)

Now I was afraid that I had brought that flu germ back to my household. I did not want to postpone my in-laws' visit. Part of their reason for coming was to help with the kids to give me some time to spend at the library updating my resume and to watch the boys for an evening so Hugh could take me out for our anniversary. I was determined to will this away. Then I felt like the urge to regurgitate was overtaking my resistance so I ran to the kitchen to grab a bowl. I sat back down on the bed trembling with dread. My heart was racing and when I leaned over to get it over with, nothing came out!? Gobs of sweat, however, were pouring off of my face into the bowl! And my hands suddenly couldn't keep a grip on the bowl. They were swelling up and becoming stiff. It seemed like my fingers were stuck together like I just had two pudgy claws. This sight scared me even more so I yelled for Hugh to rush me to the hospital because I was afraid that I was having a heart attack. We hastened the boys into the car and took off. When we got to the hospital, the lobby was full. The clerk estimated that there would be about a three hour wait. She didn't expedite my admittance because by this time, all of my symptoms had subsided. I decided that we'd just return home and I'd get a complete physical the following week.

A few days later I found a doctor who could get me an appointment quickly. After a brief examination, she verified that everything physically seemed to be fine with me but she felt that the incident that I described sounded more like a panic attack. She asked if anything had been bothering me! Then once I went through my list, she offered to prescribe some anti-anxiety medication and quickly left the room.

**As I sat there waiting on that cold examination table starring up at the stark white ceiling tiles, these were the song lyrics that came to mind: "Doctor, is there nothing I can take to relieve this belly ache?...You Put the Lime in the Coconut' & drink it all up, You put the lime in the coconut, then you'll feel better"** ("Coconut" by Harry Nilsson).

Then the nurse came back in and snapped me out of that hallucinogenic melody and attempted to further council me. She said that she herself is prone to anxiety attacks and that once you have one, they tend to keep reoccurring. At that point I declined the medication, but like the radio alarm clock which kept repeatedly playing "I Got You Babe" by Sonny & Cher, in the movie, *Groundhog Day*, when Bill Murray has to live out the same day over and over again, until he can learn from his mistakes,

**this was all a wake up call for me. And I began to realize that maybe I'd better reprogram the messages I was listening to and find a way to *change my music*.**

I had to find my way out of the dead-end road I seemed to keep ending up on. On the drive home from the doctor's office, I decided to take a route with as many quiet side streets as possible, in order to maintain a calm temperament. I guess one of the reasons that I'm so open to the messages of songs on my car stereo is because when I'm driving, I allow myself to justify the fact that I'm not responsible for getting any other tasks done. Like everyone else, I sometimes break this rule and slip in a glance at my phone while at a red light, but for the most part, when I have my hands on the wheel, I take a break from my to-do list. And in this way, I actually kick back while in the driver's seat! So on this day, I seemed to slip into automatic pilot (like Adam Sandler in the movie *Click*) as the outside world slowly faded away. And in the stillness, I heard the voice of Zac Brown through the car speakers. I heard Zac telling me:

**"There's a song in my ear that I want you to hear ...Get Away to Where the Boat Leaves From. Takes away all of your big problems. You got worries; you can drop them in the blue ocean but you gotta get away to where the boat leaves from".**

Then I remembered how in one of my very favorite Buffett ballads, **Jimmy says, "I come down to talk to me when the coast is clear...** Hello Mr. Other Me, it's been a long, long time. We hardly get to have these chats. That in itself's a crime. Tell me all of your troubles. I'll surely tell you mine. Let's laugh and joke and cuss and smoke and have a glass of wine". **The cool thing about this love song is that this one is dedicated to himself.** And I believe it's in a very healthy way. It lets us in on how even this partying Peter Pan has a very serious introspective side and like he does in the song, it's okay and sometimes best, for us to be our own best friend. In his "Jimmy Dreams" song, he actually says, **"What a joy when you are your best friend"**. In "The Dock of the Bay", Otis Redding says, "Looks like nothing's gonna change. Everything remains the same. I can't do what ten people tell me to do so I guess I'll remain the same. I'm just sitting on the dock of the bay, watching the tide roll away, ...wasting time". This singer's frustration with trying to please everybody else has him escaping to the ocean too. And eerily, hopefully it's there that he found some peace, because just three days after recording this song in 1967, he suddenly died in a plane crash.

**So now I began to think to myself, if I were to take these singers' advice, how would I indulge myself?** As my own best friend, what favor or kindness would I bestow upon myself? And just like them, the answer was, **I would treat myself to a day at the beach.** After all, Jimmy says "The ocean is my only medication"-"Knee Deep".

# So now I thought, maybe it was time for me to find my way back to the beach-

Photo by Les Criscillo

This is one place where things always seem to make more sense. Walking along the shore or sitting and staring out at the waves always gives me new perspective.

So after dropping the kids off at school the next morning, I decided to play hooky from my daily drama. I turned off the ringer on my phone and headed out to Bowman's Beach on Sanibel Island. This is one of the prettiest beaches I've ever seen. It's a very private spot. The walk over the pedestrian bridge from the parking lot makes you feel like you are truly entering a new land. And **it only took a few minutes of breathing in the salt air that day, to begin the cleansing process** for me. The sun shining on my face, like it was shining on the water, seemed to serve as a mirror of reflection for me. Lee Ann Womack sings, **"I hope you still feel small when you stand beside the ocean"** in "I Hope You Dance". And being in the presence of nature's vast waters with a multitude of mystery beneath and a continuous rolling tide controlled by the moon, can have that affect on you. Being there can give you the sensation that you are part of something bigger and that **maybe not everything is in your control.**

On the surface **it seemed as if it all was coming down to two things: time and money** —and I began focusing on how I needed to economize both of them. **Deep down, I knew that there was a whole lot more to it than that.** However on a daily basis, my quality of life seemed to be directly correlated with how sensibly I spent these two commodities. Of the two, we all know that time is the most important, but making the most of it and really living in the now when you're worried about tomorrow, is easier said than done. **When my finances were in serious jeopardy, I had to face the nagging question of how I was going to make more money, but I also had to examine how I was spending it. When it gets to the point when every dollar counts, you have to make sure you're not wasting a penny. With my recent health scare, I had to reiterate those same questions regarding time.** More importantly, when every minute counts, you have to make sure you're not wasting a second. Especially after witnessing my sister's battle with cancer, I reckoned with the truism that when you don't have your health, nothing else matters. Without physical and mental well being, you're out of options. You are powerless to make the most of your money which doesn't seem to matter if you're out of time. And now I was beginning to question my mental and emotional health.

**How did I become this person sitting in a doctor's office having it cautiously explained to me that I was developing an anxiety condition?** How did I become such an offensive person as to attract such a wretched incident in the grocery store? I could fake it for everybody else's sake, but deep down, it scared me when I thought to myself, "Who was this person I was becoming?" And as I plopped down on my towel in the sand, I heard David Essex, singing in my head, "And where do we go from here? Which is the way that's clear?' from his hit, "Rock On". I began to suspect that, "I'm dying inside and nobody knows it but me" (The Tony Rich Project's "Nobody Knows").

**It wasn't about me feeling sorry for myself, it was more about insecurity, not financial but the self esteem kind-**all of the things that I used to pride myself on (like being a good mom & having an active balanced lifestyle) were in jeopardy because I felt like I no longer knew how to think straight-I was letting all of the deficit in the one area of our life throw me so out of whack that I felt stifled. **And again, I have to emphasize that I was not so attached to all of the material goods** but letting go of the lifestyle, the image, the previous definition of success and ultimately all of the disappointment & defeat was the harder lesson - and **probably more so because there was no new normal for me to embrace.** As I've expressed, in my past life (& by that I mean Ft. Lauderdale) before all of this upheaval, I thought I had it all figured out-like I said, my motto was work hard & play hard. But now it seemed I needed to join Don Henley in saying, **"The Things I thought I figured out, I'm learning again"** ("Heart of the Matter"-this song may be the only one I actually love possibly even more than any of Buffetts! - because **its just packed with lyrical life lessons—**

159

(re: others on my list of songs with good msg.'s, *RTA*). I didn't know what I was supposed to be doing now. But having been raised by a very ambitious feminist mother, **doing nothing certainly didn't feel right-but neither did trying to force something to happen.**

**Then I though about Jimmy Buffett's song,** "Good Guys Win" from the *Hoot* soundtrack, especially as he sings, "Good guys win every once in a while, **full grown men get to learn from a child**". At that point, I was feeling weak & defeated so I figured maybe I should try to think like a child again.

When my boys were young and I was with them full time, I knew exactly where I was supposed to be and exactly what I was supposed to be doing at all times: taking care of them! Now I just wanted to go back to those days. I felt like Kenny Loggins as he sings, "Help me if you can. I've got to get back to the House at Pooh Corner by 1:00. You'd be surprised there's so much to be done: count all the bees in the hive, chase all the clouds from the sky...back to the days of Christopher Robin and Pooh". When I was pregnant with my second son, my first son and I must have watched his Winnie the Pooh video a hundred times. When my second little guy was born, I picked out a small plush Pooh Bear to give his toddler brother as a distraction while mommy was in the hospital. Now I just wanted to go back and relive those simpler times when I didn't know that the future would involve me abruptly uprooting my children from their home.

It's very disheartening when you start to sit back and shake your head thinking, "how could I have been so wrong?" **When the direction of your life takes an unexpected turn, you have a hard time considering that you may have been heading in the wrong direction all along.** It's like when someone you admire betrays you and you're forced to acknowledge that everything you believed in could have been a lie. Being from Chicago and a life-long baseball fan, My dad always used to repeat the line, "Say it aint so, Joe", from a movie called, *Eight Men Out*, which is the story of how the Chicago White Sox conspired with gamblers to throw the

1919 World Series (we even have a distant cousin, John "Lefty" Sullivan, who was a Rookie pitcher for the team at the time). There is a scene in the movie when a young boy approaches the legendary Shoeless Joe Jackson and begs him to deny the charges that got him and seven other players banned from baseball. The rumor is that Joe was innocent and played a no error game, but still got charged. The bewildered child was left feeling so disillusioned by all of these guys that he had looked up to. Styx has a line in the song, "Show Me the Way" that says, **"The heroes and legends I knew as a child, have fallen to idols of clay and I feel this empty place inside, so afraid that I've lost my faith"**. It's very difficult to reprogram your whole mindset when something takes you by such surprise. At this point in my life, I just kept thinking, "how could I have been so mislead?"

**I felt as lost as that infamous "shaker of salt"** (in case there is anyone on the planet who doesn't know, that's from Buffett's "Margaritaville!").

And as he also sings about in "First Look", "I was feeling like a missing link". This feeling seemed to become amplified as the words to Dr. John's 70's hit, "Wrong Place", began ringing in my ears: "I been in the right place, but it must have been the wrong time. I'd of said the right thing, but I must have used the wrong line. I been in the right trip, but I must have used the wrong car. **My head was in a bad place and I'm wondering what it's good for**....Slipping, dodging, sneaking, Creeping, Hiding out down the street. See my life shaking with every who I meet. Refried confusion is making itself clear. Wonder which way do I go to get on out of here".

As I sat there meditating by the shore, I glanced up at a nearby wooden sign post, like you often see in dockside settings, displaying a vertical succession of attachments with the names of different destinations in each direction with corresponding arrows painted on them. And **I remember thinking that if one of them said "My Life" on it; it probably would have been heading in the wrong direction!** I also remember wishing that one of them would just point me clearly toward my future. I thought about Five Man Electrical Band's seventies hit, "Signs", with the words, "Signs, signs, everywhere a sign, blocking out the scenery, breaking my mind, **do this, don't do that.** Can't you read the sign"? **At that point, I would have welcomed such an instructional sign.** I thought about how neat it would be to see one of these posts with the destinations,

## "Margaritaville", "Kokomo", "Thunder Island", "Penny Lane" and "Fins" on it.

I felt like I was already on "Penny Lane", only it was no longer the pleasant utopian suburban village that the Beatles sing about. In my reality, it was for people like me who were counting every penny! I felt like the life that was my daily drama was my form of "Thunder Island", only that too was not the fun romantic place that Jay Ferguson sings about. It was instead a manifestation of my stormy state of affairs. Since I felt unsure about which way to turn, I felt like I did sense "Fins to the left, Fins to the right", with sharks dangerously circling. I longed to go to the place that the Beach Boys describe in "Kokomo" or

**ultimately, I just wanted to find "Margaritaville"**-because as I said earlier, when asked, **Jimmy Buffett always says that**

## "Margaritaville" is not a state, but rather a state of mind.

In this song, at first Jimmy starts off being tempted to cast blame... "Some people claim there's a woman to blame, but I know it could be my fault". But by the third refrain, he has a cathartic realization ... "It's my own damn fault". This ability of his to take responsibility, in my opinion, is the first step in any healing process. So I don't think that he's "Wasting away again in Margaritaville". It's actually quite the opposite.

## I think that "Margaritaville" is a representation of a place we all can go to initially run away, but then to face the truth, and consequently to find freedom.

When something's bothering me, Hugh always know he's most likely to get it out of me after a few drinks. I think we've eased into this method of saving our serious discussions for a time when we can sit face to face, away from the kids & away from our clients, yet out in public so nobody can raise their voice! And in this way we still manage to keep some of the *happy* in happy hour! So as my mom always said, "The truth always comes out". And **no mater what problems come up in life, getting to the truth is key.**

So I began to realize that it was time for me to find a way to put my mind's eye in that direction. As I walked along the shore I thought, if Bob Dylan was right and the "answer is blowin' in the wind", "what is the wind telling me?" And my immediate instinct was that it was whispering to me to look within for some answers. I thought about the scene in *The Lion King* when Simba goes to wise Rafiki for some guidance. He expresses to him how he wishes he still had his dad around to tell him what to do about his problems. That's when Rafiki tells Simba, "He lives within you". **As hard as it is, sometimes we're the only ones who can solve our own problems.** The beauty of this quiet retreat with the surf blocking out all the negative noise of daily life left behind, helped me to begin to acknowledge that a lot of this could be "my own damn fault" too. **No, I was not entirely to blame for the situation we were in, but I was responsible for how I was reacting to it and how I was letting it affect me.** And then I heard Tina Turner telling me, "This is time for letting go" ("I Don't Wanna Fight"). After the shopping rage incident and the panic producing nausea, I knew it was time for this quiet contemplation. **The Eagles sing a song called, "Learn to Be Still"** and instead of forcing the issue and trying to make something happen, I felt it was time to follow that song line.

Then I thought about that song on the radio the day before that lead me here. I thought about how fate delivered such an apropos song dedication and I wanted to say, "Ok, well here I am and you're right Zac, it is starting to help". It's a good thing that a boat didn't come along at that moment because I just may have been capable of jumping in it in hopes of sailing away and leaving my cares behind! I could probably conjure up some lyrics to justify such an escape like Styx' "Come Sail Away…a gathering of angels appeared above my head. They sang to me a song of hope and this is what they said: Come Sail Away with me…". **But I sat there putting my dilemma out to the universe and feeling again like Styx, as they sing, "I keep on hoping for a sign,** so afraid that I just won't know. Show Me the Way. Take me tonight to the river and wash all of my illusions away… Give me the strength and the courage to believe that I'll get there someday. Please show me the way". Then I thought about how Zac Brown chose his words carefully in his song. He did not say, "get away in a boat"; he seems to indicate that it's good enough to **just get to where the boat leaves from.** Just standing at the water's edge can get you far enough toward transformation. It seems to be a place of possibility, a place for releasing anxiety. And for me that day, it also just may have needed to include **a cold slap of water in the face to snap me out of my self sabotage.** In "Cowboy in the Jungle", JB sings, "Forget that blind ambition and learn to trust your intuition, plowing straight ahead, come what may".

"Hmmm," I thought. "Maybe there's a message in a bottle floating out there somewhere that'll tell me what to do?" Maybe like The Police, I could, "Send My SOS to the World" and find "a hundred million bottles washed up on the shore".

**Maybe the answers to my problems will surface with that infamous "lost shaker of salt-?" Or maybe I was just becoming delirious as I sat there in the sun with that *Landshark* bottle!**

Before I drove myself any crazier, maybe I just needed to let life continue to unfold at its own pace. Maybe it was time to listen to Zac Brown telling me "know you're not the only ship out on the ocean, **save your strength for things you can change, forgive the ones you can't, you gotta let 'em go"**. (And this one makes we want to hear "The Serenity Prayer" with a very similar message, put to music). And back to Jimmy, I thought about how he declared, **"I'm rearranging all of the guilt in my mind"** in "Smart Woman w/ A Real Short Skirt". So then I thought that maybe our profession no longer being viable was life's way of telling me that being *laid off* in this way was a sign for me to live a more *laid back* life. Maybe it was time to exercise that- **"License to Chill"** (JB, Mac MCAnally & Al Anderson).

**By the way, I've been wondering, are you more qualified to exercise this license when you've finished your work, or when you've demonstrated an ability to avoid it?**

One of the things I love so much about song lyrics is how cleverly they can make a play on words. Literally, I love words and honestly find learning new vocabulary enjoyable. Then there's the second part to *word-play*, "play" itself. **And who doesn't prefer play over work? So isn't it nice how we *play* a song? We'll never have to *work* a song!**

165

And in this way, songs can *play* a very nice part as they help us *play*-out the stages of our lives! When Todd Rundgren sings, "I don't want to work; 'I Just Want to Bang on the Drum All Day"(also recorded by The Calypso Nuts), and Bruno Mars sings, "Today I don't feel like doing anything", in the "The Lazy Song", it seems to pay off pretty nicely for them! At this point, there was no career path that I could clearly see. There was no visible source with my future mapped out on it. However, it was time for me to return to the mainland and pick up the boys.

And when I got back to the car, I realized that I had parked right next to a big coconut tree so I tossed a few of the fallen ones in the back and decided that **on this bare bones Christmas, we would give painted coconuts to family members as personalized gifts**. And our relatives in Michigan were delighted with the tropical scene we painted on theirs when it was delivered to their door (By the way, the post office will mail coconuts unwrapped with proper postage). And we didn't realize that this would be the gift that would keep on giving but the one that we decorated to look like a Miami Dolphins football for my brother's family, later sprouted a baby Palm Tree!

*Anyway,* on my drive over the Sanibel causeway leading through Ft. Myers, and then back over the bridge into Cape Coral, I couldn't seem to find much on the radio other than talk programs. Then it occurred to me that at other difficult times in my life, in addition to soothing songs, I have benefited from self-help books. I took this as a cue to stop off at the local library on the way home. With the boys in tow, I picked up a few popular titles promoting problem solving and since all of my music listening had trained me to be an auditory learner, I got them in audio whenever possible. Now, armed with advice from these authors, I was determined to get out of my rut.

As I delved into this world of self-help, the first book, which was one of Oprah's recommendations, was called, *A New Earth, Awakening to your Life's Purpose*, by Eckhart Tolle. As I began playing this audio during my daily runs and walks, a concept seemed to leap off the page and strike me between the eyes, or because I was actually listening to it and not reading it, it seemed to start ringing in my ears. There was a term the author referred to as a "pain body". In my interpretation, this refers to the idea that when you go around with a chip on your shoulder, you attract others with resentments of their own and as you come in contact with one another; your attitudes comingle resulting in compounding effects. This is a subconscious, yet powerful process. Have you ever met someone who just bugs you? I once had a neighbor who usually said and did all of the right things, at least to my face, yet somehow every time I encountered her, I walked away shaking my head saying to myself, "I can't put my finger on it but there's something about her that makes me uncomfortable". It goes along with Jeff Olsen's (author of the Slight Edge), reference to each person's own music; the body language and energy they carry, which can say more than spoken words. So the woman who threateningly followed me home from the store was probably just allowing her pain body (whatever in her life that it may have been attributed to at the time) to chase after mine. On the surface, I honestly did not say or do anything in the beginning to warrant her to stop in her tracks and scream across the store at me. But she must have tuned into the heavy body of pain that I was dragging around that day. I guess it's also like "two wrongs don't make a right." This incident reinforced to me, the concept that negative thoughts and feelings lead consequentially, to more negative circumstances. So I started really trying to be more aware of my attitude.

I then discovered that my brother, Jim also owned a book by this author, called *The Power of Now*. Jim leant me his book and as I read that one, I began focusing more on the whole issue of time again. The irony here is that as good as that book was, the first message I got from it, was that I felt guilty for not living in the moment enough, so I put it aside before finishing, in order to attempt more "Quality Time" with my family, (which is also the theme of a song by Bankie Banx, recorded with Jimmy Buffett called, "Stuck in Paradise"). **So now songs about time caught my attention and there were plenty of them.**

**In songs, time is often sung about with a tie-in relating it to water.** For example, from my senior year in high school, when I knew that many of my friends and I would end up going to college all over the country and that life would never be quite the same, the song, "Time" by The Alan Parsons Project became meaningful. It had such an eerie melody that haunted me throughout that year and its words kept replaying in my head now: "Goodbye my friends, Maybe forever. Goodbye my friends. The tide waits for me. Who knows where we shall meet again if ever. But time keeps flowing like a river on and on, to the sea, to the sea---"

**Then of course, in my Jimmy Buffett stash**, there was the lyrical advice: **"Roll with the punches, play out all of your hunches, 24 hours, maybe sixty good years, it's not really that long a stay"** from the song, "Cowboy in the Jungle" and songs saying: "Life's Short, Call Now" & "Only Time Will Tell" & "According to my watch, **the time is now**...this watch is never wrong." ". I once had one of my boy's teachers give me a gift for being room mom. It was a clock that also had several openings for pictures. I've put some of my favorites of our boys in this frame but was disappointed one day to realize that the metal hands of the clock had become broken off (probably in all of our moves). Anyway, still cherishing this keepsake, I decided to paint the word "Now" in the circle where the hands were, taking a cue form Jimmy of course!

And then there were the words to, "Mademoiselle Voulez-Vous-Danser": "We all have so little time, won't you put your hand in mine. That last one made me think of holding my kids' hands and how children are so good at living in the moment and how I vowed to realign my priorities by getting more in touch with my inner child. There is nothing like a baby, starting with their newborn cry, to force you to respond and take care of them **now**. Only it's not just answering their survival needs that requires immediate attention. In my opinion, it is next to impossible to concentrate on anything else when in the presence of a child under the age of four, so my philosophy always was, "if you can't beat them, join them". What I'm referring to here is the masterful way a child can demand attention and force you to join them on their level and spend time with them in their world (all kidding aside, NO part of that statement was referring to beating in the violent sense!)

When I was a preschool teacher, the motto implemented in our program was, "Children learn through play. Play is children's work". And the Curriculum Specialist that the school board periodically sent in for on-site visits, always encouraged us to concentrate on the *process not the product*. It didn't matter if a child's clay creation while at the art station looked like a goopy brown (since they always mixed all of the other colors to result in one color=brown) volcano, if they were learning in the process, and wanted to call it a ski resort, we were to play along.

There are some precious songs in appreciation of childhood (which make excellent baby shower playlists-RTA). But for now, I'd like to share some personal experiences about my own children because I think Jimmy is so right to encourage us grown ups to sometimes learn from a child (in his "Good Guys Win" mentioned above). When my oldest son started preschool, we had no idea that the first kid that walked up to him would bring new life-long friendships for us all. When 3 year old Ryan Hamilton walked up to my toddler who was about to be out of my presence for one of the first times in his life, I was so grateful that he distracted him enough with the jungle animal toy set so I could quietly retreat from the classroom and attempt to give his younger brother some one on one mommy time. Coincidentally, Ryan had a younger sibling the same age as my younger son, Eric. On that first day of school, I guess his mother, Teresa (a very nice woman but not **the** "Mother Teresa"!) & I thought alike because she showed up at the same playgroup with her daughter where I had gone with Eric after we dropped the older guys off. And after we began chatting we realized how much we had in common (especially since she and my mother have the same maiden name, Hart) so we instantly hit it off and spent many days together with all of the kids and eventually she and her family joined us for their first trip to the Florida Keys. They have since relocated back to their hometown in Canada and someday we'll make good on our promise to let them introduce us to their part of the world.

Once again jumping forward, I heard Jim Carrey in an interview speaking about a children's book he's now written. He shared that reading bedtime stories is one time in a parent's day, when they get to plop down and connect with their children. These few moments are sometimes the only time in the day that is set aside to just be together. And he wrote his book because he wanted to be part of that tradition in people's lives. **During our kids preschool years, we loved books that rhyme, which were mostly more like long poems, much like songs. So in this chapter, as I reflect on how I was attempting to regain the optimism of a child, I am going to share some of my favorite poems (that I'd love to see somebody record to music!?...)**

As I explained above, Teresa's family and mine spent some special years together and we were constantly spending time at each other's houses. One day while we were all hanging out at her place, I noticed a precious plaque in her guest bathroom. It brilliantly pointed out the importance of **really** spending time with your kids with this poem:

"Excuse This House" (Author Unknown)

Some houses hide the fact that children live there.

Ours boasts of it quite openly, the signs are everywhere.

For smears are on the windows, tiny smudges on the doors.

I should apologize I guess, for toys strewn on the floor.
**But I sat down with the children
& we played & laughed & read.**
Even though the doorbell doesn't shine,
their eyes will shine instead.
At times I'm forced to choose the one job or the other.
I want to be a housewife, but first I'll be a mother".

Okay, most of us have additional jobs on top of the two mentioned above, but what an outstanding reminder of the importance of prioritizing any free time that we may have. And sometimes we all need a dose of the simple joys that children are so good at embracing. At a parenting seminar I once attended, the speaker advised us to try to say "yes" as much as possible. Like Jim Carrey, in one of my favorite movies, the hilarious, *Yes Man*. And you may be surprised how easy it is. I do know parents whose automatic reaction to their kids' requests is, "no". Some of them have expressed that this will help them develop into self disciplined adults. I have witnessed these same parents not applying this rule to themselves as they've expressed statements like, "it's easier to ask for forgiveness than permission". As far as their argument about self discipline, I think that self esteem is even more important; which is why I am a big proponent of giving children plenty of praise. And my preschool teaching days also helped me to learn that the more specific the praise, like explaining what it is specifically that you like about a child or how you admire what they've done, the more meaningful and memorable it is for them.

And I've found plenty of material reinforcing this principle. In an article in SELF Magazine, titled, "Energy, Grit, Love", one of the 8 traits on their **"happiness list" is gratefulness**, even more specifically, naming what precisely you are grateful for. The article suggests giving details about how exactly you benefitted when thanking someone. It says, "Let your sister know how thrilled you are about the **playlist she**

**downloaded** on your iPod, being sure to mention a few of the songs you rocked out to most. You'll get an added lift from taking pleasure in the little things"(interesting how they used music in their example!!).

Jimmy Buffett has a song called, "Quietly Making Noise" where he speaks of how "pissing off the old killjoys starts with kindergarten toys", and I think he may be referring to the theme of the following popular poem: (again wouldn't these lines make great lyrics put to a simple upbeat melody?)

### "All I Need To Know I Learned in Kindergarten"
(By Robert Fulghum)

Most of what I really need to know about how to live

and what to do and how to be, I learned in kindergarten.

**Wisdom was not at the top of the graduate school mountain, but there in the sandpile** at Sunday school.

These are the things I learned: Share everything. Play fair.

Don't hit people. Put things back where you found them.

**Clean up your own mess.** Don't take things that aren't yours. Say you're sorry when you hurt somebody.

Wash your hands before you eat. Flush.

Warm cookies and milk are good for you.

Live a balanced life-

**Learn some and think some and draw and paint and sing and dance and play and work everyday some.**

Take a nap every afternoon. When you do go out into the world, watch out for traffic, hold hands and stick together

### Be aware of wonder"

On my bulletin board in my home-work station, I have a few of my favorite pictures of my boys in action as they encountered sea creatures up close during one year's Mother's Day trip to the Mote Aquarium in Sarasota (BTW, what a treat that the place that I picked to go that day, was letting moms in for free!). I didn't necessarily snap posed pictures of them that day. Instead I have action ones like them putting their hands up to the glass as 2 mammoth manatees (1 named "Buffett" & 1 named "Hugh-manatee"!-honest!) glided by us.

I also have one shot, taken from the side, of my younger son leaning over the rail almost too far, as a giant sea turtle swam up and lifted its head as if to stare back in Eric's eyes. Another photo in this collection has my boys standing in front of a telescope on an observation deck at Bass Pro Shops, as they are pointing out at the water in Key Largo. A magazine quote that I attached to theses pictures says,

"See the world through little eyes".

And another way I've seen it put is, "Allow your inner child to come out and play instead of always being an A-**Dull**-T".

Who would have ever known we'd spend the rest of our lives trying to master Kindergarten lessons?! And again, apparently Jimmy Buffett may be doing better than the rest of us at it!---

In "Jimmy Dreams", he says, **"He's a child to the end...the world's still a toy if you just stay a boy...** You just spin it again and again... There's no bigger kick than just rhyming again and again". So again, maybe nursery rhymes and fairy tales may not be so disillusional after all. Jimmy Buffett also produced a song back in the 80's, on his *Floridays* album called, **"I Love the Now"**. A quote on my present day wish board says, "We are not born all at once, but by bits. The body first, and then the spirit later" (cut from a magazine article by Mary Antin). This tag line is accompanied by an adorable toe-headed toddler in overalls hugging a tree. Some people may not relate to this philosophy but others share how they've had cathartic moments throughout life when they sense they're discovering something they already knew. JB sings, **"Who knows why we start rediscovering our heart, we just do it again & again-**Jimmy Dreams). It's kind of like Deja-Vu, a phenomenon described in Dionne Warwick's hit song by that name, when she sings about feeling like she's been in a certain place and even known certain people before. I think this is the soul reawakening like in the above quote & like John Denver describing, "He was born in the summer of his 27$^{th}$ year, coming home to a place he'd never seen before-Rocky Mountain High". In Jonathan Butler's very melodic "Sing Me A Love Song" he says, **"My soul remembers this"**. And **Jason Mraz asks, "How old is your soul?" in "I Won't Give Up" (likely the most moving song video on Youtube, I've ever seen!-hard to watch & listen to this one & not improve your thinking even just a little)**. Many people buy into the philosophy that we meet the people we're supposed to meet on this Earth and they'll come in and out of our lives for different reasons. If this is the case, than insisting on planning everything in a regimented way is pointless (although I'm not condoning throwing out structure all together, just like Lucy Buffett stated). But Jimmy's whole theme about living spontaneously or on "Island Time" may be the smarter thing to do and it is so well put in the following poem (given to me by a fellow teacher in the early 90's, but **is it ever relevant today!**

### "Someday Isle"

(By Dennis Waitley)

There is an island fantasy, a "Someday I'll", we'll never see

When recession stops, inflation ceases

**our mortgage is paid**, our pay increases

That Someday I'll where problems end

**where every piece of mail is from a friend**

Where the children are sweet and already grown

Where all the other nations can go it alone
**Where we all retire at forty-one
playing backgammon in the island sun**
Most unhappy people look to tomorrow
to erase this day's hardship and sorrow
They put happiness on lay-away
& struggle through a blue today- But happiness
cannot be sought, it can't be earned, it can't be bought
Life's most important revelation is that
**the journey means as much as the destination
Happiness is where you are right now,**
Pushing a pencil or pushing a plow – It's knocking on doors
and making your calls -**It's getting back up after your falls**
It's going to school or standing in line
Tasting defeat, tasting the wine
If you live in the past you become senile
If you live in the future you're on Someday I'll
The fear of results is procrastination
**The joy of today is a celebration**
You can save, you can slave, trudging mile after mile
But you'll never set foot on your "Someday I'll"
When you've paid all your dues and put in your time
Out of nowhere comes another Mt. Everest to climb
From this day forward make it your vow
**Take Someday I'll and make it your Now!"**
My husband thinks that someone should record this poem being sung to a reggae beat which would probably give it just the right tempo. The line about Mt. Everest reminds me of

Miley Cyrus' "The Climb"- a very inspiring song about how we need to remember to enjoy the journey & not always just focus on the destination- "There's always going to be another mountain. I'm always going to want to make it move. Always gonna be an uphill battle. **Sometimes I'm going to have to lose.** Aint about how fast I get there. Aint about what's waiting on the other side. It's the climb. The struggles I'm facing. The chances I'm taking. Sometimes **might knock me down but no, I'm not breaking**. I may not know it but these are the moments I'm gonna remember most. Yeah, just gotta keep going. And I gotta be strong. Just keep pushing on".

And another song about not postponing joy, is one that George Strait recorded with the lyrics: "Folks are always dreamin' bout what they'd like to do. But I like to do just what I like. I'll take a chance, dance the dance. It might be wrong but then again it might be right. There's no way of knowing what tomorrow brings. Life's too short to waste it. I say bring on anything. I aint here for a long time. I'm Here for a Good Time".

These many lines of poetry and lyrics can be summed up very adequately with another apropos quote stating, "Yesterday is history, tomorrow is a mystery, **Today is a gift which is why it's called the present.**"

In 1973, I a saw a TV movie called, *Sunshine*, with a storyline similar to *Love Story*, with a young newlywed woman who is dying. In it, there's a tear jerking scene accompanied by Jim Croce's (another artist who died in a tragic plane crash) "Time in a Bottle" & that song, especially hearing it at such a young age, riveted me to the core. I was only 8 years old watching that movie (back then, we had one family TV set so I watched whatever my older siblings had on). But I remember having to leave the room and cry myself to sleep after it ended. There were scenes with the mom, who happened to be married to a struggling **musician**, got the idea to make a journal of tape recordings for her young daughter to listen to throughout the rest of her life so she could feel like she knew her mom. It was heart wrenching to watch as this parent was helpless in getting the one thing that she desperately wanted and **the only thing that seemed to matter anymore, more time.**

Rod Stewart has a song called, "Young Turks" including the lines: "Because life is so brief, and time is a thief, when you're undecided. And like a fistful of sand, it can slip right through your hands". Another stanza alludes to his advice to young people as he sings about not letting others "push you down or push you around or change your point of view. Young hearts, be free tonight". It is a shame how that childhood spirit does become suppressed in most of us. I think the song to replay for us all, is Frank Sinatra's "Young at Heart!" –especially the lines: "For it's hard you will find to be narrow of mind if you're young at heart....You can laugh when it seems your dreams fall apart at the seams....**For as rich as you are, it's much better by far to be young at heart".**

On his 1974 "A1A" album, Jimmy Buffett has a song called, "Life is Just a Tire Swing". In it he reminisces about the carelessness of childhood. He refers to himself as a "tranquil little child" and recalls that back then he "never knew a thing about pain". When I hear this one, I can picture myself pushing my boys on the swings at the park. I admit, especially during the fall when the weather turns crisp but the sky is still bright and sunny (like Joe Nichols "Sunny & 75") on days like these, I long for those few years that I spent as a stay-at-home mom with my boys. I found them to be all consuming therefore I did a pretty good job of devoting most of my concentration to them. I knew I wouldn't be good at handling the stress of chores that required brainpower during those hectic years, so I didn't set myself up for failure with unrealistic expectations. This did make it harder to keep the bills paid however. Of course, there was the obvious lack of income on my part, but also literally, balancing the check book and any other household paperwork usually waited until the kids went to bed, or until daddy could run a little interference. With two active boys less than two years apart, it was sometimes challenging enough just getting through some of those exhausting and frustrating days, especially like the ones when cases of stomach flu or painful ear infections or simply toddler temper tantrums seemed to be possessing our home. And the rest of the time, it was tiring enough just chasing after them from sun-up to sun-down. But I now realize that it was a luxury to be able to give most of my focus to them and

## I will always be grateful for every minute that I did not miss.

If I could dedicate a song to them at this point, it would be Rod Stewart's, "Forever Young" with the lines, "May the good Lord be with you down every road you roam. And may sunshine and happiness surround you when you're far from home. May you grow to be proud, dignified and true. And do unto others as you've have done to you. Be courageous and be brave, and in my heart, you'll always stay, forever young. May good fortune be with you, may your guiding light be strong. Build a stairway to heaven with/*as* a prince or a vagabond. May you never love in vain, and in my heart you'll always remain, forever young. And when you finally fly away, **I'll be hoping that I served you well**. For all of the wisdom of a life-time, no one can ever tell. For whatever road you choose, **I'm right behind you** when or lose, forever young".

Country singer, Phil Vassar has two hits on this topic, both of which reflect on what he calls, "a realization that you have to come to terms with". In a TV interview, he explained how he wrote, "Don't Miss Your Life", after meeting an older businessman on a plane who shared with him how his career took him away from so many important moments in his kids' lives. This may have not happened if he had listened to Don Henley's, "Heart of the Matter", telling us, "Pride and competition cannot fill these empty arms and the work I put between us, you know it doesn't keep me warm". One of the last lines in Vassar's song says, "I heard some words that hit me hard last night", referring to the warning from his fellow passenger about how you can never get **those ordinary, yet special, moments** back. In "Just Another Day in Paradise",

Phil sings about all of the everyday minutia of running a household and raising a family and how he chooses to cherish this time instead of resent it. Just like in the previously mentioned Trace Adkins song with a young mother apologizing to her father for the chaos when he drops by her house for a visit, and then he reminds her that **"You're Gonna Miss This"**. And Billy Joel sings, "These are the Times to Remember cause they will not last forever". Just like Kenny Chesney's , "The Good Stuff", a song about how a bartender points out to a patron who orders "the good stuff", that if he has a family at home, then "the good stuff" is already waiting for him there: "…he walked up and said, what'll it be. I said the good stuff. He didn't reach around for the whiskey. He didn't pour me a beer. His blue eyes kinda went misty. He said you can't find that here. He grabbed a carton of milk and he poured a glass. I smiled and said, I'll have some a that. We sat there and talked as an hour passed like old friends…" Then the song ends with the bartender's advice for this man to turn around and go home and, "look into those eyes so deep in love and drink it up, yeah man, that's the good stuff".

When I look back on our years as new parents learning to cope with the stress of daily situations, certain memories shine through. I vividly remember some days when Hugh would get home to find me and our toddlers dancing and prancing around the house with an upbeat Disney music CD on full volume. We had an open pathway through our family room and kitchen that formed one big circle so we would parade around & around. It was always with pure delight that Hugh would drop his keys and briefcase at the door to join our parade as we all shook off our cares and celebrated getting through another day.

**When I look back on that time, I like to give us and that energetic music we relied upon, some credit for teaching our children how to get in touch with, and express their joy.**

But allowing me to be able to spend quality time with our sons back then, had my husband working two jobs, usually relying on me to handle all errands and it goes without saying that all household chores were still up to me too. And I am not complaining about any of this. I am just pointing out that *stay-at- home moms* still have very big jobs too! And before I leave the subject of raising kids and music, if you'll allow me one more digression before I conclude this chapter, I'd like to turn to the topic of: **Sex, Drugs and Rock & Roll…**

Ok now that I really have your attention, I feel compelled to give some praise to Country music and how it has evolved from decades ago when the themes seemed to be more raunchy and full of "whooa is me" to today's mostly upbeat empowering songs. For example, **an interview I saw with megastar Taylor Swift, put her on an eternal pedestal in my eyes.**

When asked about her thoughts on the responsibility of being a role model, she gave a glowing answer, pointing out that **all singers on the radio need to realize that they are raising the next generation.** What an old soul, ahead of her time, truly deserving of all of the awards she's gotten!! I say Amen to this Angel! When I was teaching elementary school, I used to cringe at the folders, notebooks, backpacks and lunchboxes that second graders would bring in with a popular teen singer of that era, in a tight half shirt, exposing her bare mid-drift, strutting a provocative dance pose, **so** strongly sending them the wrong message! I couldn't be more proud of Ms. Swift's mature attitude while her songs make powerful impressions on her youthful audience, which makes her work even more appealing to those of my generation. And in an article that I read in **Vogue**, Taylor Swift had this to say on the subject of relationships and heartbreak, **"The only way I can feel better about myself-pull myself out of that awful pain of losing someone-is writing songs about it to get some sort of clarity"**. And I think that she helps many others do the same with her therapeutic lyrics. My son has shared that he feels she could be gentler with all of the lyrics about what the men in her life have done wrong, but I think that life has just taught her to be very assertive in standing up for herself. I feel that she is such a breath of fresh air at a time when this world really needs one! In a very on target subject matter for her target audience, her **"Mean"** song is simply brilliant. I *mean*, it is so simply states, "Why you gotta be so mean?" with candor, as it shames anyone who'd actually attempt to answer this question & justify being mean! The statement I always repeat to my kids whenever they come home with gripes about how a certain kid or occasionally it's unfortunately an authority figure, is making demeaning statements to them is:

   **"All Negativity Stems from Fear".**

I also like: **Be Happy in front of people who don't like you- it kills them!"** ☺☺☺

& similarly, **"Living Well is the Best Revenge"**

I know this is easier said than done. I try to advise them as I had to learn as a teenager at my first job at McDonalds, when a customer was being unreasonably rude, killing them with kindness really did kill their mood. It's a hard lesson to learn. It's hard not to get our feelings hurt but we have to remember for another to act so unkind, they are masking their own insecurities (my grocery store woman for example) & the way Taylor Swift calls them out on it is so boldly refreshing.. I've also seen it put this way: **Someone who hates you normally hates you for one of three reasons:**

   **They either see you as a threat,**
   **They hate themselves or**
   **They want to be you.**

Taylor, I'd like to be the first to say, that if there were anybody silly enough to hate you, you can rest assured that in your case, it's always got to be the third reason! And good for you for *not* being ashamed of being like Adam Ant's "Little Miss Goody Two Shoes!" But then my husband would argue this point with the quote, "Women who behave, rarely make history!"-

since he was so delighted with the t-shirt with this message that he found at a booth at the boat show for me years ago!

But speaking of artists that are getting all of the CMA awards, not to name any names- **Blake Shelton**, you too will always be a shining star in our hearts wherever you go because we remain ever grateful to you for giving (literally) us a surprise free concert (one where you were truly present & truly sharing your talent & love for country music with us for over 3 hrs!) in the heart of our small town & we will never stop wondering if it was actually you that we encountered on the sidewalk by the tour bus (since the office where we worked at that time shares a parking lot with the Dixie Roadhouse, where our local station, Gator Country, booked you) earlier that day. And when you sing about being Country Proud by telling those who don't like it, that they can kiss your country ass, it's still a far cry from the explicitness of some other genres. And even with all of your wonderfully romantic ballads that make us all swoon; I still appreciate your wit in "Boys Round Here" and recognize your Buffett affinity because of the line in "Some Beach" when you admit that **you were singing "Margaritaville"**!-only now, you could certainly afford to be the one driving the Benz—still we know you'd never be rude like the guy in that song! ;-)

In a very different genre, it's apparently a challenge to "stick to your guns" (or more accurately not include violence) when delivering messages to today's youth. As some very honest young people have candidly pointed out to me, many talented current artists , seem to get overlooked unless they drop a few "F bombs" in their lyrics to get the attention of kids today. They seem to be convinced that we adults are too quick to write off songs of this type because we can't overlook the profanity & see beyond it to some decent messages that may be there, like they apparently can. I guess our generation was just not trained to lend a deaf ear to it like today's kids, who seem to be numb to it. Many of these performers' songs become more about venting than problem solving, but this is still a way for people to express themselves and may just be a necessary stage in their progression toward working out aggression. Again fast forwarding, my sons are now appreciating the efforts of a new artist called Logic, whose mission is to bring peace, Love & positivity back. And I couldn't be more grateful for that!

The beauty of singing is that it allows singers to express themselves instead of holding in their feelings which can be toxic. In one year's CMT top artists count down, a commentator shared his observation about how Curt Cobain of Nirvana, excelled at relating to and expressing what many people of his time were going through. My teenagers continues to plead the case with me, assuring me that many lyrics are not to be taken literally. They report that many of today's popular artists are only portraying a fictional role to sustain the life of a made up character and that their real life personas are much different. To back up their point, I will share that during a recent meeting with the director of the Southwest Florida Make-A-Wish Foundation®, **we were assured that when kids request to meet Eminem, he is a real gentleman who welcomes the opportunity to brighten their day.** The woman who spoke to me said, "He's a real family man". I have heard all of the compassion for his daughter come through on many of the songs that my son has shared with me. My sons also point out that their favorite songs by these artists are usually the ones about empowerment and overcoming adversity. I'm also grateful that these teenage sons of mine and I do have some common ground in our appreciation of music. We mutually agree that we generally like most Reggae (for a list of pop hits that have been re-recorded to Reggae, *RTA*) and most eighties rock classics (especially The Cars) & the 90's Red Hot Chili Peppers.

However, unfortunately, there are still some messages being given airtime that may not be what we would prefer for our kids to be listening to. Andy Samberg has a hilarious spoof on such resistance themed songs called "I Threw it on the Ground" which was recently shared with my household by a twenty-something neighbor. Watching this video is a refreshing way for anyone to recognize it in themselves, if they may be listening to, or putting out, negativity. And to counteract those ones that are, I suggest listening to John Mayer as he tells us, "Bad news never had good timing, but then the circle of your friends will defend the silver lining. Pain throws your heart to the ground; Love turns the whole thing around. No, it won't all go the way it should, but I know **the heart of life is good"**. This was once my older guy's favorite and I will always cherish it, not only for that reason but because it is so **full of optimism!** The music world also offers plenty of humorous songs (*RTA* for my list w/ some throw backs from the 70's like Ray Stevens' "The Streak" & Jim Stafford's "Wildwood Weed") and then there are countless ones that make great work-out music as well as ones that make great **make-out music!**

And to segway between those 2 categories, I say "If you prefer to get your heart rate up in other ways, there are plenty of romantic love songs & much (not so subtle) **Mood Music -** Back in the 70's, Jefferson Starship's, "Miracles" got my attention with its powerful melody and persuasive lyrics. Hot Chocolate's "I Believe in Miracles, You Sexy Thing" said pretty much the same thing, just less romantically! And for a sampling of more mood music from that era, there was: "I Wanna Kiss You All Over" from Exile, "Feel Like Making Love" by Bad Company, "You Better You Bet" by The Who, "Paradise by the Dashboard Light" by Meatloaf and "The Way I Want to Touch You" by Captain & Tennille. More recently, Katy Perry's "Teenage Dream" has the words, "Let's go all the way tonight" just like Sly Fox's, "Let's Go All the Way" & The Raspberries' "Go All the Way" which all get right to the point! There's "Oh What A Night" by The Four Seasons, Rod Stewart's "Tonight's the Night" & "Baby I Like It" by Enrique Iglesias. But getting even more points for directness are the following: "I Want Your Sex" by George Michael, Tina Turner's "What's Love Got to do with It", Rod Stewart's, "If You Want My Body", Fergie's "Fergalicious", Olivia Newton John's "Let's Get Physical", Donna Summer's

"I Love the Way You Love Me" (which actually includes some moaning by her), Shakira's "Hips Don't Lie", Marvin Gaye's "Sexual Healing", Jimmy Buffett's "Why Don't We Get Drunk and Screw", Trop Rocker, Captain Josh's "She Threw Me a Room Key", Peter Mccann's "Do You Want To Make Love or Do You Just Want To Fool Around?" & Frankie Goes to Hollywood's, "Relax" with, "Relax, don't do it,..." followed by extremely explicit lines that got this song banned by the BBC in 1984!

It never ceases to amaze me how songs on this subject matter have gotten so uncensored. I look back to my days in second grade when one of the top hits constantly being played on the radio was Sammy Davis Jr.'s version of "Candy Man", which actually hit #1 in June of 1972. Maybe I was just too naïve in those days but to me, this song seemed to be full of nothing but sweetness (sweet thoughts about sweet candy). Now it leaves me shaking my head wondering how in my lifetime, we've come from such popularly played innocence, to the decadent lyrics of the more recent "Candy Shop" by 50 Cent. It's impossible to miss the metaphors this rapper uses to create graphic images. In this way, his talent for painting a picture rings through. And to his defense, he's only delivering what his audience, a large portion of today's generation, seems to want. Then there's, "Sex and Candy" by Marcy Playground, with a very appealing vibe, along with Michael Frank's "Popsicle Toes", which are additional examples of overlapping childhood and adult subject matters. Then just this morning, I heard an old John Mellancamp, not so romantic yet blatantly honest, "I Need a Lover Who Won't Drive Me Crazy, someone who knows the meaning of, hey hit the highway, a girl who'll thrill me and then go away". Then there's "Your Body is a Wonderland" (and he's not talking about Disney) by John Mayer. And Katy Perry's, "Last Friday Night" describing some pretty worldly activities (that most teenage girls of my generation probably wouldn't have understood) along with her "I Kissed A Girl", which is a far cry from the Disney movie, *Little Mermaid's*, "Kiss the Girl"!

Speaking of Disney, what's up with childhood stars/singers going out of their way to prove their "Not so Innocent" like Britney Spears sings- ?

As far as real love songs, I think the best ones are those that make you want to be the person they're singing about like Tom Petty's "Here Comes My Girl", Jesse McCartney's "Your beautiful Soul" or Blake Shelton's "God Gave Me You".

**Ultimately I think we gravitate toward music because of the way it makes us feel & hopefully that's a good feeling**

*Anyway*, back to our regularly scheduled program... or at least to my point for taking this unusually extensive digression...

**All of this reflecting on raising kids, caused me to have** what life coach, Heather Christie calls**, a blinding flash of the obvious.** This being**, that if I really cared about my boys' future, I had to do something about the only thing I could seem to control at that point in our lives, my attitude and the example I could set for them.**

By now hopefully you can see that I am not normally such a melancholy person. And as I sat on the beach in Sanibel that day, I knew that the past several months' upheaval had not brought out the best in me.

**I thought about James Taylor as he sang, "Going to Carolina in My Mind" and I was pretty sure that it was time for me to go to "Margaritaville" in my mind**.

With all of this in mind, **I started paying more attention to songs with empowering messages.** I needed to shift from songs like Zac Brown's, "I'm going to put the world away for a minute, pretend I don't live in it" - "Knee Deep" with a bit of a denial attitude, to giving attention to songs like, Garth Brooks' "Unanswered Prayers" when he says he thanks God for such, because God's plan turned out better for him. Darius Rucker also helps point out this theory with the song, "This", when he explains how all of the things that he thought went wrong in his life, were part of a grander path to true happiness: "All of the fights and the tears and the heartache, I thought I'd never get through. And the moment I almost gave up, All lead me here to you".

At that point, I didn't want to admit it, but somewhere deep down, I began to suspect that this phase in life could also possibly deliver me and my family to a better place. Maybe that perfect course we were previously on wasn't ultimately the right path for us. Up until now, all I wanted to do was get our lives back on track and I yearned for the reassurance that I was in control of my life again. This dominant thought had me feeling like I was constantly banging my head up against a wall. But songs like these, now had me contemplating the idea that maybe I was supposed to stumble off course, maybe my journey was supposed to go in a different direction…

**Then songs about letting go began flooding my mind. Whether you need to let go of control issues, anger or someone you love, òther people have been through something similar and fortunately for listeners like me, they've chosen to sing about it.**

And I realized that the message in most of these songs was one of encouragement to take inventory of all that I did have going for me in life. Like the one sung by one of my favorite Trop Rockers, who reminds me so much of Kenny Chesney,

"There's a whole lot of ocean; there's a whole lot of white sand. **I don't have a whole lot of money but I'll never be a poor man, as long as I'm grateful for what I got and don't want for what I've not**, down the road there's a sunny day; I'll never be far away from **My Favorite Spot**". Wes Loper

So now as Christmas approached,
learning to focus more on gratitude
became the best gift I'd get that year.

...................And as you will see, we're almost there-
Margaritaville is just around the corner!
Continued life lessons about gratitude,
attitude, simplifying & humor
are tucked into tunes that
will get me through
this final stretch
on my road to
recovery -
kinda like
the 7 mi.
bridge!

"It's not having what you want, it's wanting what you've got. I'm gonna soak up the sun, I'm gonna tell everyone to lighten up. I'm gonna tell 'em that I've got no one to blame. For every time I feel lame, I'm looking up...I've got my 45 on so I can Rock On!" (Sheryl Crow & yet another song referencing sunscreen!)

# 7

# My LOT in Life

("please celebrate me home" Kenny Loggins)

As the holidays past and the New Year was underway, I was eager for more positive renewal in my life, so next I checked out an audio series promising, *Your Best Life Now*. That sure sounded like something I could use! It consisted of a collection of daily devotions by Joel Osteen, a popular Texas pastor. Oddly enough, the way that this pastor interprets the selected Bible verses, is surprisingly similar to *The Secret* DVD mentioned in Chapter One. It was comforting to hear how Osteen believes that God wants us to be happy, healthy and successful. He pleads his case to convince us that abundance in all ways is achievable and it all starts with your belief system.

I played these "Best Life" daily devotions every morning as the boys and I traveled across town to their school and consequently started having some revelations of my own. And they didn't want to admit it, but all of those kind words packed full of hope and encouragement were having a positive effect on the boys too. One of my favorite quotes was, **"Don't tell your God how big your problems are, tell your problems how big your God is."** (The following Christmas, I gave my Ft. Lauderdale family members plaques we made that said, "Good morning, this is God. I'll be handling all of your problems today. I do not need your help so have a good day!") This reminder seemed to be just what the boys and I needed. I wish there were more personal development materials marketed toward kids. Anyway, I knew that my inner child was keenly listening to this calming voice on these CD's everyday, and that this was a healthier addiction than any that

I previously had in place. After each session, I was always glad I had tuned in. So my second lesson in self-help gave me further reassurance that "God really does help those who help themselves". And it was time for me to take my first step in that direction. As I allowed myself to rely on the wisdom of these authors and songwriters, I began to pull myself out of that rut and come to terms with the inevitable. It must be similar to the stages of grief that people go through when they lose a loved one. I think that the disbelief causing a delayed realization of how life is going to have to change, is a significant part of the struggle.

**But in order to make room in my life for future happiness, I had to let go of old disappointments.**

In another quote by Andy Rooney, who's known for saying so much in so few words, he says, "I've learned that

## When you Harbor Bitterness, Happiness will Dock Elsewhere".

I finally began to see that in order to regain energy for any challenges that I might need to rise to in the future, I had to drop the victim mentality that was weighing me down now. I had to have faith that a better plan was in store for us, but it wasn't going to reveal itself **until I found a way to recognize all of the blessings that I already had.** I had to stop resisting our new circumstances and find a way to adapt. A popular email that was circulating several years ago comes to mind. I found it today on an online blog by a woman called, "Momma Clem". It has a pertinent line saying, "I've learned that you can tell a lot about a person by the way he/she handles four things: a rainy day, the elderly, lost luggage, and tangled Christmas tree lights". The point is that I had to learn to **rediscover my joy, despite my challenges** like my bother, Jim's favorite quote:

> **"Life is not about waiting for the storm to pass,**
> **It's about Learning to Dance in the Rain!"**

like those "Barefoot Children in the Rain" that JB sings about and I believe that some simple songs played a big part in helping me to do it- Like "Earth Wind & Fire" telling me: "If you feel down & out, Sing a Song, it'll make you're day... If you sing a song a day, you will find a better way". And in this spirit, Joel Walsh invites us to sing along with him as he declares, **"life's been good to me so far"** (this one has my vote for best song to conduct your own personal air-band to; although my son would argue for Phil Collins' "In the Air Tonight").

With the following lyrics, Rodney Adkins also recognizes how music can transform you: "Sittin in six lane backed up traffic, horns a honkin, I've about had it. I'm lookin for an exit sign, gotta get outa here, get it all off my mind and like a memory from your grandpa's attic, a song comes slippin through the radio static, **changin my mood-**A little George Strait 1982. And it makes me wanna take a back road. Makes me wanna take the long way home. Put a little gravel in my travel. Unwind, unravel all night long. Makes me wanna grab my honey. Tear down some two lane country. **Who knows, get lost and get right with my soul"**.

So **I began realizing that in order to get back on my road to recovery, I too should let the music change my mood.**

I thought about Bon Jovi's words, "We gotta hold on to what we got. It doesn't make a difference if we make it or not. **We got each other and that's a lot"**, (Living on a Prayer). It was true. I had my health. I had my family.

## Perhaps I had to stop thinking of this situation as my *lot in life*, and instead begin appreciating that I still had a *lot in life* to be grateful for.

I think the thing that eventually kicked into focus for me during this post housing market crash identity crisis, was Tony Robbins' pleasure/pain principle. He says whichever one takes over, the desire for a certain pleasure, or the dread of a certain pain, is what drives all of our decisions. For me, it got to the point that I think I could no longer even stand to be around myself. There were many days that I didn't want to be in my own skin. I just wanted to as they say, stop the world and get off. Even at night my mind would race. Sleep started becoming a rare luxury. **I just wanted Gary Wright to send me his "Dreamweaver"** because he sang about how it could, "Take away my worries of today,... help me to forget today's pain,... fly me away to the bright side of the moon,... meet me on the other side", and I wanted to join him in singing, "I believe you can get me through the night. I believe we can reach the morning light". This thought of the morning light which is supposed to represent relief and rejuvenation in each new day, *made it dawn on me* that **it was very unlike me to be so miserable for so long**. I finally started wanting to find a way out of my rut more than I wanted to remain wallowing in self pity. **Kenny Chesney has a song called, "I'm Alive", which can be instrumental** (pun intended!) **in helping you examine your priorities and realign your attitude**. It says, "So damn easy to say that life's so hard. Everybody's got their share of battle scars. As for me, I'd like to thank my lucky stars that I'm alive and well. It'd be easy to add up all of the pain and all of your dreams that you sat and watched go up in flames, dwell on the wreckage as it smolders in the rain, but not me. I'm alive and well; and today you know that's good enough for me...

### Breathing in and out's a blessing can't you see?"

And as Kenny goes on to vow to make today the first day of the rest of his life, he reiterates the helpfulness of a simple breathing exercise **just like in that Buffett song** that I clung to through my journey. Similarly, when you don't know what else to do, Anna Nalick sings, "Cradle your head in your hands and breathe, **Just Breathe**".

A wonderful clip called, "Extraordinary Life", sent to me recently by my brother, Jim said, "Breathe deeply and often". It also had this to say about money: **"Be a friend to money, not a slave to it"**. And a long time ago, the Beatles said, "I don't care too much for money. Money Can't Buy Me Love".

So it seemed I'd been getting the same messages over and over from various sources. My morning audio discs also explained to me that if I had suffered some disappointment, it was okay to acknowledge it but then I needed to move on.

## "IF YOU WANT TO FEEL RICH, JUST COUNT THE THINGS YOU HAVE THAT MONEY *CAN'T* BUY

Just like the singer, Jewel as her song, "Hands", describes her recovery process through economic and emotional challenges… "Poverty stole your golden shoes, but it didn't steal your laughter and heartache came to visit me, but I knew it wasn't ever after". The Eagles put it not so gently in their song, "Get over it". Maybe these lyrics were just the splash of cold water that I may have needed: "I turn on the tube and what do I see? A whole lotta people crying, 'don't blame me.' They point their crooked little fingers at everybody else; spend all of their time feeling sorry for themselves. Victim of this, victim of that,.Your mamma's too thin and your daddy's too fat. Get Over It! All of this whinin', cryin' and pitching a fit, Get Over It! You say you haven't been the same since you had your little crash, but you might feel better if I gave you some cash. You don't wanna work but you wanna live like a king. The big bad world don't owe you a thing. Get Over It! And again, "Here for a Good Time" by George Strait, puts it this way: "I'm not gonna lay around and whine and moan Cause somebody done me wrong. Don't think for a minute that I'm gonna sit around And sing some old sad song **I believe it's half full not half empty glass** Every day I wake up knowing it could be my last".

But sometimes you really do have to just start all over. In another song together with Zac Brown, Jimmy and he put it like this: "When you lose yourself, you find the key to paradise"(Knee Deep).

**I guess they're saying that sometimes it's necessary to let go before you can recognize what is actually worth holding on to.**

I know "Don't Worry, be Happy" by Bobby McFerrin, is more easily sung, than done. **I do realize that sometimes you have to get all of the *"blah, blah"* out of your system before you can be receptive to the *"rah, rah"* stuff.** Another up and coming performer who seems to get this concept is Paul McDonald, who placed #8 in Season 10 of American Idol. Fast forwarding again a bit here, I had the pleasure of meeting this performer who just comes across as such a genuine guy, at that Songwriter's Festival on Ft. Myers Beach, which I previously mentioned. He was first up in the line-up of performers at one of the waterfront host bars on a Sunday morning. As I was sitting there nursing my Bloody Mary, taking in the breeze, I had no idea of what a powerful performance I was about to take in too. Paul sat on a barstool and explained to the crowd that what he was about to share was a song that he rarely includes in his concert tour playlist but was nonetheless, very special to him. He went on to give a very heartfelt delivery of a song with the message, "Thank you for the Misery". And he was not at all sarcastic about this. He went on to say that for him, unpleasant and even painful circumstances have been meaningful life lessons. And to me, he seemed like a guy very wise for his years!

As far as the power of attitude and the subconscious, I want to share a story about how **the answer to a nagging question once actually came to me in a dream.** Several years ago, I misplaced my driver's license and gym membership I.D. I retraced my steps and checked every place I could think of, to no avail but continued hoping that they'd show up. After a few weeks, I decided that I'd probably have to make an appointment at the DMV to replace the license and then pay the fee to replace the gym I.D. The next morning, while I was still somewhat in a dream state, I awoke with a vision in my head of my hand reaching into a small black purse (that I rarely use) and pulling out both items. So when I got up, I immediately began searching for that black purse. I found it in the back of the closet on a cluttered shelf and as I reenacted the scene from the dream, I pulled out both items!! My only explanation for this incident is that my subconscious knew all along where to look. But somehow, I was never able to retrieve this information with my conscious mind.

As I've mentioned, in "Stranded on a Sandbar", Jimmy Buffett sings about being "stuck in a fairly nice maze". I think that our dominant thoughts sometimes have us blocking out more helpful thoughts and that **sometimes getting another's perspective through a song line can help us to look at things differently.** And again in dreams, anything is possible. Heart's song, "These Dreams" says, "The sweetest song is silence that I've ever heard. Funny how your feet in dreams never touch the Earth." This song goes on to depict several other unexplainable visions that somehow seem totally realistic in dreams. The silence that Ann and Nancy Wilson are singing about, I think is the quieting of all of the naysaying and distractions that our conscious minds have trouble blocking out. **And this is why I see that the verb, "dream" has taken on a second meaning referring to visualizing your goals and believing in the possibility of something even if you can't explain it.**

Even Aerosmith tells us to "Dream On-dream until your dreams come true"! And in an article about her in <u>SELF Magazine,</u> Fergie explains how she visualizes her dreams. She explains how getting a Grammy came about after she saw this as a goal, visualized it in detail and made it come true!

**So just as I had to retrain myself to be able to get some sleep, I also had to remind myself that it was okay to dream in this way again too.**

And before I could do that, I had to find a way to consciously **block out negativism.** If I encountered negative people, I started making it a mantra to tell myself (yet mentally directing the statement toward them**), "Don't Bring Me Down"**, like the song by Electric Light Orchestra. Another way to think of it is, **don't let anyone steal your music.** If you've ever attended a motivational seminar or inspirational meeting, and gone back into an environment where coworkers or family members don't share your new found enthusiasm, it can really drag on you. And Don Henley's "Heart of the Matter", says, "There are people in your life who've come & gone. They'll let you down. You know they'll hurt your pride. **You better put it all behind you baby; 'cause life goes on. If you keep carryin' that anger, it'll eat you up inside".** So I realized **that I needed to repeat some simple yet meaningful lyrics in my head** instead of jumping on the bandwagon every time I heard someone else gripe. **In order to regain some optimism,**

**I needed to focus on some uplifting theme songs and make them my mantras. I started with Jimmy Buffett's "Jimmy Dreams"**

"count all your blessings
and remember your dreams".

Then the lyrics to an outstanding song by Michael Franti and Spearhead called "Let it Go" came to mind:

"I know a place out on this Earth called home

> After a thousand miles of road you've gone, you finally see the light that lets you know-whoa whoa- And I say Hey there holy roller, Hey there broken daughter, don't you know, we'll get you to the water... to the place to heal your soul -So please remember what you said to me all those years ago and I'll say it back to you, Just let it go ... If all the things that you stood for were burned to ashes at your door, would you stand trial so more? What if the Love you gave was starin' at you from the grave, would it make your heart explode? Just let your heart go"

The above profound lyrics are put to such an uplifting beat and like I said, nothing happens all at once; but I started craving being a happy person again. On a daily basis, I was longing for that *everything's going to be all right* feeling. In "Golden Slumbers" The Beatles sing, "Once there was a way to get back homeward...Sleep pretty darling, do not cry and I will sing you a lullaby". Like a child, I had to find a way to self soothe. **I thought back about when I wanted to correct a bad behavior in my classroom; I would use the practice of substitution (ie."instead of doing this, do that").**

That parenting seminar that we once attended, suggested that we try this strategy with our children too. For instance, if a toddler is screaming, instead of saying "don't scream", we should say, "use your inside voice". The speaker claimed that saying "don't___" only registers as, "do___" in young minds and like I said, **this time period became about reprogramming my thoughts.** Thinking back to childhood, I remembered that when my sweet grandma, Ruth once accidently flicked an ash from her cigarette onto my arm, after apologizing profusely, she tried to help me get past it by encouraging me to use the word, "cigarette" in place of other expletives anytime something bad happened. And if you ask anyone who knows me well, I still do this type of substituting. Just like the adorable Xfinity commercial w/ the dad turtle, realizing that he uses the "F" word, "fast" way too much in front of his son! And one year when we went on one of Hugh's business trips with him, our boys were shocked to see an interstate sign with the city of "Flagstaff" on it, because they'd been hearing me use that one all of their lives and they assumed I had made it up!(& sorry for anyone who may live there, it's nothing personal, just what came to my mind, like when others use "fudge" or "frick", etc.) And today, I caught myself saying, "Oh Tabloids"(but seriously, that one is more deserving of this disparaging use) and another common one of mine is, "skunk butts"!

*Anyway,* I've read that putting your energy into resistance, only blocks the passage for what you do want to come into your life. There is a Trace Adkin's song that says "Say a prayer for Peace" which puts a positive spin on a troubling situation in this same manner. Instead of "stop fighting", "say a prayer" puts out **a proactive message**. Similarly, I once heard a talk by Wayne Dyer referring to Mother Theresa. He said that when asked about how she felt about war protests, she replied that she didn't want to be part of any resistance groups. She instead said something like, "tell me when there's going to be a peace rally, and I'll be there!"

**So every time my eyes flew open in the middle of the night, instead of making endless mental lists of my problems and my *to-do* list in my head, I'd start silently singing myself my own lullabies...**

"Don't worry about a thing, **every little thing is going to be alight**"("Three Birds" by Bob Marley) or "Good things will come your way, **you'll find a brighter day**"("The Key to You" by David Benoit) or The Beatles' "Here Comes the Sun" or "It just takes some time, everything will be alright" by Jimmy Eat World & one of the very best:

**"Quiet Your Mind, take it all in, it's a game you can't win, enjoy the ride"** (Zach Brown).

For this method to work, you have to be so familiar with the tunes and at least a few lines of the songs that you choose;

because you have to be able to hear the refrains in your head effortlessly. This allows you to go into a relaxed meditation mode. **I'd recite these lines over and over again until I could doze back off & hopefully wake with a better attitude.** And speaking of waking up, I changed my alarm clock too. Instead of being startled awake each morning by that anxiety producing annoying buzz, I got a recordable clock and recorded my two boys singing, "Mama Pajama, roll out of bed-we love you" to the tune of Simon and Garfunkel's, "Me and Julio Down by the Schoolyard". So my wake-up call became that message being played from their loving voices instead. As a result, most days my husband and I wake up laughing and I whisper to the air that I love them too. After months of sleepless nights, actually waking up feeling rested, can make you feel so grateful. And remembering what it felt like to genuinely feel grateful was a powerful part of my transition.

**I started recognizing that leaning on these soothing lyrics in this way, had me feeling grateful to my friend, music for coming through for me once again.**

If I could say something back to this friend, I'd borrow a line from Debbie Boone, and say, "You light up my life. You give me hope to carry on. **You light up my days and fill my nights with song".** I continued to attempt to implement these subtle changes **in order to use my conscious mind to convince my subconscious mind**, and eventually somewhere along the way, it worked. Like so many real transformations in life, **maybe I had to hit rock bottom** before I could stop looking down in fear of falling and begin to look up again. In "A Pirate Looks at Forty", Jimmy says, "Down to rock bottom again, just a few friends". And like I said, it's times like these that you find out who your real friends are.

I also avoided watching the local news or dysfunctional daytime TV. I tried to watch only national news or educational TV (and by watch TV, I mean have on in the background as I worked on the computer, etc.) And if the national news was addressing the economy or war, I'd try to block my ears & start singing loudly!! In Mac McAnally's "Until Then" he says, "looking forward to the day I'm not afraid to watch the news". In "Show Me the Way", Styx reminds us how all too often, the news can bring us down: "Every night I say a prayer in the hope that there's a Heaven & every day I'm more confused as the saints turn into sinners…as I slowly drift to sleep, for a moment **dreams are sacred.** I close my eyes and know there's peace in a world so filled with hatred. Then I wake up each morning and turn on the news to find we've so far to go". Because we all know, all too often the news is full of local crime stories (which can make you feel likes it's hitting too close to home), and as Don Henley says, plenty of "Dirty Laundry". Mentioned several times throughout this book, "Heart of the Matter" recorded decades ago also by him, is still so timely today as it includes the lines, "trust and self assurance that lead to happiness, they're the only things we kill I guess…These times are so uncertain, with a yearning undefined & people filled with rage. **We all need a little tenderness. How can Love survive in such a graceless age"?** And in that Mac McAnally song, he also sings, "The last six thousand years, they say the end is coming soon, but 'Until Then' I keep smiling". And in "A Lot to Drink About", JB says, **"I can't take another doomsday minute".** I guess it was getting to that point for me too. I thought, if doomsday really is just around the corner, I believe some people will still rise above it, and I'd rather be one of them!

But it was becoming apparent to me that in order to do that, I'd need to start improving my thinking. And it was mostly songs reminding me to do this instead of continuing to worry, like in the graduation speech put to music, "Everybody's Free to Wear Sunscreen" recorded by Baz Luhrman: **"Don't worry, or worry. Just know that worrying is as effective as attempting to solve an algebraic equation by chewing bubblegum. The real troubles in life are apt to be the things that never crossed your worried mind, the kind that blindside you on some idle Tuesday".** It's ironic how that line came to my mind on Tuesday, September 11, 2001. Reflecting on that subject, can certainly help put it all in perspective.

And I'd like to add that as unproductive as worrying is, so equally are playing the guilt and/or blame game. The sooner I could release these toxic practices, the sooner I could get past this hurtle. And even if some of this did prove to be "my own damn fault", it was time for me to take accountability, learn from it and find some positives to focus on. Thankfully, there are *some* positive stories in society and I appreciate any news outlets that make a point to share them, especially in music venues like The Bobby Bones Show and the John Tesh Radio Show. On that topic, Just like Bob Marley said, "One Love, One Heart, Let's get together & feel alright", Lucy Buffett was quoted in an article about her restaurant as saying, "That's why I started the 'One Love-One Ocean' campaign. **We humans have to learn to take care of each other"**. Then when being asked how the economy has affected her, Lucy responded: **"Gratefully, burgers, margaritas and beer are recession proof**....We make the best of the inevitable "acts of God" that also occur. After Hurricane Ivan hit, we were one of the first businesses to open. We welcomed relief workers and residents and offered free cheeseburgers to everybody". Also, in that publication, when speaking about life lessons, LuLu shared that she believes that when you're not sure what to do in life, just take the next small step.

So, back on the path to my recovery...**I believe my turning point finally came** when it occurred to me that years before, I had read a wonderful book called *Simple Abundance* by Sarah Ban Breathnach, explaining and recommending the process of **recognizing joy in everyday simple pleasures**. And I recalled reading an article in Redbook, that claimed that researchers discovered that grateful people are more satisfied with their lives not because they ignore the bad stuff-but because they're just better at appreciating the good.

**I then reflected on how usually, the hardest part in breaking bad habits and replacing them with better ones,**

is finding a starting point or substitution. Just like JB says, "all you need is a place to start"!

For me that point was when I got the idea to start a Gratitude Journal

"Fill your life up with so much **Positivity** that there will be no room for negativity" (Positive Inspirational Quotes)

So I bought a small silk lined journal and began writing down items that I was grateful for in this new city.

I recorded: "smaller house to clean, lower electric bill, lower crime rate, west coast sunsets, Bob FM," with each item put on a separate line. When the boys got home from school that day I told them that I had some new homework for them. I showed them our "Cape Coral Gratitude Journal" and offered them $1.00 for each additional item that they could add to my list. I was praying that this would prove to be a justifiable expense! I was careful to instruct them to only include good things, places or people that we found as a result of our move here. The boys' reaction was surprisingly enthusiastic. My oldest one, Hugh said, "Give me that. I can add some". He then wrote, "burrowing owls, skate board ramp (at vacant house down the street), ping pong table, pet parrot". Seeing how profitable this could be, his younger brother Eric, was also quick to join in. He added, "fishing pier, Tiki Bar restaurant, Wii video game " (The parrot & new video game were guilt gifts because their birthdays fell during the time of our move and I thought they needed some consolation for all that they were giving up). Both boys were anxious to fill up the whole page until I reemphasized that all entries needed to be unique to this city or presented to us directly as a result of this move. However I was pleased that the 3 of us were getting such a good start with this list.

Later, I explained it to "Big Hugh", as we all affectionately call their father. His first submissions were: "less traffic, the Caloosahatchee River and Tequila Tom". He was enthusiastically on board with this project because he believes that if mom's not happy, nobody's happy! And I couldn't allow myself to be happy until I was assured that we hadn't just screwed up our kids' whole lives! I couldn't bear the thought of what lesson they may be absorbing from our bad example. By the time you're in your forties, you're supposed to have your act together, right? Well, for now maybe it was better to bury our heads in the sand. After all, we had just moved to a beach town! For as long as it would take, maybe we needed to indulge ourselves in a little healthy denial. Sometimes you have to start out fooling yourself. This was one of those "fake it until you make it" situations. Action Coach, Heather Christie stresses how we all can use our conscious minds to emphasize positive thoughts in order to eventually convince our subconscious minds and bring about self improvement, success and happiness. Practicing this principle **from that day forward, we all began looking for the good in all that we encountered as we came and went throughout our new surroundings.** And songs like, Louis Armstrong's "Wonderful World" and Colin Hay's "Beautiful World" (BTW, I love the msg. in his "Finding My Dance" tour theme-see his website) made great accompaniments for this project! (to see adt'l gratitude theme songs, RTA).

Many of these journal entries involved tangible items, but some referred more to shared experiences. We began learning about this small town's resources, local events and friendly population. During its development starting in the late 1950's, people were flown in from all over the world to invest in this "Waterfront Wonderland". So now there are German, Greek and Irish Festivals regularly held here. Being a popular vacation and retirement destination with lots of people who have time for hobbies and recreation, there are car, boat and art shows. We found fishing tournaments on the pier and sunset celebrations (held on Wednesdays, not just weekends) at the city marina better known as the Yacht Club; which we learned is also the meeting spot for the Cape Coral New Residents' Club. We were invited to participate in the annual waterside pirate parade and we learned about the downtown Christmas Tree lighting ceremony. We partook in periodic city sponsored "bike nights" as carnival style food booths & crowd pleasing bands (one particularly popular one, now called *Push*, has a lead singer named J Jaye Steele, formerly with the group, *Head East* who recorded the hit "Never Been any Reason" and who was also to become our son's football coach and our good friend, also mentioned in this book's dedication) took over Main Street while hundreds of Harley owners admired each other's rides and swayed in the streets as they danced & cheered on the band. We rode through town on old fashioned trolleys & observed the local atmosphere through the windows of many "mom & pop" places like Annie's restaurant, The paint Escape, The Twisted Conch Seagrille (now known as Cork Soakers) and The Monkey Bar (I'd absolutely Love to have Sunny Jim, one of the best known performers in the Trop/Rock world, perform his hilarious "Monkey Party" someday at The Monkey Bar!). We treated ourselves to fresh produce from the Farmers' Market, homemade fudge from the Candy Station and tasty treats from the ice cream shop. We attended our first "Burrowing Owl Festival". Even our dog was happy when he sniffed out the nearby dog park and all of the pet friendly places throughout town, like Cape Harbour, which sponsors an annual "Most Patriotic Pet Contest", since he won the grand prize the first time we participated!). Like tourists, we took boat rides to the city's surrounding island beaches and dockside plazas, with "Buffettesque" places like, Rumrunners, The Joint & Longboards(now Fathoms, which sponsors live music & block parties for the whole town every Tuesday), Islands (an eclectic surf shop whose main inventory includes tropical attire straight from Margaritaville, mixed with an extensive "Life is Good" line). We watched the opening of Marker 92 & The Nauti Mermaid, which are the on-site hospitality spots within the Westin Resort at Marina Village, ( & previously the site for this area's local version of "Meeting of the Minds" & if Hugh & I have anything to do with it, will be again!). We paddled along with kayaking tours through the mangroves toward places called Picnic Island and Beer Can Island & observed live conch, horse shoe crabs, dolphins & manatees up close! We discovered the community performing arts center featuring live performances by some of our neighbors. We discovered Sunsplash, the local water park. We followed winding paths through beautiful city parks that we somehow now had no trouble finding. These places had boardwalks with scenic observation towers over mangrove preserves, athletic facilities, outdoor movie nights & symphony performances & jazz concerts under the stars. When we visited the Cape Coral History Museum, we learned that one of our favorite neighborhood walking routes guided us through the former site of this city's "Waltzing Waters" attraction, a porpoise & fountain show originally set up to entertain prospective investors & future residents as they came to look at the area. One day I even stumbled onto the old entrance wall, now in a condo development. I've also learned from one of this city's founders, that for the stage design of this show, the developers of Cape Coral, the Rosen Brothers brought in the designers from Radio City Music Hall. So they too, understood the value of making the music connection. At that museum, I also learned that our neighborhood, called "The Rose Garden", was once a public place for visitors to enjoy lavish botanical sights and smells. While being treated to aerial views of this future city, they were encouraged to drop a bag of flower on the plot of land that they were interested in buying. The founders also shared a photo from those days featuring "The Santiva", which was the mailboat that made rounds through our area and went on to Sanibel & Captiva as the only form of mail service before there were bridges connecting these areas. Of course this reminded me of Jimmy's lines, "The whistle blows in Congo town, Mailboat's in" from "That's What Living Means to Me". There is also the obvious tie in to his "Mailboat Records" company. And every time we take a ride over or under the bridge to Ft. Myers

Beach, I look at all of the **"shrimp boats tied up to the pilings"** just like the ones mentioned in his "Tin Cup Chalice". **I finally found a way to connect with the best this city had to offer** & all of these discoveries became journal entries. Mysteriously, **now fun seemed to be falling at our feet.**

**Suddenly as we looked around, we felt like we were in the middle of a Norman Rockwell painting exuding small town charm.**

John Mellencamp sings praises for his "Small Town" calling himself "another boring romantic". I guess every place has its advantages and disadvantages so it becomes more about whether you see the glass half empty or half full. I once heard Hillary Clinton say, **"I believe in blooming where you're planted"**. Just like tropical Soul does in their "Backyard Tropical Vacation" and The Boatdrunks do in "This Aint Duval Street"! And **if only Phillip Phillips' song would have been out sooner to tell me "…as we roll down this unfamiliar road, settle down it'll all be clear, don't pay know no mind to the demons they fill you with fear, the trouble it might drag you down, if you get lost you can always be found, just know you're not alone, I'm gonna make this place your Home"**. But somehow I finally **decided** to implement this positive philosophy of those who went before me on their life journeys.

Clearly, it did not happen all at once But when I say I decided, that's actually how it had to happen. I don't know how to explain it except to say that it was a choice. My husband always says that **happiness is a choice**. In an article in <u>Ladies Home Journal</u>, one of my favorite actresses, Valerie Bertinelli said, "I wake up every morning and before I even open my eyes I say a prayer of gratefulness for the life I've been given. **Being happy is a choice**". I know that this is easier said than done. So once again, let me repeat it in the words of a song: "Don't waste time on jealousy. Sometimes you're ahead, sometimes you're behind. **The race is long and in the end,** it's only with yourself"-again, "Everybody's Free to Wear Sunscreen". To me, this line kinda slaps you in the face saying, "all that time you were making yourself miserable, thinking that you had something to prove, was just wasted time, never to be retrieved, like Jimmy says in "Carnival World"- "There's no rewrite in this carnival world". Another of his precious ballads "Bring Back the Magic" says: **"Once you see that no one really wins, then the magic begins. Nothing can tear you apart, if you keep living straight from the heart. You will know when to stop and to start, if you keep living straight from the heart. Bring back the magic, don't make life so tragic. Though you know that you're gonna hurt some, the magic will come".**

And much to our surprise, once we started sharing about how much we really liked this area, we became the envy of many of our previous neighbors! One after another, those families & friends that we abruptly left behind were anxious to come and visit us. Our place became a popular vacation destination for friends & family as the word got out about all that this area had to offer. There were days when we barely had time to change the sheets as one set of guests departed & another arrived! -Very much like Lenore Troia's "Everybody's got a Houseguest in KW" song! Even though we could only provide cramped quarters and it was more like a camp-out for them, they all started thinking of our place as their beach house get away. During one visit, my sister & her family piled in our minivan for a day trip with the 4 of us & our combined 3 dogs (which brings to mind the group, "Three Dog Night!"). Throughout that trip, we had several destination outings but it is the memory of the hours together in the car (that became smellier as the day went on) **singing**, laughing & bonding that I most cherish. Evenings were spent gathered around the fire pit or at the kitchen table. Our kids learned a few new very amusing games (Balderdash is our favorite) and a few new vocabulary words-mostly PG! Those hours provided much belly laughing for us all and this laughter surely was the best medicine. **What a relief it was to not take life so seriously**

**for a while.** We all now share many inside jokes and many pleasant memories, and nobody had to spend any extra money!

Regarding things that have been known to help improve one's attitude, humor has got to be at the top of the list. The summer before Diane and I had to part, we made each other scrapbooks. Mine was filled with magazine cut out quotes (mostly from <u>Seventeen Magazine</u>) like, "Look at them, aren't they the silliest ever?" & "I can't wait to grow up but I love the now" & our mutual favorite: "Among those people I like, I find nothing in common-**Among those I love,**

**I find they all make me laugh.**

And my husband certainly is no exception to this rule! I'll save his antidotes for the book he's going to write someday. But let me just say that like Buffett, I too, "wish that we could sit upon a bed in some hotel & listen to The Stories He Could Tell!" This concept is also expressed very convincingly by John Bon Jovi in his song, "You Wanna Make a Memory". When I was a teenager, I could often be quoted saying, "come on let's, ... _____ "(fill in the blank with a series of stupid or more often just silly actions) because it'll give us something to remember this time by". We used to have a school club called Exchangettes that would initiate new members by showing up unannounced at their homes in the late hours of a weeknight & escort them to the local 24 hr. grocery store so they could race them down the aisles in shopping carts in their pajamas. I remember highly valuing being so silly & spontaneous, especially when it seemed to be creating such sentimental memories. I guess that's what the popular phenomena of "planking" (laying face down with arms by your side & an uplifted head & arched back in the most bizarre & inappropriate places, like this kid ) may be all about!

So along with other measures, attempting to interject more humor & playfulness in our day was another factor in my attitude adjustment. We began making a point to catch the "Phone Taps" on the nationally syndicated, *Elvis Duran Radio Show* with the kids' carpool in the mornings & watching shows like *Ellen* (who certainly incorporates music & goodwill into her show) and *Impractical Jokers* (which I call today's version of *Candid Camera*) & reruns of *Frasier* (whose final episode showed him reciting a poem about how it's **the things in life that you don't try that you regret!**) and *Scrubs* (my favorite scene of all was the one when Turk, the main character's best friend, quotes the lines & dances to "Safety Dance" by Men without Hats, while in the middle of a conversation!) These shows reminded me to not take life so seriously and to start thinking about the benefits of living more simply.

I found a greeting card that I framed that said: **"Very Little is needed to make a Happy Life, It is all within you, in you way of thinking"** & another that put it this way:

# "JOY IS NOT IN THINGS; IT IS IN US!"

When my sister, Anne came to visit, she brought us the perfect housewarming gift, a canvas with this quote:

> **"Our family is about remembering what matters,**
> **Letting go what doesn't, laughing, loving,**
> **& knowing life is good because we have each other".**

And it can be refreshingly liberating to realign your priorities in this way. It may not be easy at first. When you have to downsize, everything can feel like an uncomfortable sacrifice. **You may just have to look differently at the value you attribute to things.** Once I could bring myself to doing this, I'd be able to make new room in my heart and in my life for appreciating all of my intrinsic blessings. **"Keep it simple, stupid" is how Jimmy Buffett put it** as he explained that all he really needs is "Six String Music".

In a more tangible example, I reflected on how I actually got a dose of this lesson on simplifying, while taking a walk on Bowman's Beach that day. I love collecting seashells but I wanted to get some exercise and keep my heart rate up, so I did not bring along a bucket for collecting since I knew it would tempt me to keep stopping and lose my pace. I was able to honor this intention during the first half of my walk, however on the way back, I just couldn't resist all of those perfectly shaped treasures that seemed to be calling out to me. I've seen this beach on the Travel Channel being described as one of the best sea shell collecting places in the world. So I proceeded to pick up one & then another here and there. Before I knew it, every time I bent down to greedily grab an additional shell, one of the ones already in my hand would drop. Finally, the irony of that situation occurred to me. I could not keep adding new shells unless I was willing to let go of some of the ones I already had. I've since called upon this lesson when trying to teach my boys about greed. They used to drag me to fast food chains obsessively in quest of kids' meal toys. These restaurants are smart. They bring these toys out in themes but only release one in the series per week, while advertising the complete collection just so we have to keep going back. One theme included over twenty mini plush characters.Well, when I realized that as a result of this obcessive-ness, the boys' stuffed animal inventory seemed to leave little room for them in their own beds, I remembered my sea shell incident. Then I announced to the boys that if they wanted any new toys/stuffed animals, they'd have to choose one to get rid of. This actually led to some gratifying donating experiences for all of us.

Then I remember leaning back with astonishment, when one particular old friend who happens to run a successful podiatry clinic and lives a glamorous life in Ft. Lauderdale, said to me, "I tell you for me, coming here and being in this small seaside town with such affordable waterfront, I feel you're living my dream". This was further affirmation. It seemed as if everything had turned around. But **we knew that it was not the town that had changed; rather, it was how we perceived it.**

## The more good we looked for, the more good we found.

Another funny thing is that I actually took a cue from Jim Carrey again, while the boys were watching his movie, *Ace Ventura* on TV. For anyone who may not remember, the story line involves a former kicker named Ray Finkle, who has a long-standing grudge against Miami Dolphins player, Dan Marino. It is up to Ace to solve the mystery of who has stolen the Dolphins' mascot, a live dolphin named Snowflake. In the movie, one day while studying news clippings, Ace's pet Yorkie sits on top of a photograph of Ray Finkle and the dog's hair ends up framing this guy's face to make him look like a woman. That's when the light goes off in Ace's head that the local police chief, a woman he knows as Lois Einhorn, is actually the villan, posing as a woman. My point is that until he could see the image of these two people superimposed on one another, he could not put 2 and 2 together. The way this scenario played out for me involved refrigerator magnets: one brought back from Key West, one purchased from the Margaritaville store, & one given to us at one of the booths at a Cape Coral street fest. One day as I went to open the fridge, I glanced at the Mile Marker type magnet from Key West & then my eyes glanced over at the one of the pier in Cape Coral. I then reached for the second magnet and centered it on top of the first as I thought,

**"it's time for me to embrace this place & make it my "Margaritaville"**-Then as I took a good look around, it occurred to me that this small town of Cape Coral, ironically does seem to lend itself to a closer version of what "Margaritaville" is probably supposed to be all about, much more so then the place I was so heart broken to leave behind". So I then cut out the Margaritaville logo and added a "#1." (to indicate that we have reached the gateway to our destination) & created this symbolic representation to serve as another daily reminder for me.

While it is second in the state in geographic size, its population is mellower than where we came from. It provides some of the most affordable access to Florida's waterways, which in turn provides ample access to nature and all of its seaside creatures. Around here, if you don't have a boat or at least a kayak and live by the water, you know someone who does. And if you're just visiting, you can find an affordable place to rent or charter a boat. There are plenty of city-run & privately owned marinas, some of which actually allow full time residence aboard your house boat!

**Here, we do not have much glitzy night life but most people don't need to go out when they have the Gulf of Mexico in their backyard.**

Being a place that attracts retirees and vacation home owners, social gatherings in this town are of a folksy nature. My husband refers to Cape Coral as a biker/boater town. I love those t-shirts I've seen in other small tourist towns that say, "A small drinking town with a fishing problem!" Public places here for the most part, have quaint atmospheres and since most people are coming in from their bikes and boats, it is refreshing how almost any attire is acceptable. This is no South Beach, like the one in Miami, where people often dress to impress. Although it is tough to go out to those popular dockside plazas, like Cape Harbour and Tarpon Pointe and not run into several people you know. But if you choose to get dressed up, there are a few formal spots in these promenades that Hugh and I prefer to declare for special occasions.

Hugh and I actually learned about the local dress code (or refreshingly, the lack of one) by accident. When we first got to town and were exploring the lay of the land, we wandered into a popular spot called, The DEK. They had a sign out front that said, "A pitcher & a large pizza for $10." So that enticed us through the door. But once inside, we realized that we might be out of place. Hugh was dressed like he was still on the east coast in pastel linen pants and a brightly colored polo shirt. Like most women, who have plenty of black in their wardrobe because of its slenderizing qualities, I was way more in line with the local attire. As we rushed through the doorway and set our eyes upon the small room encasing only one large circular bar filled with denim and leather clad bikers, there was nowhere for Hugh to hide. Unfortunately for him, just about then, I urgently needed the restroom, and as I left him standing there in front of all of them, I said, "You're going to get killed in this place!" Fortunately, I was very wrong. Our faux pa hadn't even phased most of them enough to even look up from their beer mugs and if any of them did, they were mostly smiling (or more likely laughing)! So we learned our lesson that night and we were ready to heed Kenny Chesney's advice in his song telling us to, "Be as You Are". In this one, he makes references to how it doesn't matter if you're "a tourist, a beach bum or a star" and after that night, we knew that **this was a place where it was safe to "be as you are"**.

And the casualness doesn't stop with appearances. The senior citizens who come here seem **active and happy**, not bitter, almost like the spunky ones in the movie, "Cocoon"-*Come to think of it, I have heard them talk about the powers of the natural springs nearby in Bonita Beach??-hmmmm-* But seriously, there is a **refreshing lack of pretentiousness in this town** and I've had many guests comment to me about it. Most of the people we've come in contact with seem to really be *salt of the earth-hmmmm-maybe they've been hording that salt shaker all of this time??*

And it seems easier to keep an **"island attitude"** around here. This place reminds me of another song by Kenny Chesney called, "The Life", as he says: "Somewhere over Texas, I thought of my Lexus and all of the stuff I worked so hard for, all of the things that I've gathered by climbing that ladder didn't seem to make so much sense anymore. For a while I thought that I had it made, but the truth is that I'm really just dying to live like Jose, and **just fish and play my guitar and laugh at the bar with my friends,** go home to my wife and pray every night I can do it all over again" (my older son, in humor, always says, "why do they have to be so mean to the bar?" LOL).

**I used to think of our old backyard as our own "Margaritaville". Now I realized that living here, a truer version of "Margaritaville" was all around us & most of those we encountered here, seemed to be like minded "Margaritavillians"!**

The bigger house & fancier cars began fading in comparison.

In another song by Mac McAnally, it is said that,

**"If You Hang Around Long Enough, you can have a good time when times are tough, you get around to figuring out what you can do and do without, you'll recognize the real stuff".** I say, wow -This song may just need to be our new national anthem!

As far as the business owners around here, because there is a common mindset to "Keep it in the Cape" (promoting city rebounding growth), those I've met are usually very approachable and love to hear ideas and comments from the locals. When things started taking such a sharp turn for the better, I began to wonder if we were living out a scene from the Chevy Chase movie, *Funny Farm*, where a couple, desperate to sell their home which they considered to be a money pit, come up with a scheme involving paying the local town's people to do neighborly things like singing carols and baking each other treats, in an effort to disillusion perspective buyers into thinking that this was a place they just **had** to be. The predictable consequence was that this couple ended up falling back in love with their own place after all. Unlike them, we didn't pay the locals to make this new town shine, we just learned to start looking with open eyes & more importantly, open hearts. Many people believe that when the student is ready, the teacher will appear; a concept that likely came into play here. It's like when you learn a new vocabulary word or a new popular slang term and suddenly something that you were not aware of one day, seems to keep popping up every time you turn around. It's unlikely that your surroundings have dramatically changed. It's more likely that you are now just more in tune with any references to this new knowledge.

**So, what you focus on, does seem to manifest itself more into your life.** This place was growing on us and-

**something had clicked inside of me. I suppose I could call it my *gratitude meter* and tuning into it became the most profound of all of the gifts in the form of a lesson that this situation had bestowed upon me.**

"There is Always, Always, Always

## Something to be Thankful For"

So gratefulness begets growth, but there were a few areas of our new life that still had room for improvement. As wonderful as it was sharing all of these new discoveries among the four of us and with old friends, it was time for us to branch out and make some new connections. They say it takes a village to raise a child, and it was time for us to figure out where we fit in. I've previously stated Jeff Olsen's theory that you become a combination of the five people that you spend the most time with. If this is true, than associations, especially at a young age, are crucial.

With this in mind, we felt that the boys' new school was not proving to be a good fit. It seemed like all of the nice families we met around town were in the school with the longest waiting list. This was not a private school, but a publically run city charter school. We were just counting down the days until summer, when at last, I got a call from that sought after school! The application that I had filled out to substitute teach there had finally reached the top of somebody's in-box and they wanted me to come in for an interview! When I met with the principal, his words were, "You're highly overqualified for this position," but fortunately that wasn't a problem for this $9.00/hour job. As much as I needed the money, my real reason for seeking this position was for the boys' sake. They could now move through that waiting list more expediently with my employee status! So that's just how it happened. I immediately began subbing there. I'd have to drive across town and drop off the boys at "before care" at their present school in order to arrive on time for my shifts at what was hopefully going to be their new school. It was tough juggling it all, but at least now we had a plan. The more people I met and the more research I did, the more I knew that this was the school community where we belonged and I continued to do everything in my power to make it happen. After a few more months, it finally did. And on their first day, the boys pointed out a familiar sight-

**As if to once again to give his blessing, Jimmy Buffett showed us a sign.** A sign literally that is, in the form of a bumper sticker featuring a fin (the universal sign of Jimmy Buffett fans), on the back of one of the vehicles in the staff parking lot. The owner of that minivan, no doubt another kindred spirit among the realm of Parrot Heads, would prove to be another blessing in our lives as she became the fifth grade teacher for each of the boys successively. Later I would also learn that one of the school's coaches (who wears a swim suit to basketball practice) is an officer in the local Parrot Head club.

About the time of our transfer to Oasis Elementary School, (a place that continues to live up to its name; truly serving as an "oasis in the desert" of our move-metaphorically), the boys registered for sports teams and we joined a friendly church congregation. Just recently, the pastor of St. Katherine Drexel, Father John Deary, gave a sermon suggesting gratitude journals as an additional way for us all to give thanks and praise. That day after mass, I went up to him and introduced myself and thanked him for such a pertinent point. I gave a brief summary of my story and told him that as he was delivering the sermon that day, **both of my boys and my husband leaned forward and titled their heads toward me with a grin and a nod of approval. I couldn't be more grateful that they heard his message that day and that hopefully this will be a lesson that we'll all never forget.**

After much research, we also found a better neighborhood with sidewalks, nearby parks, families and a friendly landlord who was willing to look past how we looked on paper. This was a major turning point. As we signed this new lease, all of the pieces were finally falling into place. And speaking of falling, during the housewarming party that we threw for ourselves, all of our new neighbors were very concerned about our musical entertainer falling into the pool. Local "Coastal Cowboy", Mr. John Friday treated us all to many Buffett cover songs and his relatable originals until the wee hours of the morning all the while with his bare feet in the hot tub!

So with the boys in a healthier environment, and a little bit of extra money trickling in from my substitute teaching job, I could turn my attention to some of my own needs, like making some new friends of my own. While on a break in the teachers' lounge one day, I came across a family community newspaper. In it I read about a local ladies' empowerment group which addresses the challenges of achieving balance in life. So I contacted the director of the group, Stacie Harmon and forced myself to show up for the next meeting. There, she explained to me that being from California, she relates to surfing like I relate to songs. She navigates the ups & down of life like a surfer facing the challenges of balancing on a surf board. The group is called "Ninth Wave" because this is the term surfers use to refer to the wave (in 3 groups of 3) with the most potential for the best ride. With no ulterior motives other than spreading goodwill throughout the community and supporting local businesses, these women meet once a month to discuss goals and share their success stories. These triumphs may be as big as a job promotion or as small as getting your closets cleaned out. As far as local businesses hosting our meetings, the most interesting aspect to this venue, is when these business owners address our group, the motivation comes about from hearing their personal stories about how their life has been full of twists and turns, landing them in their present positions. I'm hoping that one of our future meetings will be held at the new car dealership in town. This business owner has seemed to portray a larger than life persona since the day he who opened his doors & began simultaneously airing commercials announcing that it's going to be "HUUUge!" Last month, I was treated to a little more serendipity as a friend and I sat in a newly opened restaurant down the street. Just as we were studying the menu at The Lobster Lady, this guy and his entourage stormed through the door, shot a quick commercial on the premises (while holding up a monster lobster from the tank & encouraging all of us to cheer in the background). Then he treated everyone in the place to lunch!

The point to my women's group is to find something to celebrate every day. Upon my first meeting back in 2007, I was grateful to be there and make these new associations. I knew that these were people I wanted to spend time with. And I can honestly say, on the subject of setting and achieving goals, which is the cornerstone of this group, the energy of the members is what empowers us all. Getting together periodically, and learning by one another's (especially, Stacie, the leader) examples, does have a subtle, yet powerful affect. I do know for certain, that it was witnessing Stacie's relentless efforts in all of her various projects, that sparked me to endeavor into this writing project and I will be eternally grateful to her & this group for that!

And **finding this group became my last entry in that gratitude journal - not because of a lack of continued positive influx** in our lives but because of a lack of time. Suddenly we were all so busy and content carrying on our new lives. Acceptance of all of the changes was no longer such a forced issue. The temporary use of the journal trained us to recognize the good on a regular basis and the formality of writing it down was no longer necessary.

I finally felt that my family and I were in a town with a lifestyle and atmosphere that was better suited for us than where we started out. Believe it or not, we all became so well adjusted that we'd never go back.

**It had become ironic how we came to appreciate the serendipity in what we used to resent as an abrupt interruption. So At this point, for the first time since we left Lauderdale, I could exhale.**

And this time, as I breathed in and breathed out, I no longer needed to *move on* because:

"I Have Found Me a Home"
(Jimmy Buffett)

"We all deserve a Happpily Ever After Every Now & Then" *-JB*

# 8.
# Encore

(Bring Back the Magic)

In the words of Jackson Browne, "Here's to Lights and Virtues". And just like Elvis Costello's "Allison", I hope that as you read this book's conclusion, you'll see that **"My Aim is True"**. **This story of mine is intended to be a light-hearted way of looking at today's challenges with lots of Parrot Head perspective.** This book is the result of my seven year process of "Relapse" and "Recovery" (borrowing Eminem's words), however mine relates to economic and emotional challenges. And it's my version of **"A Parrot Head Looks at Fifty!"**

Behind **my main musical mentor, Jimmy Buffett**, who wins the grand prize in most categories in my opinion, turning attention to Honorable Mentions is something that I also Love to do. I mean, even Vanilla Ice thinks of himself as a lyrical poet, as he states in "Ice, Ice, Baby". And M.C. Hammer in "Can't Touch This", recognizes that, "Music hits me so hard, makes me say Oh my Lord, thank you for blessing me with a mind to rhyme and two hype feet", so I know that there still have to be so many others who remain *unsung heroes* at this point. But in the words of Rihanna, **"Please Don't Stop the Music"**!

One night my husband shared a Utube video with me (that had been posted on Facebook by *Godvine*, which is, "A Christian website that focuses on uplifting, encouraging and inspiring you in your daily life"), titled, **"Alive Inside, Old Man in Nursing Home Reacts to Music From his Era"**. While this title gives you the main gist of the scene, what it does not do is make you witness how this elderly gentleman named Henry, literally came alive when headphones with his style of music were placed on his head. It's worth watching this transformation. This guy goes from being non responsive to the point that you suspect severe brain damage, to talking a mile a minute about his favorite Cab Calloway songs and sharing memories of dancing and romancing as he snaps his fingers and speaks with wide eyed alert expressions. A therapist in the video fights back the tears as she describes another patient's similar reaction. When Oliver Sacks, the M.D. involved, comments on Henry's experience, he refers to philosophy he's read about **music being the quickening art**. Dr. Sacks says that Henry is being quickened, or brought to life with this music. After ten years in this nursing home, apparently this is the first time Henry remembered who he is and thus reacquired his identity through the power of music. Dr. Sacks indicates that **music can bring those who are "out of it" back into it! When Henry is asked what music means to him, he says, "Love"**. Among many others, *Godvine* also has a video showing a homeless man singing with lots of talent and lots of joy.

The August, 2012 Good Housekeeping Magazine contains an article titled, "New RX: Tune In - From rap to rock to Mozart, music's surprising health payoffs. This article states: "If you've ever crooned a cranky baby to sleep or pumped up a flagging workout with Top 40 hits, you know the power of music. **Now new research has documented impressive health benefits locked within the tunes you love best."** Namely, lowering blood pressure, soothing tension and even easing (along with practicing breathing exercises for 30 minutes a day). Joke Bradt, Ph.D., is an associate professor in the creative arts therapies department at Drexel University and a board-certified music therapist. The article quotes her explanation: "Music does more than provide distraction. It's first processed in the brain's medulla, which controls basic functions like breathing and heart rate. That may explain the blood pressure and cardio payoffs. Music also reduces activity in the amygdale, an area that regulates negative emotions, while acting on neutral systems that stimulate pleasure." She reported that any kind of music that you enjoy and find relaxing works. But she cautioned that, "So many of us play music all day as sonic wallpaper, but that won't work here. Save a favorite song or two. Then sit down or lie down, and really listen to it purposefully." **So I say, maybe it's really a *song* a day that keeps the doctor away!** But if I had a personal doctor like Joke Bradt, giving advice like that, I'd probably want to get her prescriptions as often as possible! And apparently one place I can find it is on the hotline that John Oates along with his musical partner, Daryl Hall have set up so you can phone in and hear a variety of Hall & Oates tunes if you find yourself needing a fix! There is also now Hall's show, "Daryl's House" which gained great popularity with other artists and fans alike. I've heard him explain that the success of their 70's hit, "She's Gone" was due to the fact that **the lyrics turned a simple idea into a universal expression.** He talks about how this realization hits him in the morning as he no longer sees her "toothbrush in the stand" (one more example of tying in music to health, only its dental hygiene this time!)

And just like Trace Adkin's experience with his formerly suicidal fan, Chynna Phillips who was one of the writers of Wilson Phillips' hit, "Hold On", shares a similar experience in the book, *"Chicken Soup for the Soul, The Story Behind The Song"*. She said, "When we did interviews at radio stations, people called in and said things from, "I was going to take my life when this song came on and it saved me" to "I love listening to this song when I'm driving" (which I think is a true test of a good sing along, especially if you stay in your car once you've reached your destination just to hear it til the end!).

BJ Thomas announced his thoughts on the subject back in the seventies, with his song, **"I Believe in Music"** including the lines: **"Music is Love & Love is Music** if you know what I mean…**Music is the universal language**, and Love is the key to peace, hope and understanding and living in harmony". And in this singer's song mentioned in the baby shower category *(RTA)*, he says, "Nothin' moves my soul like the sound of the good old **Rock and Roll Lullaby**".

Also from that era, I absolutely love Tom T. Hall's "I Love" song, especially the lines: "I Love honest open smiles, kisses from a child, tomatoes on the vine and onions. I Love winners when they cry, losers **when they try, Music when it's good, And life"**.

In a recent TV interview, I heard rocker, Gene Simmons of the group Kiss, point out how **our nation sees itself through musical terms**. For example, **when someone excels at a sport or profession, we call them a "Rock Star"**. And I thought about how when we pass a test with flying colors, we say we "aced" it, which I think, could be a reference to Simmons' fellow Kiss star, Ace Frehley--?? He also went on to say that we are the country that invented flight and first put a man on the moon but we are also the ones who invented the blues. (And Neil Diamond says, "If you take the blues and sing a song, you sing them out again, Song Sung, Blue, Blue").

And now with Simmons' restaurant chain devoted to the theme of music, he is willing to put his money where his mouth is! After twenty eight gold albums, we can trust that he probably knows what he's talking about. A Kiss performance according to Wikipedia, might include anything from fire breathing, levitating drum sets, pyrotechnics, and a variety of other flamboyant displays by band members with make-up and costumes designed to give them the persona of comic book-style characters. However, I am getting into uncharted territory here, because in **"Manana", Jimmy Buffett advises, "Don't try to describe a Kiss concert if you've never seen one"**! I told you,

## there's a Buffett lyric for everything!

I feel like quoting the cell phone commercial that says, "We've got an Ap for that. We've got an Ap for that,...etc., etc." And my version would be, **"We've got a lyric for that....!"**

And speaking of giving credit where credit is due, during a Guitar Legends TV Special, Hugh and I were so impressed to hear John Mayer's comments about how he acknowledges that every guitar player learned through the legendary talent of Eric Clapton.

And speaking of other legends of our time, in "Piano Man" Billy Joel says, "The manager gives me a smile. He knows that it's me they've been coming to see to forget about life for a while...We're all in the mood for a melody and you've got us feeling alright". I think we all agree that music can draw a crowd but maybe it can also serve as the foundation for much more. Jefferson Starship says, **"We built this city on Rock and Roll"**. There are Hard Rock Hotels, Grand Ole Opry Hotels, and Margaritaville Hotels. There is Radio City Music Hall, **The Rock and Roll Hall of Fame (And I am not alone in supporting getting Jimmy Buffett recognized there-an idea a phellow phan, Garry Myrwold** has brought to my attention), and Graceland. There is also now Toby Keith's "I Love This Bar". And what would Las Vegas, Branson, Missouri and Nashville be without musical acts?

Whether its local cover bands or headliners, I think we all do actually agree with Gary Portnoy & Judy Hart Angelo's lines to the show, "Cheers" theme song: "Making your way in the world today takes everything you've got. Taking a break from all of your worries, sure would help a lot...Sometimes you want to go where everybody knows your name and they're always glad you came'. And in our town, these neighborhood type places we go to for cocktails and camaraderie, recognize that *music is key* in bringing us all in. I think that we need background music to keep others from noticing when we may not realize that we're talking too loud or inversely, we need music to direct our attention to, when nobody may be talking to us!

In another expert's opinion about the power of songs, accomplished songwriter and producer, Lamont Dozier, shared the following comments in the above mentioned book, *Chicken Soup for the Soul, The Story Behind The Song* :

"I can remember special events by songs I've heard in my life. **I believe that a song marks history just as much as a political event or birthday celebration.** Why is it that we can hear a song and remember exactly where we were at the time we first heard the song and the feelings we were experiencing at the time, or see a face from the past? **A song can evoke all of these memories and feelings in each and every one of us and that stays with us all forever".**

In the same above book, Christina Aguilera says: "I wanted my songs to have positive empowering messages, especially to women so they could feel strong and speak for themselves.

**I try to write lyrics and music that people can relate to and that help them to find personal strength. I try to communicate universal ideas and thoughts that help them get through the day or the year a bit better."** In her, **"Blessed"** song, she says, "Do my best with every breath that's in me" and I believe she does indeed!

Also in this book, an excerpt by Greg Camp of Smash Mouth, explains his motivation for writing the song, **"All Star"**, made even more famous by the movie, "Shrek". Camp says, "We realized that a lot of kids were troubled with their family situations, parents who weren't great at parenting, older siblings, school, friends. **They thanked us for our music, saying that it helped to get them through the tough times. It made us realize that we do have a voice and we can help people.** The song was 100% for the fans. I wanted to give something back to them for letting us know that they were actually listening to us and I wanted them to know that we were listening to them. It was my gift to them".

Melissa Ethreridge's entry in this book, about her song, "Come To My Window", explains how some eerie irony in one of the lines came to play out in her life. When she wrote the song, she was going through a difficult time in a relationship. It wasn't until years later that the line, "Nothing fills the blackness that has seeped into my chest", took on a new meaning as she became aware of her diagnosis of breast cancer!

Also in this book, Liz Phair in speaking about her "Divorce" and "Whip-Smart" songs, says **"there's a magic to songwriting. It usually comes in one piece, free form. It feels like channeling.** What you write often becomes reality." And Darius Rucker in speaking about his "It Won't be Like this for Long", says, "The song really came out of the simplicity of everyday life. That's how all great songs happen". Richie Sambora speaks of the song, "Livin on a Prayer" which he co-wrote with Desmond Child and john Bonjovi, saying, **"A songwriter wants to write songs which transcend time."** And that one sure served me well in this phase of my life.

Music, as a form of self expression, allows singers and songwriters to share a piece of themselves and **ideally, their contribution is for the common good.** In the same book, the following is shared by Mick Jones who wrote "Waiting for a Girl Like You"( recorded by Foreigner): **"That's when I realized there was something spiritual about writing a song. It comes from somewhere above; you're just the conduit. You have to be in a space where you can accept it**. The minute I wrote it, I got full of melancholy. It had sort of a strange hold over me. It made me sad when I heard it. It was very powerful. When we recorded it, I had difficulty keeping it together. I had to leave a few times during the session. While we were recording, a girl we'd never seen before wandered into the studio. She was beautiful. She stood against the wall and when Lou went into the vocal booth, he sang for her through the glass. When we turned around, she was gone. She was the inspiration for the vocal. He captured it with such emotion, and on one take. So many people tell me how powerful this song was for them as well. Once it was completed, we played it for several couples, all of whom were in various stages of break-up. By the end of the night, they were all cuddling. It was always very mysterious and still is for me." For more inspirational type of songs (RTA).

I feel the way he talks about songwriting is probably how another of my favorite artists, Steve Winwood likely approaches it. I just love all of the positivity in his songs "Higher Love" and "Finer Things". And the lyrics to Jeanne Newhall's "Glide" are similarly one big breath of fresh air, just like my favorite by Brittany Kingery, "Teach Me to Breathe".

To include one more excerpt from that same *Chicken Soup* book, I'd like to share some lines from a song that Joss Stone cowrote and recorded with one of her idols, Lauryn Hill, called appropriately, "Music". She writes it from the perspective of music being her boyfriend:

"Nothing in this world got me like you baby. I'd give up my soul if I could sing with you daily. I'm not the only girl in love with you its crazy. I appreciate your groove now. I know I owe everything to you. Music, I'm so in Love with my music...Higher vibration energizing entire lands with something to stand with or stand for...fueling entire societies, making economies, stimulating generating inspiration synonymously, entertaining expression, intangible invisible but undeniable, plays the language of excitement on survival...some say collectively everything". I have to say that based on those lyrics, I may have met my match in the recognition I give to music. **Could it be that maybe this artist and myself had the iHeart Radio App somehow automatically programmed into our DNA?** It does seem to be in our blood to REALLY Love music! And speaking of pumping blood, Huey Lewis says, "The Heart of Roll and Roll is still beating"!

Moving on to thinking about our reasons for being alive, I agree with Social Distortion's, "Story of My Life", when they sing, "Life goes by so fast. **You only want to do what you think is right**". I've heard it said that the definition of

**wisdom is knowing the right thing to do in every situation**, a skill that usually comes with age and experience. Another venue that delivers this theme is the show, "What Would You Do", in which host, John Quinones uses a hidden camera to test unsuspecting people's reactions to ethical dilemmas. Author and speaker, Les Brown says, "Evil prevails when good men and women do nothing." And John Mayer sings about, "Waiting for the World to Change" but those who do what is right even when it is not what is popular, are real heroes. A local church called Vineyard, that operates from a store front in downtown Cape Coral, advertises the message, **"Be the change you want to see in the world"**. With a similar message, my favorite Michael Jackson song is "Man in the Mirror". I believe all that was good in him came through in the lines, "I'm starting with the man in the mirror. I'm asking him to change his ways. And no message could have been any clearer. If you want to make the world a better place, take a look at yourself and change". And my musical hero too actually has a song stating the sad truth in the lines, "Be good and you will be lonesome. Be lonesome and you will be free. Live a lie and you will live to regret it. **That's what living is to me"–Jimmy Buffett, Pretty good intrinsic values, huh?** As he sings this one, he shares that he found that inspiration in a Mark Twain book.

Another icon who was instrumental in spreading the popularity of music and for spreading goodwill was Dick Clark, host of "American Band Stand". Upon his recent death, of the many news commentaries, the one that caught my ear was one explaining how this guy got this job as a result of the original host being arrested for drunk driving and he was at the right place at the right time. It went on to say that as a DJ, he had a good ear for music but more importantly, as a person, he had a good heart and **a way of doing the right thing.** For example, he was responsible for changing the show's rules in order to include black teenagers as guest dancers on this after school show. Ryan Seacrest was quoted saying, "Without Dick Clark's work, a show like "American

Idol" would not exist today". I'll add that most likely, line dancing venues probably wouldn't exist either. It's really interesting to watch some of the old clips from that show with bell bottom teens having the time of their lives doing The Twist, or The Bump, or The Locomotion, or The Hustle (just different versions of The Electric Slide, or The Macarena, or any of the numbers from the *Dirty Dancing* movie or any country bar). There probably wouldn't be a show like "Dancing with the Stars" either.

While none of us can claim to be perfect, I like to share Linkin Park's sentiment when they sing, "When my time comes, help me leave behind some reason to be missed. Don't resent me and when you're feeling empty keep me in your memory. Leave Out All the Rest". And I do believe that the human memory can be very resilient in overcoming unpleasant memories and remembering the good. Otherwise, how could anyone ever give birth for a second time??

And speaking of growing up, I love how some songs can so strongly conjure up nostalgia, like Kid Rock's "All Summer Long" and Dave Matthews' "Old Dirt Hill". In the previously mentioned, "Springstein" Eric Church says, "Baby, is it spring or is it summer, the guitar sound or the beat of that drummer, you hear sometimes late at night on your radio, even though you're a million miles away. When you hear 'Born in the USA', you relive those 'Glory Days' so long ago...".

So like the theme song of "That 70's Show" recorded by Reunion and written by Norman Dolph (which according to Wikipedia, is perhaps the earliest recorded rap song) as it rattles off a tribute to dozens of artists of that era in the fastest monologue imaginable,

**"Life is a Rock"** does kind of sum it all up!

And speaking of being *between a rock and a hard place,* Jimmy Buffett sings, **"There's nothing soft about hard times..**A fool and his money are bound to part and what goes up must come down...Take care of your needs and watch out for your greeds or that wolf'll be at your door. I Used to Have Money

One Time". **Oh Jimmy, why didn't I listen more to that one??!**

While trying to come up with some promotional captions for this book, I came up with the following phrase:

> **Just when you think you have it all, the storms of life can come crashing in. That's when it's up to you to sink or swim and if you choose to swim, you just may find that a better you emerges.**

I will say one thing that this whole experience has taught me is that in the future, whatever I may need to change in my life or whatever I cannot change and must learn to live with, I will try to do all of the sensible things but I will also still put my dilemma out to the universe and again watch for signs. **I believe it's likely that many of those signs will come to me in the lines of a song!** And I will do my best **to** remember Earth Wind and Fire's advice, "If you feel down and out, Sing a Song,

**If you sing a song a day, you will find a better way".**

I once heard a commercial for Metro, referring to "your life's soundtrack" just like jazz artists, Mindi Abair sings, "Let the whole world know and sing a song". I will always try to emulate Judy Andrews Joy as she focused on "A Few of her Favorite Things" in *The Sound of Music*. And always try to return to a state of gratitude.Speaking of which**,** as I approach my conclusion of this story, I want to share that I've realized that I may have abandoned that Gratitude Journal a little prematurely because more good things have continued to come our way, which I will list to follow-

1. Since first self publishing in 2012, sharing this book **has brought so many interesting people into my life** and sharing our common appreciation for music and song lyrics has brought me **such joy!** One stmt. that I heard from Jimmy Buffett & also from Kenny Chesney, is that "you never know who is going to help you along the way"- These additional recognitions are being devoted to those who've shown up to

help me in my initial journey with this book- **Namely, DJ Jeff Allen of BeachFront Radio, Artist Koz of Green World Gallery, Jack McKissock of Power Chord & Jenny Craig of Live Your Power and The Grateful Ring Movement.**

I first met DJ Jeff at an event held at Koz's shop on Duval St. in Key West. At that time, my book had just been printed & upon reading it, 3 different **Ph**riends, within a 3 day period, suggested that I go see Artist Koz. Feeling that the universe must be trying to tell me something, I made a point to see what would happen if I did. What I witnessed upon walking through the doors of Koz's Green World Gallery for the first time reinforced to me that I was right to believe in "signs". You see, that morning as fate would have it, Trop Rockers from all over the world were present for a ceremony honoring Koz for the way he gives back to the Trop Rock community. I had to stop in my tracks to take it all in; as DJ Jeff & his partner, Carol were presenting Koz & his wife, Pam with a symbolic personalized watermelon ukulele. People were passing around Mimosas & making toasts with bittersweet tears as they described how so many people came together to produce the "Taking Care of Our Own Fund" spearheaded by "Phins to the West". One after another, they shared how Koz pays-it-forward by not only supporting worthwhile causes(that's an interesting pun!) but by giving so many budding artist like me, a start by inventorying original Trop Rock music & unique "parrot-phanalia". Looking around that room, and observing not only all of the special items on his shelves, but all of the smiling faces there that day, I remember thinking to myself, "This must be Parrot Head Heaven"!-and that is why I like to refer to his shop as a "magic shop"!

Then it was time to honor DJ Jeff and celebrate all he does year-round to keep this community connected. At that point, being ignorant to any of his pre-existing conditions, I was just thrilled to have the chance to meet him and give him a copy of my book since he was mentioned in it. I had copied one of his Facebook posts that fit perfectly into some of the subject matter discussed in the book. I did not find out until later about Jeff's own health challenges. Once I became more aware of the extent of this whole Trop Rock world and started tuning in more often to DJ Jeff's online radio show, I learned about his struggles but more so, I learned about his strength. To listen to this guy host his "Amish Beach Party" daily on the radio, it took me by surprise to hear how the energy in his voice and the attitude of his comments was consistently as uplifting as the songs he chose to play! No matter what he was going through, Jeff showed up and celebrated everyday with us. I actually had to remind myself that he was dealing with serious issues because of his poise. So I was humbled.

I am also somewhat embarrassed about the pettiness of the problems I bring up in this book because I am sure that DJ Jeff & J. Harold Lowry (author of Key Lime Floats) & Hillbilly Beach's Hugo Duarte & J Jaye Steele (lead singer of SW FL's band,"PUSH") would trade with me without hesitation. And these are just four fine individuals that I happened to know, in a sea of so many more, facing life's challenges with exemplary courage. And all I feel I can do is to humbly cheer them on (**Rock On**!) and thank them for adopting me into this Trop Rock **Ph**amily and attempt to learn from them; just like the "song gods" continuously help me learn so many lessons.

Also, big **Thank Yous** to **Jack Mckissock** for giving me my 1st broadcast interview on his **Power Chord Radio Show,** found on iTunes/Yoo-Rock, followed by **Jenny Craig** who had me as a guest speaker on her **Live Your Power Radio Show,** focusing on gratitude (PS: this is not the weight-loss lady although if you partake in any of her programs, I can attest that you will feel some weight lifted in your life!)

Thank you again to BeachFront Radio for inviting me to participate in one of the "Welcome to Key West" celebrations hosted by Smokin Tuna Saloon, and have one of my first book signing events; which was truly a magical experience for me. And this is where I also got to meet **Howard Livingston** of The Mile Marker 24 Band, the troprocker with his own fastly growing fan club, The Coconut Castaways.

And Thank you once again to **Artist Koz** for also hosting a book signing event for me that year and for now making space on your wonderful shop shelves in order to carry my book! And speaking of coconuts and shops, **I'd like to thank Denise Ahlstrom of Karma & Coconuts**, a Cape Coral boutique featuring local artists, for carrying this book too!

2. Our Hometown of **Cape Coral has become** noted in national publications as being:

   -among the **Top Markets** for housing recovery

   by The Wall Street Journal

   -among the **Best Places** to retire

   By Forbes magazine

   -among the **Happiest Seaside Towns**-( Nearby Sanibel Island)

   By Coastal Living

3. **We're back in business!-** With so many Baby Boomers coming to town to "Go Coastal on us"(like Kenny Chesney's song), the local real estate market is bouncing back and in the spirit of Zig Ziglar's quote, **"You can get what you want in life if you help enough other people get what they want"**, Hugh and I delight in helping newcomers house hunt by boat and plan their best dockside happy-hour routes or day-trip destinations. A recap of some of our typical days goes something like this:

'Recovering from a long wkend...when everybody else is off, that's when we go to work---delivering the Florida lifestyle dream that is! And this past one was no exception--picked up Illinois clients @ airport on Sat. morn, took them to lunch @ Rumrunners, spent day viewing waterfront condos, treated them to a cocktail @ the "World Famous Tiki Bar," got them settled into their accommodations @ The Resort at Marina Village/Tarpon Pointe, picked them up by boat Sun. a.m. with Bloody Marys and this time viewed properties by boat, put in a bid for their top pick, took a ride through Matlacha Pass for some grouper @ Bert's Bar, continued the sight seeing cruise toward Pine Island, got the news that they won the bid for their vacation place, stopped to celebrate with a Margarita toast at Woody's Waterside; sparked by a portrait of Captain Tony on the wall, got caught up in a discussion on how much this town of ours is like Key West and how if you let it, it can seem to take on a Margaritaville persona;----then it was back on the boat, escorted by dolphins playing in our wake, we made it back in just enough time to drop them back off at the airport with visions of palm trees swaying in their heads........For us, just another day at the office, but in the words of these new friends and new Florida property owners, "something to look forward to!" I Love my job...how lucky we are to be delivering the dream!"

**4. We found a way to bring MOTM to us-**

One Sunday evening, as we were settling our tab at Bert's Bar in Matlacha, the trop-rocker performing that night spotted Hugh's "Meeting of the Minds" commemorative t-shirt. So he quickly switched his playlist to The Boat Drunks' "Hollowman" followed by several Jerry Jeff Walker originals that only those in this inner circle would recognize! Of course, Hugh & I leapt from our seats at the bar & ran to get a front row seat to cheer this guy on. Then we proceeded to make requests of songs by various "MOTM" artists & of course, reopened our tab in order to send this singer drinks. Before the night ended, we felt like we were being treated to our own private concert. When his relief arrived & his set ended, he joined us for a toast at the bar & we all bonded, sharing "One time @ MOTM"stories! & now anytime we need a little dose of MOTM, we get to wherever **Scott Bryan** is playing, because he sure can deliver it!

**5. We eventually did sell our previous home via short sale** but this was still in the time when banks did not release deficiencies; however **we've learned to take it day by day & dollar by dollar-**

6. In the time that's passed throughout 3 rounds of revisions on this book, **both of my sons have gained an appreciation for musical artists of their generation with** relate-able yet still mostly **positive messages!**

7. In "Piano Man", Billy Joel makes reference to someone who is a "Real Estate Novelist". I'm not really sure what that is, but since I'm in real estate and I hope to be a novelist, I like the ring of it!

In an effort to stay active in the writing process, I've been thrilled to become a freelance writer for TropRockin.com and **I'd like to thank Tammy Camp**, that site's founder, for that opportunity. And to add icing on the cake, I've additionally had the very rewarding experience of becoming a regular contributor to *PHlockers* Magazine, a global vehicle that allows us all to stay in touch on a monthly basis. **And I like to thank Katy Waugh**, this publication's founder, for all of the ways that this vehicle contributes to all of our lives!

8. I've **Finally** finished this thesis and in the process, gathered enough information about the power of music to start a second book! For a sneak peak, go to: www.**LeaningOnTheLyrics.com**, and **please feel free to share your music related stories with me there too!** I'd LOVE to be part of a **"Tequila Shots for the Parrothead's Soul"** collaboration!?...

And now at last, it is time for me to **"put this book on the shelf with my heart in it, never wasting time, finding the right way home"**, "Incommunicado" Jimmy Buffett

### AND IN THE END

### THE LOVE YOU TAKE

### IS EQUAL TO THE LOVE YOU MAKE

(The Beatles)

## About the Author

*\*Clean\* Funny Pics's photo.*

**Linda Hebert** is a real estate agent in Cape Coral, Florida where she lives with her husband and two sons. She's a native Floridian and life-long Parrot Head who claims after once being lost, she's now found Margaritaville & she invites you to meet her there-

**She says, "When the student is ready, the teacher appears & so often, my teachers have turned out to be singers & songwriters.** As a matter of fact, I enrolled in a life time course of "Summerzcool" with my musical mentor, Jimmy Buffett at University of Margaritaville, a long time ago!--Only now I've graduated to become an adjunct professor at the *Cape* **Coral Reefer**(rette!) satellite campus & around here, it's always Friday, it's always 5 O'clock, it's always Sunny & 75, and we don't need to see your excuse to "Take a Holiday!"

*RTA=*"Refer to Appendix"online @

**www.LeaningOnTheLyrics.com, for categorized playlists & short stories on various song subjects.**

**Freelancelinda@yahoo.com, to submit reader reviews/correspondence**

**www.MoveCoastal.com, for information about SW FL**

# Readers' Reviews:

**Kokomo Joe-** President, SW FL Parrot Head Club:

I never realized how much song lyrics made such an impact on the way I think and act. Linda also introduced me to some old (new to me) music that I had no idea even existed.

**Lynne Eaton,** WINGS:

Delightful read with lots of self help messages throughout. If you were not a Jimmy Buffett fan previously, you will be after you read this book. Many of his songs are more meaningful than just the mainstream ones that earned him a beach bum image. It doesn't take a rocket scientist to relate to this book! Linda's insight as to how to deal with everyday problems along with monumental ones may be just what the doctor ordered. I am sure you will be buying Jimmy Buffett albums to help soothe your mortal soul once you have read her book.

**Jack Owens-** former driver for the band, Chicago

If you're experiencing any kind of pitfalls in life these days, or know someone who might be, this book is a life preserver. Ms. Hebert's talent for sharing her personal story in a whimsical way makes you realize that tough times don't last, tough people do. It's been a blessing to me as I've leaned on it to get through the recent loss of my wife, Diane. And if you're looking for song suggestions for a theme party or particular purpose, her online Appendix provides a plethora of suggestions!

**J. Harold Lowry,** author of **Key Lime Floats:**

Leaning on the Lyrics by Linda Hebert releases your mind. Allowing you to relive memories the only way song lyrics can. Linda takes you into her (and your) life through the lyrics of the songs that have touched each of us in so many ways.

The one quote of hers that stands out is "A song can evoke all of these memories and feelings in each & every one of us and stays with us all forever."

Leaning on the Lyrics is not your typical Jimmy Buffett love fest. For through her book, she provides insight exploring the lyrics of many different artist and genres. With everyone's Ipods and smart phones being filled today with songs where we have or are ourselves, Leaning on the Lyrics, this book is and will be a true **delight to read even for the second and third time!**

**Steve G**-Fort Lauderdale businessman & Music Fan**:**

Ms. Hebert has done a really good job of capturing the feeling of a normal person swept up by the economic crisis. Her occupation and location placed her family on the very leading edge of the housing collapse forcing them into turmoil long before being in turmoil was cool. Her story is great and will cause you to reflect on your self and your situation even if you have escaped this recession relatively unscathed. She has obviously put a lot of thought into her thesis that musical lyrics can speak to us and help us in bad times (and good). Her encyclopedic memory of songs from my era (teenager in the '80's) as well as a shared devotion to Jimmy Buffett made this book very enjoyable for me.

Made in the USA
Charleston, SC
02 March 2016